# Invisibly
# Yours

# Invisibly Yours

## C.D. Payne

ISBN  1453854118

EAN-13  9781453854112

To the friends of Nick

Special thanks to my agent Mickey Freiberg and to Till Hack for his editorial assistance.

# Chapter 1

The first time I "dematerialized" I was taking my dog to the pound because I could no longer afford to feed him.

Now this mutt I had always pegged as more lovable than intelligent, but he had the smarts to perceive that this place was bad news for canines. He didn't want to get out of the car and then halfway across the parking lot he slammed on the brakes. So I say his name and yell out a command.

A weird queasy feeling comes over me. "Queasy" hardly describes it. More like someone had touched an icy metal bar to every one of my internal organs. That's when I noticed that my legs and feet had disappeared. Along, I quickly spotted, with the rest of me.

I'm a fairly rational guy. So I jump to the only logical conclusion.

I'm dead.

Stone dead from a stroke or something. Damn, that sucks.

Well, at least I went out owing a ton of money. Not in Judy Garland's class, who checked out a cool $4 million behind the eight ball. But still, I'd finished ahead of the game.

So this is what it's like to be dead.

Kind of surprising. Not what had always been advertised.

Your body disappears, but your mind continues on.

Wow, who knew?

But for how long does your mind continue to function? For a few seconds until your brain finally chokes off from lack of oxygen? For a minute or two? What?

I assumed I was deceased, but I could feel my heart pounding in my chest.

Something wasn't adding up.

I look around. There's my dog still pulling against the leash, which extends up from his collar and hangs–apparently unsupported–in mid-air.

If I'm dead, where's the body? Shouldn't at least some visible part of me be sprawled lifeless on the asphalt?

My dog is just as panicked as I am. He nearly pulls me off my no-longer-visible feet. Without thinking, I yell out his name and repeat the command.

*Poof.* My ears tingle strangely, vivid magenta stars twinkle and pop before my eyes, and suddenly I'm back.

Wow, I'm not dead after all. I check myself out. There are my legs extending down nicely from my crotch. There's my beer gut, my scuffed sandals, my funky cargo shorts, and all the rest of me. Yes, my body had returned to the visible world. I gaze around the deserted parking lot. Apparently, no one had witnessed my dramatic departure and reappearance.

By now I'm shaking all over, but I make it back to my car and collapse in the seat. Being not yet deceased is a very welcome and exciting development. Thirty-seven, I decide, is way too young to croak. Good news for my pup too. His abandonment was now temporarily postponed.

So how does a 37-year-old college grad arrive at a state where he can no longer afford to provide for a 30-pound mixed-breed dog?

It's the usual story of ambition and sloth.

I'm a journalist by training, employed until two years ago by a metropolitan daily in a second-tier midwestern city.

I liked the work. I wasn't shackled behind a desk all day. I even won a few of those awards they hand out like peanuts at press conventions.

My job as a reporter took me frequently to hospitals to interview folks who had been shot, mauled by pit bulls, mangled in machinery, sucked out of trailers by tornadoes, or rendered unwell in some other newsworthy way. In the city hospital near downtown I frequently encountered Rachel, the nurse with the amazing green-blue eyes. Lovely Rachel had a much-despised surgeon boyfriend, but the persistent journalist persisted doggedly. Not quite six years ago we got our names in the paper under the matrimonial listings: Axel Weston and Rachel Burke. United forever. Or so I thought.

As you may have heard, all is not golden these days in the newspaper biz. Our chain was still making money, but every year or so they would rotate in a new publisher. Each one was more of a corporate suit and less of a journalist than the previous one. Then they started the layoffs. Not good for morale or one's dedication to the cause.

Still, my job seemed pretty secure. They needed at least a few bodies in the newsroom to cover the shootings and factory closings. Rachel and I bought a modest house in a semi-genteel neighborhood, and there was some preliminary discussion of ankle-biters. At least *I* regarded them as pre-liminary. A puppy arrived on the scene as a test of our nurturing skills.

And then three senior reporters got called upstairs and were offered buyouts. For my 13 years in the saddle I was offered $93,742 to go away permanently. Rachel and I mulled it over for two days, and then I went in and signed all the termination forms. I cleared out my desk that same morning. No going-away party, but a few of us met later that day for a long, boozy lunch. For the first time since I was four years old I didn't have school or a job to go to.

I was a free man with a big fat bank balance.

Three months later we had sold the house and moved

to Los Angeles. Rachel got a job in about two seconds as an ICU nurse with a big increase in pay. Housing prices were a shock, but we found a two-bedroom condo in Glendale that we (foolishly) bought because it was close to her hospital and within walking distance of a dog park. The second bedroom I would be using as my office. In that 10 by 12 foot box overlooking our midget patio, I was to produce best-selling mystery novels and the occasional blockbuster screenplay.

That was the plan.

But L.A. was an exciting new place to explore and I was a guy with a big fat bank balance. Besides, hadn't I earned a nice vacation? And that rusty beater that had towed the rental trailer from the Midwest wasn't cutting it in L.A., where You Are What You Drive. It got traded in on a sporty import. And then April 15 arrived, and what was left of my termination wad got axed in half by the tax man. No unemployment compensation coming in, of course, since I had left my job voluntarily. Still, I had a gainfully employed wife, and you can't rush the creative process.

I did manage to excrete a screenplay. It was not great, but how many great movies was Hollywood turning out these days? If anything, today's producers seemed to hone in on mediocrity. I even managed to get a few agents to read it. They declined to take me on, but a couple asked to see my next effort.

My next effort. Right. And what was that going to be?

So there I was living on a bleak street in Glendale with no friends except for a few acquaintances I'd made at the dog park. I took to showing up with a six-pack of beer in a cooler. Then I got a bigger cooler. That one I charged on my credit card because the fat bank balance was long gone.

And then a few months later the lovely nurse was gone. That shook me up enough to send out some résumés. What newspaper wouldn't want an award-winning reporter with 13 years of experience? Lots of them as it turned out.

Then our bank started sending registered letters with

foreclosure notices. Like they really expected me to scrape up $2600 every month for a crummy overpriced condo that the slob owner never even bothered to clean. Fortunately, by then the whole housing bubble had popped, swamping the greedy bankers with a tidal wave of condo deadbeats. Nearly a year had passed since I'd made a payment, and I was still waiting for the sheriff to toss me out on the street. Meanwhile, I was parking my sporty car six blocks away; I was late on those payments too. The calls from bill collectors came in 18 hours a day (I turned my phone off at night).

One by one, my credit cards got maxed out. Then the day came when I was flat busted. No money for beer–or for dog food. That was the day I discovered this universe has a few surprises up its sleeve.

So there I am sucking wind in my car as my heartbeat edges back from the Red Zone. Had I really just dematerialized like Captain Kirk beaming away on the Transporter, or was I still impaired from the previous night's debaucheries? I certainly felt sober. Too sober, in fact. What I really needed was a nice cold one.

OK, had I hit rock bottom at last? Was I ready to abandon all pride and resort to panhandling in the offices of the county dog pound? Could I cadge a few quarters from those animal lovers if I said I needed to buy dog food? I looked over at my pup, gazing adoringly at me in his usual servile way. All those endless hours of dog-park fun had earned a lifetime of loyalty from that mutt. Too bad he wasn't showing a few gaunt rib bones.

And then the beer-besotted remnants of my ace reporter's brain ticked over. It occurred to me that I had never before uttered that particular combination of words to my dog. Nor, likely had anyone else. In a moment of nostalgia, I had named that squirming puppy after my first childhood pet–only with the letters reversed. Everyone at the dog park remarked on my dog's unusual name.

So what did I have to lose? I looked around the parking lot. Still deserted. I took a deep breath and said those words again. The icy metal bar again goosed my pancreas and spleen. My visible form immediately disappeared from view. I reached over and pulled out the cigarette lighter. Interesting, my clothing had disappeared with my body, but the object in my hand was visible floating in space. I felt for my shirt pocket and stuck the lighter inside. It could no longer be seen. Hmm, a very interesting effect. I removed the lighter; a couple inches from my shirt it slid into view. I cupped my fingers around it and it disappeared.

I said the phrase again.

No ear tingling this time. I was still invisible!

Fuck!

Had I said it correctly? I tried not to panic, and concentrated on remembering the exact order of the words. My fourth attempt worked the magic. I was back in view. I scrambled for a pen in the glove box, and immediately wrote down the phrase.

The whole experience took less than 10 minutes. In that flash of time I had discovered a way to render myself invisible. I had discovered a portal out of the visible world.

# Chapter 2

I drove slowly and cautiously back to my grungy condo. It would be just my luck to die in a car crash the same day I had made that monumental discovery. Risking repossession of my wheels, I drove into my garage and loaded up all the stacks of empties. These I cashed in at the local recycling center for a voucher that bought $9.83 of beer and dog crunchies at the adjoining market. I even got $2.37 back in change that I could use to splurge on actual food should I feel peckish later. I stashed my car in its usual spot and strolled home with the groceries and pup. I hadn't felt this good since I nailed the mayor in a page-one story over that expensive lot he had sold to the redevelopment agency in a quiet (he wished) sweetheart deal. The contract was in his granny's name, but I had long since learned it pays to know such details.

I spent the rest of the afternoon checking things out in the bedroom in front of the mirrored closet door. Anything within about two inches of my flesh was invisible, except around my earlobes, fingers, and dick. Guess they didn't have enough mass to project invisibility very far, which is not to suggest I'm not respectably hung. OK, so I wouldn't be wearing pendulous earrings or prancing around naked with a large metal stud through my pecker. Not a problem. Gloves disappeared nicely on my hands, which would be helpful for not leaving fingerprints. My long raincoat, however, showed alarmingly around my knees, which was bad news for concealing bulky items. Also my feet made visible impressions when I walked on carpet. In my new life as a sometimes invisible person, deep pile and thick shag would be my enemy.

Mr. Invisible (as I now thought of myself) decided it would be a wise idea to rename my dog Bob. No use risking having someone else say those magic words. (Not that likely since another factor in my discovering the words has gone unmentioned by me. A good reporter knows how to keep a secret.) Bob seemed OK with the change, although he still barked nervously every time Mr. Invisible did his disappearing act.

I also decided that Mr. Invisible should pay a surreptitious visit that night on my wife to see how she was getting on. We had an appointment for later that week to go over the final papers of our amicable, do-it-yourself divorce. Rachel had kissed off her share of the condo down payment and wasn't demanding any alimony from my sorry ass. People who daily tend to the sick and dying are realistic about such matters. Funny, all through our marriage I thought of her as "Rachel," and now that we were getting divorced I could conceive of her only as "my wife."

Rachel had moved a few miles away to Burbank's dreariest stucco apartment building. It had been built long ago in the 1970s when unadorned, discount, soul-withering ugliness was at its peak. It had roaches too, which my sweet wife claimed she didn't mind. Still, one couldn't help blaming that loser who had taken her away from her sparkling midwestern home.

It was just getting dark when I parked a block from Rachel's building. I locked my car, ducked behind some bushes, said the words, and strolled invisibly toward her building–setting off fierce barking from every mutt I passed (all, fortunately, confined behind fences). I followed a guy with a limp as he got buzzed through the welded-steel lobby door. Some Young Singles were having beer and take-out barbecue around the blue-illuminated pool in the center of the concrete courtyard. Rachel wasn't among them, thank God.

To my surprise I followed the guy with the limp all the way to Rachel's door and then through it. Exclaiming, "Hi, Peter," she embraced him with an alarming lack of restraint. The cad then proceeded to kiss her brazenly on her lips.

Holy shit, what was going on here!

Come to think of it, I remembered Rachel mentioning a few months back some patient of hers who got badly tore up in a motorcycle crash on Sunset. He almost lost a leg. The guy was a film editor named Peter.

Hey, no way could it be ethical for a medical professional to be socializing in such an uninhibited way with a former patient. Plus, the guy was an obvious horn dog. Didn't my wife have any standards?

"Care for a glass of wine, darling?" she asked.

"I've got a better idea," he replied, picking her up bodily and carrying her off toward the bedroom.

Were these provocations to be endured? Had the lout no respect at all for the institution of marriage?

Exercising all his formidable powers of restraint, Mr. Invisible followed them.

Disgustingly intertwined, they fell upon *my* marriage bed (that I myself had helpfully carried into this very apartment) and proceeded to grapple and writhe upon its hallowed surface while struggling to remove each other's garments.

Yes, the evidence before my eyes could not be denied: Peter the Presumptuous proposed to screw my wife, a woman the law still recognized as my lawful spouse.

The disrobing continued. It became apparent that Peter had not spent the last six months on the beer and pizza diet. Hey, I could have abs like that if I wanted to devote all those hours to mindless exercise. And where was Rachel's institutional white nurse's bra? How come she never wore sexy lingerie like that for me?

My wife suddenly paused while unhooking her lacy Victoria Secret special. "Peter, have you been drinking?" she inquired.

"No, darling. Why do you ask?"

"I smell beer. It smells just like my ex-husband in here."

Well, excuse me for breathing!

While Peter was caressing my wife's now liberated breasts, Mr. Invisible slithered over to the night stand and discreetly pocketed the waiting condom. A few minutes later its sudden absence caused some momentary exasperation, but resourceful Peter retrieved a reserve rubber from his wallet. This he handed to my wife, who proceeded without embarrassment to unroll it over his excessively flamboyant erection. OK, now matters had definitely crossed over the line.

Having treated many rape victims over the years, my wife was the sort of gal who took precautions. I waited until they were thoroughly distracted, then reached under the bed and retrieved the aluminum baseball bat that Rachel wisely kept close at hand for protection. This Mr. Invisible raised far over his head and brought down as forcefully as possible–Tanya Harding style–on what he gauged to be the former patient's still-tender leg. This action produced a very loud, prolonged, and satisfyingly blood-curdling scream of agony, during which Mr. Invisible dropped the bat and made a hasty exit from the apartment. On his way out of the building he paused to push several of the more obnoxious-looking Young Singles into the pool. No, he was not a fellow to be trifled with.

# Chapter 3

I awoke the next morning profoundly depressed. My wife had a boyfriend. Well, she was an attractive woman, and I'm sure guys were always pestering her for dates. I myself had devoted many frustrating years to that very activity. It should not come as a major shock that she had hooked up with someone new.

Fuck!

The only thing I ever wanted in my entire life was Rachel Burke. All the rest I could dismiss with a casual wave. I had her too and then I blew it big time. Life had handed me a window of unstructured time and I couldn't handle it.

Somehow I crawled out of bed. I shuffled through the condo and looked around. It would take a hard-working crew scrubbing for weeks just to get this place back merely to squalid. It smelled rank–nearly as rank as I did. Nowhere in its 958 square feet was a stitch of clean laundry. Even Bob looked depressed. After two days of inactivity, he was going into dog-park withdrawal.

OK, it was time to Face Facts. I was on an express train to Skid Row. If I didn't hop off now, in a month or two I could be sleeping in a doorway somewhere and sucking my nourishment out of a brown-paper sack.

It was time to put Mr. Invisible in charge of my life.

It was time to wrap his invisible fingers around great wads of cold cash.

Let me emphasize here that never before had I contemplated a life of crime. As a reporter I covered many trials and encountered many criminals. With a few exceptions they were a dreary lot of mental dullards. The guys who committed property crimes usually had records as long as their tattooed arms. Yet somehow they optimistically assumed they would get away with that next perfect robbery, burglary, or stickup. They seemed genuinely surprised when things went awry, and the cops nailed their sorry asses. They rotated in and out of prison like rubber ducks in a carnival game. So, how was I any different?

Well, call me egotistical, but I believed I had just bit more on the ball. And I had the services of the most invisible accomplice in the history of crime.

Like the immortal Willie Sutton, I decided to go where the money was. Naturally, I chose the closest branch of the stuffy, exploitative, and foreclosure-happy bank that held our condo mortgage. It occupied a major corner in downtown Pasadena. Best of all, it was floored throughout in expensive and unyielding (like a banker's heart) terrazzo.

Mr. Invisible waltzed in behind a little old lady. My invisible shirt was unbuttoned down to my navel and firmly tucked into my cargo shorts. I had plenty of places to stash tidy packets of $100 bills. On my hands were rubber gloves I'd found under our kitchen sink. Long ago, believe or not, I'd actually washed dishes with them.

The bank was not bustling. There were a few customers at teller windows and only the little old lady in line. No guards in sight. Pasadena was not a hotbed of crime. The first problem was getting beyond the counter; access to which was through the usual locked door controlled by a buzzer release. After waiting nearly 20 minutes for someone to go through the damn door, I said fuck that, and laboriously and silently (I hoped) climbed over a vacant teller window. Geez, who did they think Mr. Invisible was–Douglas Fairbanks?

Jackie Chan?

After getting my breathing under control (this was the most exercise I'd done in months), I slithered over to the vault, the impressive polished door of which was invitingly ajar.

Yes, the vault was open, but everything inside it was LOCKED up like Fort Knox. You'd think they'd leave a few thousand out in the open for convenient access by the tellers. Too bad Mr. Invisible didn't know how to pick locks. OK, I'd have to help myself to the tellers' cash.

This, I soon discovered, was easier said than done. In between customers, the tellers locked their fucking cash drawers. Damn, the paranoia ran deep in this bank. It appeared that no one trusted anyone. And these were the people we tried to negotiate with when our adjustable condo loan reset to an even more usurious rate. Talk about wasting our time.

Having come this far, I wasn't about to settle for a complimentary ballpoint pen. I waited until a teller had his cash drawer open, then pushed over a stand holding a large laser printer. *Crash!* While everyone looked over to see what the commotion was about, I grabbed as much cash as I could and headed toward the access door. A concerned bank official got buzzed through and I charged out the other way. For several long, scary minutes I had to cool my heels beside the big bronze entry door until the next customer came through and I could sneak out.

Damn, crime is nerve-wracking. I committed a major felony, but all I netted was a measly $712. To make a decent living at that rate, I'd have to knock off a bank a day. And how long would it be before all the banks started bolting down their office equipment? At least I got out of the bank without grabbing any of that booby-trapped loot they have in reserve to hand over to more-conventional stickup artists. So far, my $712 hasn't blown up and sprayed me with caustic blue dye.

I blew some of my take on soap, shampoo, and laundry

detergent. Time to heave another load into the dryer. Only about 18 more to go. I briefly eyed the vacuum cleaner, but decided things had deteriorated far past its ability to perform anything useful. I did take out quite a bit of the accumulated garbage. Some of the overflow I had to dump in my neighbor's can.

Over 24 hours now without a beer. Jesus, sobriety can be a trial. Considering that booze had sent both my parents to an early grave, I probably never should have taken that first drink. But how many teetotalers do you find in city newsrooms?

After a shower and shave, Mr. Invisible made me walk nearly a mile to Denny's for a hearty breakfast. My crime made Page 4 of the *L.A. Times* Metro section. The headline read: "Mystery Bank Robbery in Pasadena." The story reported that an undisclosed "but reportedly large" sum of money had disappeared from the bank without any of its employees or customers having spotted the alleged bandit, although "suspicious activity" was seen later on one surveillance video. (Probably the $712 rising up and disappearing into thin air.) The "mystifying circumstances" were now being investigated by the FBI.

Great, now I've got the feds on my trail. I patted my back pocket. Nope, I hadn't done anything spectacularly stupid like dropping my wallet while bounding over that counter.

I got a long-overdue haircut, then dropped by the dog park with Bob. The regulars were happy to see us, but quite a few of them objected to Bob's "boring" new name. I told them to ferk my gherk and stretched out on my favorite donor lawn chair. I reached down automatically for a cold one, then remembered my new regimen of sober enterprise. So I leaned back in the sun and contemplated my next criminal act.

OK, if I sent Mr. Invisible into Tiffany's, he could (probably) snatch a major gem or two. Then what? How would I fence them? Hanging out all day at the Glendale dog park is not the best way to cultivate underworld connections. I could drop a dazzling zircon on my wayward bride as a reconciliation gesture, but she'd want to know where I got the funds to buy it.

Or, Mr. Invisible could loiter in some swanky store until after closing time, then heist furs, Rolexes, gold coins, and other marketable items at his leisure. Except these stores have sophisticated security systems. Mr. Invisible's flesh may be invisible, but his skin was still warm to the touch. No way he could go undetected by infra-red and motion sensors.

Unfortunately, these days invisibility didn't really offer that much of a leg up to your wannabe master criminal. Sure, it helps you duck the cops. Yes, it's handy for spying on adulterous spouses. But it doesn't afford much access to those golden storehouses of treasure. For that, you're better off graduating from Yale and going into bond trading.

Damn, crime was harder than it looked. No wonder the prisons were so full.

I met Rachel at 7 pm at the restaurant she suggested: a Turkish place on Verdugo Avenue. Though she had always loved tabooli, I never felt the need to overdose that strenuously on parsley. I think I surprised her with my sharp new appearance: neat haircut, well-pressed clothes, healthy dog-park tan. Too bad Mr. Invisible couldn't have managed a selective disappearance of the beer paunch. I surprised her even more with my beverage choice: sparkling water.

We chitchatted through a pleasant meal. I told her I had made some contacts and was in line to do some consulting work for a major media corporation. I didn't want to jinx things by being any more specific, but said I was well past the preliminary negotiations. I added that they sounded impressed so far with my ideas and suggestions.

I'm not sure Rachel bought any of that, but for a change she seemed upbeat about my prospects. I poured on the old

Axel Weston charm and even ate most of my falafel, although I knew I was risking a major gas attack later.

As we were finishing up with cups of Turkish coffee, Rachel reached into her oversized nurse's purse and brought out the dreaded papers.

"They're all ready to go, Axel. I've marked where you should sign them."

"Right. Good work, Rach. I was thinking we could, uh, postpone this. Say for a month."

I'd seen that frosty frown many times before.

"Axel we've discussed things and we've agreed this is for the best."

"Right, I know. It's just we had a good marriage for all those years. I know I screwed up lately, but I'm turning things around. I just want a second chance."

"We didn't have a good marriage, Axel. I hardly ever saw you. You were always out on assignments or off drinking with your newspaper buddies. The move to California was our second chance. It didn't work out. Things only got worse."

"I know. And for that you have my sincere apologies. I'm ready to sign those papers. In a month. That's all I ask."

"Axel, if you insist on this delay, I'll have to get a lawyer. She may not be as generous about the terms as I've been."

Damn, serious hardball tactics from sweet Rachel.

I didn't reach for my pen; she sighed, and put away the papers.

"Axel, do you have a key to my apartment?"

"No, darling. As I recall, you didn't feel your husband should have one."

"Have you been in my apartment recently?"

"Uh, not likely. Why do you ask?"

"A friend of mine was attacked the other night. He's in the hospital now."

"Well, did you *see* me attack him?"

"No. It was dark. We didn't see the assailant. He must have been hiding in the closet or under the bed. The Burbank police said in such cases it's usually the estranged husband."

"You called the cops!"

"Of course. It was a vicious assault." She handed me a business card. "Detective Myers of the Burbank police would like you to call him. That's his number."

"Jesus, Rachel, you move into a crime-infested building and all of a sudden I'm on the hook for mugging your boyfriend!"

"They just want to ask you some questions. No one's accusing you."

"So who is this guy?"

"He's just a friend."

"What does he do?"

"Uh, he's a film editor."

"Do you think he might read my screenplay?"

The guy's screwing my wife; the least he could do was read my script.

"Peter works in TV, not the movies. And he's not feeling very well disposed toward you at the moment."

"Jesus, honey, I'm Mr. Milquetoast. I hang out with puppies and dogs. I can't believe you think me capable of such an act."

"Well, who else could it have been?"

"How well do you know this Peter fellow? Perhaps it was his wife."

A flicker of doubt flashed across those arresting green-blue eyes. Interesting. Was it possible my wife was fooling around with a married man?

# Chapter 4

One of the (many) problems with sobriety is your libido tends to revive. Seeing Rachel yesterday reminded me of the innumerable luscious carnalities I was no longer enjoying. So much for my fantasy that after I picked up the check she'd invite me back to her place. Probably it was best that she hadn't. As it was, I nearly blew the roof off the condo last night digesting that falafel. No wonder Bob abandoned his usual spot at the foot of my bed.

I'm in no rush to call Detective Myers. Mr. Invisible and I are trying to stay away from policemen. I figured with their workload the Burbank cops wouldn't be devoting much effort to a simple assault with two eyewitnesses who hadn't seen a damn thing. No one gets their name in the papers for solving a case like that. Besides, is it such a crime to swat a lowlife who's nailing your wife? In some jurisdictions you could blow the guy away and receive a letter of commendation from the district attorney. Before I tossed the detective's card I entered his number into my home phone and cell phone–under "blocked numbers." I was getting more than enough harassment calls as it was.

I decided I was obsessing too much on the practicalities of crime. I was missing out on that fun and potentially lucrative category known as crimes of opportunity. And for opportunity with a capital O, I could think of no better place than nearby Beverly Hills.

By the time I lucked into a parking space around the corner from Rodeo Drive it was time for lunch. They had a spare table for one at Chez Rodeo, where I indulged in the medallion of filet mignon with lobster asparagus spring roll, gorgonzola mashed potatoes, and baby vegetables. The waiter recommended a French cabernet, but I stuck with the pricey sparkling water. I noticed Leonardo DiCaprio across the way was having the mango coconut bread pudding, so I finished off with the same. Not bad, but perhaps a little heavy. Regretfully, I couldn't linger long over my cappuccino because I had to pay a visit to the men's room, where Mr. Invisible took over. He exited discreetly to the street with Mr. DiCaprio's party. A lunch to remember and you couldn't beat the price.

I peeked into several boutique hotels, but was deterred by the sumptuous carpeting. Many of the posh designer stores, though, sported tasteful and inviting marble floors. Here Mr. Invisible felt right at home, especially in the privacy of the fitting rooms where the eager matrons paid little attention to their Gucci purses as they squirmed into that fetching $3,700 smock. The middle-aged nudity also helped to squelch my renascent libido. If that's what I'll be facing in some future bedroom, I can only hope fate strikes me blind by age 50.

In a shop called Grata I followed a woman into a dressing room only because she was young and beautiful. She had a clutch of dresses to try on and not much underwear in evidence under her clingy top. But she dumped the dresses on the bench and set to work with a small magnet to liberate a cashmere scarf from its security tag. Being invisible, I could stare at her without restraint or embarrassment. She had perfect bone structure and amazingly flawless skin as if she had been Photoshopped by God.

I had just reached into her purse when her cool hand came to rest on mind. She froze instantly.

"Oh, dear," she gasped. "Are you going to hurt me?"

"Not in a million years."

"I was, uh, going to get a mint."

"OK, I'll have one too."

We unclinched. Her long, slender hands were shaking as she unwrapped the roll and held out the exposed candy. I took one. She observed it rise up in the air and disappear.

"Are you a ghost?"

"Not hardly. Ghosts don't have warm hands."

"Are you thousands of years old?"

"I'm 37. How about you?"

"I'm 25. Today's my birthday in fact."

"Really?"

"Uh-huh."

"Well, congratulations. Say, where have I seen you before?"

"I've been in a few awful movies. I did a commercial for a mop."

"You're much too beautiful for housework."

"You could get a girl to marry you with a line like that."

"I'll keep that in mind. What's your name?"

"Desma. What's yours?"

"Axel."

"Axle like the car part?"

"Sort of. Different spelling. Are you going to steal that scarf?"

"Not steal it exactly. I prefer to think of it as a trade. I'll wear it to nice places and show off their label."

"How will you take it out of the store?"

"It's not very bulky. I'll put it up the sleeve of my jacket."

"Would you like me to carry it for you?"

"That would be very gentlemanly of you."

She handed me the scarf, which disappeared under my shirt.

"Desma, you should have something special for your birthday. This street is loaded with jewelers. Would you like me to swipe a bauble for you?"

"Oh, now you're teasing me."

"No, I'm serious. Tell me what you want and it's yours."

"Really?"

"Sure. Shall we adjourn to Cartiers?"

"Actually, there's a pin I've been admiring at Harry Weinstock."

"Then let us be off!"

We left the store and strolled around the corner. Harry Weinstock was carpeted throughout in a salt-and-pepper berber. Damn. But there was no backing out now; Desma had been promised her birthday bauble. I prayed my footfalls didn't show in the low pile. I also hoped the numerous ceiling-mounted cameras were not monitoring the infra-red spectrum. I followed Desma over to a glass showcase. As arranged, she let the corner of her new scarf fall briefly over her desired item, then sauntered away, looked casually into a few other cases, and exited the store.

It was a quite nice yellow diamond pin with a staggering price elegantly inked by hand on the attached tag. The case, of course, was locked. I moved in for a closer look. There was an electronic security dot on the back of the price tag and probably another one on the underside of the pin. Then I had a bit of luck. An older couple asked to see something in the same case, which a white-haired salesman obligingly unlocked. I reached in and closed my gloved fingers over the pin, causing it to disappear instantly. I quickly opened my shirt and transferred the pin into a small foil-lined bag that Desma had given me. Unlike Mr. Invisible, she was no amateur when it came to shoplifting. A few seconds later Desma reentered the store, casually holding open the door for her exiting accomplice. No alarms went off, no guns were drawn, my pounding heart did not burst an unsuspected aneurism in my brain.

We met up 10 minutes later in front of Bulgari; I grasped her arm lightly and we strolled down Olympic to a leafy old cemetery. We sat on a bench that overlooked an immaculately manicured lawn-bowling court being watered by energetic sprinklers. Desma clipped a bluetooth receiver to her ear so that anyone passing by would suppose she was conversing on her cell phone. She opened her purse and I dropped in the small foil bag.

"That was kind of scary, Axel. As I was leaving, I saw two big security guys detain a man and a woman."

"An older couple?"

"Uh-huh."

"They're probably strip-searching them now for your pin."

"Oh, dear. I hope not."

"Now, Desma, you have to promise me you will never tell anyone–not a soul–about me."

"Of course, I won't, Axel.  No one would believe me anyway."

Desma peeked into her purse.

"Oh, God, Axel, it's so beautiful. You know what I like about it?"

"What?"

"Those are yellow diamonds in a platinum setting, but everyone will assume they're measly citrine in white gold. I love fooling people."

"People like your husband?"

"People like my boyfriend."

"And what does he do?"

"He runs a hedge fund in Westwood. He lost a billion dollars last year."

"Wow. That must be rather stressful."

"Yeah, Tommy's kind of a mess."

Tommy was having a worse time than I was. That was comforting.

"Will he take you out tonight for your birthday?"

"I don't know. I hope so."

"Can I see you again, Desma?"

"Hey, I should be asking if *I* could see *you*."

She felt for my hand and wrote her cell phone number on my palm. The ink disappeared with every stroke of her pen. I touched her shoulder and kissed her lightly on her lips. She kissed me back with enthusiasm.

"Thanks for the greatest birthday ever, Axel."

"Don't mention it, kid. The pleasure was all mine."

When I got back to Glendale, Bob was jonesing for a walk, and a yellow notice had been stapled to my front door. According to the L.A. County Sheriff I have five days to exit the premises. Another typed notice slipped under the door advised me that the property had been sold at a foreclosure auction and that any goods or chattel remaining past the date of possession would be forfeited by me. I wondered what sort of masochistic speculator would buy my condo sight unseen. Boy, were they in for a surprise when they took possession. Now I felt entirely unmotivated to take out the vacuum–or the garbage.

I was on the Great American Countdown to Homelessness. After walking and feeding Bob, I sat down and counted the day's take. Not promising. Those affluent Rodeo Drive shoppers didn't carry much ready cash; I only scored a few bucks over $400. God, I needed a drink.

I heard a loud knock on the front door. I got up and peered out between the dusty mini blinds. Parked in front of my unit was a Burbank police car.

# Chapter 5

I could only assume that Detective Myers was pursuing the case because he–like countless other creeps–had the hots for my wife. No way was I going to open that door. I let Bob bark away by the door until the cop got bored and drove off. I suspected he'd be back.

It was time to bail.

I got my car and drove it into the garage. Then I loaded up everything I couldn't live without: some clothes, my laptop, a few file folders with birth certificate, passport, photos, college diploma, etc., some books I might reread someday, three pristine copies of my script, Bob's dish and food, and my cell phone (with Desma's newly entered number). Good-bye gracious condo living in Glendale. My last act before I left was to take a tire iron to my aging desktop computer. I found it curiously satisfying swinging away at its shattered electronic brains.

In a marginal neighborhood near Pico and Vermont I found an old building that rented out little furnished studios by the day, week, month, year, or century if you could afford it. I paid for three days in advance and had to slip an extra ten bucks to the elderly lady clerk to overlook my dog. She took a look at my car and recommended I get a steering wheel lock. Figuring it was sage counsel, I drove to Pep Boys right after I unpacked. Being car-less in L.A. is as desperate as life gets.

Settling into my tiny pad, I needed a drink in the worst way, but I resisted the urge. Someday I might want to present myself to Desma in the flesh, and I didn't want to look like the guy who swept her boyfriend's office floors. I wanted to look like the man who had dropped a high-five-figures diamond sparkler into her purse.

By the next morning I had formulated a plan. But I needed a camera. One of those thin little digital cameras that slip into a shirt pocket. The kind with a decent zoom lens and a high-resolution sensor. A video function might come in handy too, and low-light capability. Something small but expensive. Your basic miracle of technology from Japan. Most of all, it had to have a flash that could be switched off and a very quiet shutter.

I drove to West Hollywood to a big-box store called Fred's that advertised heavily in the *L.A. Times*. It's where I'd bought my laptop back when I was blowing my buyout bundle. The display cameras were all anchored to those little chains, but trusting Fred arrayed his inventory right out on open shelves. The camera I wanted was suitably small, but was packaged in a box that was–as expected–too bulky to conceal under my shirt. So I grabbed one, carried it into the men's room, removed the camera, software disc, and cables, secreted them about my person, dumped the packaging in the trash, said the words, and Mr. Invisible walked out of the store with the goods. The whole exercise had taken less than four minutes by my dashboard clock. Mr. Invisible was turning into a one-man crime wave.

I ate one of those make-your-own salad deals at a nearby supermarket, then spent some time reading in their magazine section. Before I drove back I called Desma to see how the rest of her birthday had turned out. A black man answered. He said I had called a Pentecostal church in Watts. There was no Desma at that address.

If there's one thing a decent reporter knows how to do it's find people. I took my laptop to a coffee shop with free WiFi and went to work. I found the mop commercial pretty fast and the number for the ad agency that created it. I called them and said I was a casting director looking for the pretty gal with the mop. They told me her name was Diane Phillips and gave me the name of her agent. I called that guy and identified myself as a grad student at USC film school. I said I was casting parts for a  film I was directing as my master's thesis. I told him I was impressed by a client of his named Diane Phillips and wondered if she would consider being in a student film. The guy was not dismissive, nor too eager to find out more since there was no money in it for him. He said he would pass my number to Diane and she would call me if she were interested. I thanked him and asked if he'd read a spec script of mine. He sighed and told me to email it to him. It never hurts to get your work out there.

The student-film ploy was not that much of a stretch. You'd be surprised at the number of name actors who turn up in student films. Actors want to work at their craft, and sometimes they endure long stretches when the phone never rings.

Diane called me that evening. She recognized my voice right away.

"Don't hang up. Please!" I implored.

"Hi, Axel," she sighed.

"So what's with the brush off, Diane?"

"The name is Desma. I'm changing it. Half the chicks in L.A. are named Diane."

"I thought we were friends."

"God, Axel, I was terrified the whole time I was with you."

"You were? You didn't look terrified."

"Well, I'm an actor. I mean, that's what actors do. They look calm when they're terrified."

"OK, I'm impressed with your acting skills. But why was I scaring you?"

"God, Axel you're fucking invisible! I mean freak me out!"

"Desma, I'm really quite a normal, average guy. I'm just invisible occasionally when the need arises."

"How do I know you're not trying to recruit me?"

"Recruit you for what?"

"You know–for being invisible. I work too hard to look the way I do to start being invisible. I mean, invisibility is not a look I'm trying to achieve."

"Desma, I couldn't make you invisible if I tried. I like you just the way you are. Do I sound like some kind of nut?"

"Hey, if you'd gone out with the men I've dated, you'd be cautious too."

"So are you really going out with a hedge-fund manager?"

"Nah, I broke up with Tommy a while ago. I couldn't compete with his Blackberry. I'm seeing this surgeon in Westwood who worked on my nose."

What is it with these surgeons? How come they got to monopolize all the gorgeous women?

"I thought Tommy was in Westwood."

"Nah, he's on a top floor in Century City."

"So did your surgeon take you out for your birthday?"

"Nah, Axel, my birthday's in March. I only told you it was my birthday yesterday so you wouldn't strangle me in that dressing room."

"Oh, wacko invisible maniacs don't kill people on their birthdays?"

"That was my earnest hope."

"Jesus, Desma, is there no hope for us?"

"I do sort of like you, Axel. I mean you're definitely not your boring Hollywood type. And I'm getting lots of compliments on your pin."

Desma said I could call her whenever I wanted, but she wasn't ready yet to risk seeing me again. She said invisibility made her nervous because she never knew what the guy was doing with his hands. I told her I could understand that and was fine taking things slowly. Anyway, I didn't want to meet her in the flesh until I'd worked off more of my beer gut.

My lovely wife Rachel called after that to warn me that Detective Myers was getting pissed that I hadn't contacted him yet. She also said she had spoken to a lawyer who sounded pretty confident she could secure a divorce decree entailing a "significant portion" of any and all my future earnings. I told her to do what she had to do, but I was only asking for one measly month's delay. I added that I loved her with all my heart.

"How come you never mentioned that when we were together?"

"I'm a newspaper man, Rach. Reporters bleed cynicism. We're not big on heartfelt expressions of sentiment. How's your boyfriend?"

"Peter's not my boyfriend. He's doing OK, considering. Detective Myers is checking out an employee he discharged last month."

"So his wife's in the clear?"

"His wife's Asian. She's a tiny little thing."

"Those people have connections, Rach. She could hire a thug with one phone call. You'd better be careful."

Rachel said she wasn't worried, but I sensed some uncertainty in her voice. And that I took as an encouraging sign.

# Chapter 6

After an early morning dog walk and sober breakfast, I got my stuff ready and drove up to Holmby Hills. This is part of L.A.'s "Platinum Triangle," where the elite of the elite live pampered lives that are the envy of millions. My destination was an address on South Mapleton Drive: the home of one of filmland's A-list power couples, who–the tabloids were screaming–were now riven asunder by domestic turmoil. Yeah, I know the feeling.

I parked a block away, ducked down in the seat, put on my equipment, and said the words. Mr. Invisible exited the car and walked uphill. It was risky having the car door open and close apparently unassisted, but I could think of no better alternative. The lots around there were huge and all the houses were hidden behind high walls or hedges. The street was as empty as my bank account.

About a dozen or so paparazzi were loitering around the power couple's driveway, which was blocked off by a tall electronic gate. Around their necks dangled cameras with telephoto lenses that could read billboards on Mars. These guys would do anything short of murder (or felony trespass) for a photograph. After about 45 minutes a ten-year-old Ford Escort pulled up in front of the gate. Its arrival failed to elicit any excitement, suggesting that the Hispanic-looking driver was a known employee or regular delivery person of some type. When the gate opened for the car, Mr. Invisible went up the drive right behind it.

I had examined the property via Google Earth, so I knew that the first impressive residence up the drive wasn't the main house. I didn't bother trying to get into that one. I heard some faint dog barking and hoped it was coming from next door. In preparation for possible dog encounters, I had worn my heaviest pants and filled my pockets with sausages. As a backup I had clipped a container of pepper spray to my belt.

The views across the city got more spectacular the higher I went up the drive, as did my pulse rate. Zoning board meetings back home were never this nerve-wracking. I stuck to the stone path as I circled around to the back of the main house. Footfalls in all that lush grass would be a dead give-away. I crossed a broad terrace and walked straight into the house. A half-dozen sliding doors had been pushed all the way open to embrace the morning sunshine. You could drive a truck right into their living room. Eighteen thousand square feet of luxury living, and I had yet to encounter even a scullery maid..

I found the man of the house running on a treadmill in a second-floor exercise room. He looked pretty much like he did on TV–maybe a little older, a little slighter of build. He was going at it full-tilt and working up quite a sweat. I had improvised a rig that strapped the camera flat against my forehead, figuring the lens would be pointing wherever I was looking. I reached up and got off a few shots. Not exactly exciting, but even the best pro photographers take many hundreds shots for every one that gets used.

Things got more interesting down the hall in the master bedroom. She had just gotten out of the shower and was swaddled in about ten yards of luxury toweling. A huge flat TV mounted across from the bed was tuned into a cooking show, helping obscure the sounds of my approach. Parked in front of a mirror at an immense vanity table, America's sweetheart (well, of the current TV season) was applying make-up to a vivid purple shiner. I snapped a photo, but knew I had to get closer. But how to get across that obscenely thick carpet? I tread on tiptoes, routing my way behind the overstuffed sofa and chairs. Fortunately for me, their decorator wasn't inclined toward the spare and austere. I got off three decent shots (I hoped), when her husband came into the room.

"I had Maria take photographs," she announced. "I'm adding them to your file."

"Add away, sweetheart," he said, stripping off his sweats. "But don't forget the file I've got on you."

"I would prefer you didn't shower in my bathroom," she said coldly, not glancing away from the mirror.

She didn't look, but Mr. Invisible did. I snapped several photos of the full, sweaty monty. "Don't be a bitch. You've got the only shower with a full body spray."

"What is that horrible smell?" she exclaimed. "What have you been eating?"

"I smell it too," he said, scratching his balls and sniffing the air. "It smells like garlic."

Uh-oh, had they detected Mr. Invisible's dog-appeasing sausages?

"Someone might be in the house," he said. "Where's that stupid guard?"

"Don't you remember? You fired him yesterday when he tried to halt your drunken assault upon my person?"

"I wasn't drunk," he said, following his nose in my direction. "You were the one who was falling down drunk."

Full panic mode. I backed away as the naked star of TV and screen crept closer. I couldn't believe he hadn't spotted my footfalls in the carpet.

"What *are* you doing?" she demanded.

He turned back toward her. "I'm getting a definite garlic aroma in this part of the room. Have you been screwing that damn Tony again?"

"I only wish I was! He's the only man that left me feeling really fulfilled."

"Yeah, well maybe you should have looked closer. He

was probably shoving a salami up there."

"I can't believe you just said that to me. You are the crudest man I've ever known!"

"Yeah, and you've known plenty. Let me tell you this, sister, you are . . ."

I didn't stay for the rest of the fight. Mr. Invisible backed silently out of the room and stole away. On my way out, I stopped by his room and peeled off most of a fat money roll I found in his pants. Mr. Invisible left behind the star's Rolex, his flashy ruby ring, and his Emmy. A guy can misplace some money, but if too much stuff goes missing, he'd know for sure he'd been robbed.

The photos came out better than I expected. I'd been worried that the light was too dim, but every detail and pubic hair were revealed with startling clarity. I slapped my watermark on three of the raw images and emailed them to Z77, the hottest photo agency in town. Ten minutes later a Brit named Jeremy phoned.

"Extraordinary pictures," he said, "But, of course, we can't sell them anywhere."

"I know."

"It's a prima facie case that you invaded their privacy. They'd sue in a heartbeat."

"I know."

"Extraordinary though. I recognized her bedroom from the spread in *Architectural Digest*."

"Yeah. I was up there this morning."

"And you lived to tell about it. God, that's incredible. The office here is in a complete uproar."

"That's nice."

"You don't say much, do you?"

"I hear Teresany is due this week. Any interest in some photos of the kid?"

"We could get six figures easy for a clear shot of the mother and baby."

"OK. You get me the name of the hospital, I'll get you the photos."

"Deal. Say, would you mind sending us today's photos without the watermarks? Just for our files."

"I'll send them after you pay me for the baby shots."

"Not any sooner?"

"Sorry."

"OK, I understand. And what's your full name, Axel?"

"Just call me Axel. I'll be awaiting your call."

"You got it."

I knew I couldn't sell the photos of the squabbling stars, but I figured they might help me get a foot in the door. The tricky part of the celebrity photo biz was grabbing shots that magazines could use without getting sued for violating privacy laws. I was also competing against millions of media-savvy folks, ever ready to whip out their cell-phone cameras should Reese and Jake come strolling hand-in-hand down Melrose.

With the assistance of an Emmy-winning actor, I paid for three more days of my bachelor pad. Then, to work off the flab, I took Bob for a long walk in the neighborhood. He enjoyed exploring leafy Rosedale Cemetery. It wasn't a hot-bed of deceased celebrities like other L.A. cemeteries, but we did spot the graves of Hattie McDaniel ("Gone with the Wind") and Dooley Wilson ("Casablanca"). While we were taking a break by the final resting spot of Tod Browning (director of "Freaks"), I got a call from Desma.

"I figured out why you want to be invisible, Axel."

"Oh?"

"It's because you're horribly disfigured like that guy in 'Phantom of the Opera'."

"Wrong."

"Well, then it's because you look like Boris Karloff. You're hideously ugly."

"You must have me confused with some of your other

boyfriends, Desma. I look fine. Nobody ever runs away screaming when I show up. Speaking of being terrified, if you were so scared the other day, why didn't you escape while I was busy in that jewelry store?"

"Don't be dense, Axel. The reason is pinned over my left breast."

"Do I detect some gold-digging here, Desma?"

"A girl on her own has to look out for her security, Axel."

"Right. So how's your surgeon?"

"Steven treats me like a queen."

"I'll bet he's 53 and has erectile issues. Is he married?"

"Are you married?"

"I asked you first."

"Yeah, he's sort of married. And you are . . ?"

"Getting a divorce as we speak."

"Uh-oh. Well, if she takes you to the cleaners, you can forget about me."

"You're all heart, Desma."

"Is your wife invisible too?"

"Sure. When we make love all you see is the mattress bouncing around."

"Really?"

"No. I'm kidding. So, are you working up the courage to see me again?"

"Maybe. One of these days. I never got it on with an invisible man before."

"Believe me, kiddo, you have no idea what you're missing."

# Chapter 7

My cell phone woke me in the middle of the night. It was Jeremy the Brit.

"We just got the news, Axel. The coroner has released the body of Briny X."

"Right. OK."

Briny X was a rapper, previously unknown to me, but apparently verging on superstardom, who had gone down in a drive-by a few days earlier. I had read about it in the *Times*. In my darkest days of despondent drunkenness, I faithfully read the *Los Angeles Times* every morning. It was a far better paper than the one I had worked for. Even through changes of ownership and a subsequent bankruptcy, it sailed serenely on in its majestic excellence.

"They've taken it to a funeral home in South Central on East Slauson. We could get you at least 25 Gs for a pix of the body in the box. Probably more if a bullet hole was visible."

Since rappers had a history of surviving such attacks, the still-at-large shooter had taken extra pains with Briny X. He had pumped in a total of 108 slugs. Already, there was a tribute song out titled "Mr. 108."

"What's the address?" I asked.

Jeremy gave me the number and said it would probably be a madhouse there by daybreak.

"OK, I'm on my way there now."

"Good luck, Axel. Briny's crew is out in force, so you

may have some trouble getting in."

"Not to worry. I'll handle it."

"Are you by any chance black?"

"No, but I've got everything under control."

"I admire your confidence, Axel."

"Talk to you later, Jeremy."

The funeral parlor was in a section of L.A. that not many white people drive to at 2:30 in the morning. I parked a half-block away, attached the steering-wheel lock, strapped on my camera, and said the words. Mr. Invisible took the time to lock the car door even though it meant the keys would be briefly visible. But I figured not many people would be gazing my way. Across the street it looked like a Hollywood premiere was underway: milling crowds, TV news vans, police cars with flashing lights, gangsta-types roaring up and down on throbbing Harleys. In his 23 years Briny X had created enough of a stir to go out in a very big way.

Mr. Invisible did not like crowds. People could freak bumping into someone they couldn't see. My first tactic was to circle around to the side door under the porte cochere.Only three black dudes with guns were guarding it (a phalanx of eight were blocking the front door). The low moon must have been hurting their eyes since they were all wearing sunglasses. I got past the guards, but found the door was locked. There might have been a back door, but the driveway to the rear where the funeral cars were parked was closed off by a chained gate and fence topped with razor wire. My only recourse was to try the front door.

I decided to go through the crowd where the milling throngs were most jammed together. In such a crush there might be better hope for anonymity. I edged my way through, receiving numerous rude elbowings for my trouble. One woman screamed as I slid by–pressed forcefully against her frontal curves–but I didn't stick around to apologize. When I got to the entrance, there was just enough room to slither between the stucco facade and a 300-pound leather-jacketed man gripping an Uzi.

Mr. Invisible's new theory on entering buildings: swing open the door, dart through, and leave it ajar. That way, observers might suppose a sudden breeze had blown the door open. Anyway, it worked this time; I was inside and treading on thick carpet.

I stayed against a wall and made my way down the dimly lit central corridor. The open casket was on a bier in a large receiving room. Three women and two men were huddled in chairs around it. The older woman I assumed was the mother, although she didn't look much past my age. The others could have been sisters, girlfriends, brothers, cousins, etc. They all looked stunned with grief.

As a reporter, I had become somewhat inured to intruding on families who had just lost loved ones. That was my job. But Mr. Invisible was there merely for the bucks. OK, I was a low-life creep, but $25,000 could solve a lot of my problems. And I was in a public place. Any pictures I took were legal to sell.

The room, though, was practically dark. The only light was from four candles–a pair on tall bronze floor stands at each end of the casket. The body in the casket was dark skinned. Taking a photo in this light would be like photographing the inside of my shoe at midnight inside a cave. I scoped out the situation. There were two big overhead chandeliers and a wall switch by the doorway to the corridor. Well, I had to give it a shot. I tiptoed over and flipped the switch. The chandeliers blazed with light. Before I could get off a shot, one of the male mourners hissed, "What the fuck?" and got up and switched off the lights.

Damn.

Time to go to Plan B.

As soon as I thought of one.

OK, I was now officially desperate. I needed the money, and I was thoroughly unscrupulous. Any sense of moral decency had withered away long ago. If this didn't work out, I was facing life on Skid Row. I would lose Rachel forever. I was ready for Plan B.

I reached up and activated the auto flash. I edged as close to the casket as I could get. To correct for parallax I aimed my head at the windsor knot in the late Briny X's silk tie. Holding my torso rigid, I screamed in my highest falsetto, "I see the light, Mama!" and pressed the camera button. The flash fired, the shutter clicked, and pandemonium broke out.

In the whirl of invading bodyguards, cops, morticians, embalmers, and God knows who else, Mr. Invisible was knocked off his feet. The camera rig flew off my head. More than a few people stepped on my prostrate body in the dim light. A woman was screaming, "My baby! My baby! My baby sent me a sign!" Then someone switched on the chandeliers. Still on my hands and knees, I scrambled around desperately for my camera. I spotted it at last under an L.A. cop's large shoe. I gave the cop a vicious poke, grabbed the camera, stuffed it under my shirt, and took refuge under the bier. At that moment, someone entered with a large, growling pit bull on a flimsy chain. I shot out from under the casket, knocked an elderly mortician flat on his back, tumbled over several newly arrived jumbo memorial wreathes, recovered my footing, and wove my way along the corridor toward the open door.

There's no question about it. God put the Japanese on earth to build cameras. My one and only shot of the body in the box was a winner. The lighting was harsh, but I preferred to think of it as dramatically stark. The sophisticated facial recognition software had focused precisely on the face in repose. Since the subject was deceased, no red-eye correction was required. Whoever did the make-up on the corpse had tried their best, but I counted four distinct bullet holes. Jeremy claimed he could make out six. He said he practically wet his pants when my email arrived.

Sure, Briny X was no Michael Jackson, but the bidding that morning got pretty spirited. By the end of the day, I was due nearly $70,000. Jeremy wired an immediate $10,000 into my long-languishing bank account, and promised to have the balance by the end of the week.

Being invisible was starting to pay. And not a moment too soon.

I instructed Jeremy to credit the photo to H.G. Swell. By that evening the decedent's brother had started a Facebook page titled "One Million Friends of Briny X Who Want To See the Slimebag H.G. Swell Die a Horrible Death."

# Chapter 8

The next few days I spent rising from the gutter. I paid off my car loan (the finance company was amazed), so I wouldn't have to worry about losing my wheels. I saw no reason to pay off the credit cards, since they had all been canceled and, what with the condo debacle, my credit was wrecked anyway. Perhaps next time those companies will be a little more cautious about getting $37,000 into the hole with an obvious deadbeat.

I found a decent one-bedroom apartment in a big new building in West L.A. near the border with Santa Monica. I was hoping Desma would appreciate its proximity to Westwood. It was a spec building that had been finished right as the housing market collapsed. The management was so desperate for tenants they were willing to overlook my "free-lance" employment status and credit report from hell. It helped that Claudia, the leasing agent/manager, loved dogs and took a shine to Bob. She also appeared to take a shine to me. I needed it bad, but I wasn't sure I was ready to date a woman built like an exceptionally tall linebacker.

My new apartment was the last one off a second-floor corridor. The entry door was around a corner, so no one would be able to observe me or Mr. Invisible come and go. Only two other apartments on that floor appeared to be occupied.

Of course, I had no furniture–not even a bed. Unlike

me, my wife always enjoyed shopping for furniture. I thought helping me furnish my apartment might be a good way to reconnect. Rachel didn't answer her cell phone, so I left her an upbeat message with the pertinent details. A few hours later I emailed her with my new address and asked her to call me. Then I went to Ikea and bought a futon, a knock-down desk, bathroom scale, and lamp. While I put the desk together, Bob sniffed out all the corners and plopped down on the fake wood floor in the setting sun. He was moved in.

That evening I got a curt email from Rachel informing me that her attorney advised her not to accept any more calls from me. Most important, she was not to see or meet with me under any circumstances. Typical. Lawyers like to make things ugly just so they can jack up their fees. I saw no reason for our relations to become so adversarial. I called Rachel at home to make that very point, but got a message saying her number was no longer in service.

When you're standing at the altar with your bride, you never imagine that some day it could all come crashing down to this.

Teresany had her baby a few nights later. All those years of hanging out in hospitals with Rachel paid off big time for Mr. Invisible. He knew where to go and how to sneak by security. Not only did he get many remarkable candids of mother and new daughter, he captured several dramatic shots of the newest little celebrity navigating her way through the birth canal. Best of all, I got some shots (unintentionally as it turned out) of the rumored father-to-be, who had been es-corted clandestinely in through some side entrance. Jeremy said he "tingled all over" when he saw that the fellow was heavily disguised. What a development! Jeremy insisted I tell him how I had gained such unprecedented access.

"It's all a matter of your approach," I replied. "I make a very credible-looking obstetrician."

Unlike Briny X, Teresany was so famous that even I had

heard of her. The bidding could only be described as frenzied. My share was up to $218,000, and Jeremy reported he still had offers dribbling in from places like Tasmania and Chad.

I was feeling so flush I went out and bought a king-size bed and $1800 in linens and towels. I was picking dog hair off the new duvet when Desma called.

"Axel, were you in Van Nuys recently?"

"No. Why do you ask?"

"I heard on the news some woman out there got strangled."

"Not me, Desma. I make it a point never to kill people in the Valley."

"I saw you on Youtube, Axel."

"I doubt that."

"No, Myron told me about this video, so I watched it. It was from some bank in Pasadena. You could see money rising up and disappearing."

Well, that was unsettling news. What was the FBI up to in letting that tape get out?

"Are you going to turn me in for the reward?"

"Oh, that's a thought, Axel."

"Not advisable, Desma darling. I'd have to snitch on you in for receiving stolen property. And who's Myron?"

"He's an attorney in Westwood. I went to the symphony with him last night. Myron likes to take me to classy places, unlike you."

"What happened to Steve, your Westwood surgeon?"

"Steve's in Studio City. Myron's in Westwood. And who said a girl can't go out with more than one fellow? You should hope I date multiple guys!"

"No, I just want you to date me. I'm practically in Westwood myself now."

I told Desma about my new apartment and my brand new, unbroken-in bed.

"I'm dying to take you to classy places, Desma. You know that."

"Yes, but would I be dying for real if I went out with you? Oh, I got another commercial."

"What's this one?"

"For a stain remover, can you believe that? I never, ever leave my place unless I'm totally together in this perfect package, and some account executive decides I'm a girl who looks like I have a bad problem with stains."

"Life is unfair, Desma. How about dinner on Friday?"

"I'll think about it. Myron said he's going to get me a little gun. He's worried about me, unlike you. If I get my gun by Friday, I might let you take me out."

"That's the best news I've heard all day, darling."

"It might be hard to shoot an invisible man. I hope I don't blast someone else by mistake."

"We'll work it out, Desma. See you on Friday."

"Maybe."

Even though I had a nice (though nearly bare) apartment, a brand new bed, luxury sheets, and money in the bank, I wasn't sleeping well at night. I closed my eyes, and all I could think about was my wayward wife. I realized that Rachel regarded my refusal to talk to that Burbank cop as an admission of guilt. The complicating factor was that I was indeed guilty. I had gotten into the usual neighborhood scraps as a kid, but I had never before attacked or hurt anyone as an adult. Looking back now on that night in her apartment, I can barely believe what I did. Of course, I wasn't entirely sober. But I think I was more drunk with the power of being invisible. Who has the strength of character to resist taking a free swing at a perceived enemy if they thought they could get away with it under the cover of invisibility?

I couldn't admit my guilt either. If Rachel knew for certain I had broken into her apartment, lain in wait (neither technically true), spied on her during intimate acts, and then attacked her boyfriend, she would be done with me forever. She and her divorce lawyer would demand my scalp and all the rest of my sorry hide. Somehow I had to convince her that I was innocent. What I needed was an alibi.

People call lawyers dogs, but the reverse is just as true. If you do something nice for a dog in his mind you have established a Precedent. He believes you are legally required to repeat that act every day *ad infinitum*. Bob certainly felt that way about trips to the dog park. So he was only getting what was rightfully his when I fought my way through heavy traffic for a long-overdue reappearance at the Glendale dog park. As Bob romped off with his buddies, I dragged over a donor lawn chair and sat down beside my old pal Gus.

"Hi, Gus."

"Hi, Axel. Where's the cooler?"

Gus had mooched innumerable beers off me in the past.

"I'm on the wagon, Gus. I'm getting back in shape."

"For what?"

"Uh, life I guess."

Gus Baboo was a chronically underemployed towel jockey at a car wash on Victory Boulevard. He was somewhere around my age and lived in his mother's garage with a large slobbering Rottweiler named Princess. I have no doubt with a little coaching Princess could outscore Gus on a standard I.Q. test. Gus was the last man on the car wash's reserve list. Whenever they were desperately short of towel flappers, they'd give him a call.

Like Lana Turner at MGM during the 1940s, Princess was the Queen of the Lot. All of the other dogs deferred to her. And because Princess was sweet on Bob, he got a free pass from the bigger dogs. Nobody messed with Bob.

"Gus, how would you like to make $1,000?"

"Sure, Axel. Where you want me dump the body?"

So I laid out my proposition: he was to confirm with a certain Burbank cop that on the evening of June 18 I was with him at the dog park.

"Be my pleasure, Axel. You don't have to pay me for that."

"No, I want to, Gus. Now, we need to make your story credible. You say you remember it was the 18th because that is your dog's birthday, and I'd brought her a special birthday treat."

"I don't know, Axel. Princess's birthday is in November. Anybody who looks at her can tell she's a Sagittarius. She's *always* in command."

"Right, well, I don't think the cop will be paying that much attention to your dog."

"So what did you do, Axel?"

"Uh, nothing. A friend of my wife's got mugged. I was home watching TV, but it's better to have someone else confirm my story."

"Yeah, I get it."

"Now, Gus, we don't want you to sound too rehearsed."

"What's that mean?"

"Well, when the cop asks you about June 18, you take a moment or two to remember that it was your dog's birthday."

"But Princess's birthday is in November."

"Right, but we're *pretending* it's in June."

"Oh, pretending–right, I get it."

I then amazed Gus by taking out my wallet and handing him five $100 bills.

"That's half the money, Gus. If you do what I say and the cop believes your story, I'll give you another $500."

"In cash?"

"In cash, Gus. I promise. And what are we *not* going to tell the cop?"

"That Princess is a Sagittarius?"

"Yes. And we're not going to mention the money either."

"Oh, right."

"And we're not going to tell the cop that I talked to you about what to say."

"Sure, Axel. I get it."

Just to be on the safe side, we spent the next half hour role-playing the interview where I was Detective Myers and Gus was himself. It was a stretch for him, but he was almost credible in that role.

Needless to say, Bob was incredulous that he didn't get to spend the *entire* day at the dog park. That was the precedent and that was his right. Princess thought so too. She growled and bared her fangs at me as I dragged away my protesting pup.

After another salad-laden diet lunch, I sat in my car in a Glendale strip mall and phoned Detective Myers.

"You took your time contacting me," he said, sounding none too friendly. "I was about to put a warrant out for your arrest."

"Sorry, officer. I've had a lot on my plate. My condo got sold in a foreclosure auction and I just got evicted."

I heard the sound of shuffling papers as he located Rachel's file.

"Your ex-wife said you helped her move into her place."

"Well, Rachel's not technically my ex-wife yet, but, yes, I did move most of her things."

"And you had the key to her apartment one day while she was at work?"

"Yes, I was moving her kitchen stuff that day. I was being very nice and helpful about the separation."

"So you had an opportunity to copy her apartment key?"

"Well, her building has had a problem with break-ins. As I recall, all of the apartment keys are stamped Do Not Copy."

Which is precisely why I *hadn't* made a copy of her key that day.

"OK, I'll check with Ms. Weston about that. And do you recall your whereabouts that evening?"

"What day was that?"

"June 18, hours five to seven p.m."

"Uh, gosh, that was a while ago. Well, let's see, I was probably at the Glendale dog park. I try to be considerate of my dog as well as my wife. Oh, yes, now I recall. . ."

So I laid the dog birthday party alibi on him. He had me spell out Gus's name and repeat his phone number.

"Have you discussed this with Mr. Baboo?"

"Uh, well I do recall mentioning the attack to him when I heard about it. I'm not sure he'd remember. Gus isn't the brightest bulb in the pack."

"Did you know your wife was seeing another man?"

"No, uh, I had no idea. She hadn't mentioned it. The first time I heard about it was when she told me about the attack."

"Did you suspect she was seeing someone else?"

"Not at all, officer. I understood our separation was only temporary until I became employed again, which thankfully I now am."

"How do you feel about your wife seeing another man?"

How do you think I feel about it, you fucking idiot?

"Uh, well, I guess that's her choice. I've always been something of a champion of women's rights. I wish her all the best. I always have."

"Uh-huh, well, I'll be in touch, Mr. Weston. And please, unblock my number on your phone."

"Gosh, officer. I don't know how that happened. These cell phones are so complicated nowadays."

"Right."

God, do I need a drink. I wonder how many alcoholic binges result from conversations with nosy police detectives?

# Chapter 9

My chat with that skeptical cop did not improve my sleep. After a very restless night I rolled out of bed around dawn. Although the apartment was advertised as "quiet," I could hear the din of traffic on I-405 a few blocks away. I felt like taking a walk, so I hiked into Santa Monica on Pico to have breakfast at Rae's diner. As I was approaching the restaurant, someone behind me said, "Yo, buddy." I turned around and tall guy with a greasy mullet haircut smashed a steel pipe into my left leg. He hit me on the shin right below the knee. I dropped like a stone to the sidewalk in an explosion of pain. It was a true Nancy Kerrigan moment.

A waitress at Rae's called 9-1-1. Eventually an ambulance showed up and took me to Santa Monica Presbyterian Hospital. Every jolt in the road was like a knife through my leg. I wasn't Presbyterian, which may be why the admitting clerk asked me so many questions about health insurance and finances as I writhed in agony in their emergency room. I formerly had insurance through Rachel's job, but I wasn't sure if she'd been keeping up the matching payments. I certainly hadn't. So they called Rachel at her hospital, which took a while to track her down. Meanwhile, my battered leg continued to throb and swell. At some point I passed out.

I came to in the X-ray room. A doctor said my wife was on her way and to try not to move. He'd given me an injection for the pain, so after that details began to swim. At some point, hours later, I talked to a Santa Monica policewoman. I recall she was quite attractive, but the rest is pretty much a blur.

It was past dinner time when I walked out of there–on crutches. They'd wanted to put me in a  full-leg plaster cast, but I refused. Rachel looked at the X-rays and said I was lucky it was just a hairline fracture of the tibia and not a full break. So they fitted me with one of those removable plastic cast walkers, and I hobbled out to her car.

We didn't say much on the drive to my apartment. I thanked her for taking off from her job and inquired if I had any health insurance. I didn't. She had charged my initial hospital bill to her credit card. I said I'd write her a check for the amount and added that the check would be good. Bob was overjoyed to see us, since he'd had a long, lonely wait for breakfast and a walk. He also missed his mom.

Rachel fed and walked the pup while I zoned out on the futon. Then she checked my refrigerator, sighed, and hit a nearby supermarket for two big bags of frozen microwave meals and some fruit.

She zapped a pair of Stouffers. I had no plates, but Rachel scrounged up a couple of plastic forks from the bottom of her nurse's purse. We sat at either end of my futon and dined out of the plastic containers by the light of my only lamp.

When she finished, she put down her fork and looked over at me. "The way you're getting money now, Axel, are you doing anything illegal?"

"Not at all, Rachel. I have no enemies in the underworld, if that's what you're thinking. I am not a drug lord."

"OK. I'll talk to Peter about this."

"You do that. Did you tell him my address?"

"No."

"Could he have seen any of your emails–on your phone, for example?"

"I don't know. Possibly. I've got to go. Will you be OK?"

"Sure. I'm a quick healer. And thanks for all your help."

I wrote her the check and added another $100 to the

total for the groceries. Rachel didn't kiss me good-bye. Instead, on her way out, she fished the divorce papers from her purse.

"If you sign these, Axel, I'll fire my lawyer. We can still do it the way we originally talked about."

"I'll think about it, Rach. I'm a little too groggy now from the painkillers to decide whether to terminate my marriage."

"It's already terminated, Axel. All that's left is the paperwork."

So I signed the papers.

I wasn't giving up on Rachel, but I had to get her crazed beast of a lawyer off my back.

Lots of couples get divorced and then remarry. It happens all the time. Some diehard couples do it more than once. I once wrote a Valentine's day feature story on former high school sweethearts who had split and remarried three times. They claimed they always loved each other, but had let those little nagging problems build up.

I decided to view this first temporary divorce as a means of opening the marital pressure-relief valve. I think it's working too. When I asked my wife for a pen, it was the first time I'd seen her crack a smile all day. Come to think of it, that may have been the first time she'd smiled at me in months.

I'd been hoping for morphine, but the Presbyterians were willing to prescribe only Tylenol with codeine. Still, if you swallow enough of them, you can sleep with five pounds of constricting plastic clamped to your very sore leg. I slept like a dead person, then underwent 15 minutes of medieval torture in the bathroom shower. Claudia, the outsized apartment manager, came to my rescue on Bob walks. She's volunteered for four a day. Very nice of her, but let's face it, they can both use the exercise.

The crutch, as an assist to walking, has not been materially improved since 3000 B.C. I can sort of get around, but twice I lost my balance and nearly fell flat on my face. So I spent 99 percent of the day in bed with my leg elevated. I wasn't too bored; the phone rang every five minutes.

The Santa Monica policewoman with the sexy voice called to ask if she could bring over some mugshot books of local hoodlums. I said I had glimpsed the guy for less than a second and wouldn't recognize him if he were standing next to me with a steel pipe. True, but what really deterred me was the wedding ring on her left hand. She said nobody in the neighborhood had seen him get into a car or had helpfully noted down a license plate number. And he hadn't dropped his weapon, so there was no fingerprint evidence. Who says there's no such thing as the perfect crime? I thanked her for her efforts, and said I would call her if I happened to think of anyone who might want to bash in my leg.

Then Jeremy called with a hot assignment. One of filmdom's most notorious Bad Boys had wrecked his Jag while DUI, then been whisked away to a clinic for a drying out. Jeremy wanted me to drive out to Rancho Mirage to score some photos of the star sipping his carrot juice in the meditation room, vacuuming floors, swabbing toilets, etc. I declined for medical reasons and then had to describe in great detail the attack and its gruesome aftermath. Jeremy was thrilled as usual, and is even more convinced that I am a man of mystery and danger. He told me to heal fast so I could "once again knock this town on its ass."

Next, I got a call from Detective Myers. He said he had spoken with "your Mr. Baboo" and had one followup question: Why were we having a birthday party in June for a Rottweiler if the dog was a Sagittarius?

I had to think fast on that one. Damn that Gus.

"Er, I must have misspoke, officer. We weren't actually having the party. We had gotten together that night to *plan* the party."

"You were planning a dog's birthday party five months in advance?"

"Uh, you'd understand that if you were an animal lover."

"Right. By the way, Mr. Weston, I hear you received a

swat to your own leg yesterday."

"That's right," I chuckled nervously. "I'm flat on my back with my leg in a cast."

"Well, sometimes when there's not enough evidence in a case, vigilante justice is just what people deserve."

I saw no reason to lie there and listen to some cop gloat over my broken leg.

"Is there anything else, officer?" I asked coldly.

"Nope. Have a nice day."

I had assumed Rachel's buffed film editor was behind the attack. Could it be the Burbank Police department had in its employ a pipe-swinging thug ready to do Detective Myers's bidding? Was it in any way significant that I'd been Crippled on Pico (C.O.P.)? Just how stuck was that detective on my wife?

Yesterday at the hospital I had contemplated sending Mr. Invisible after Rachel's boyfriend again–once I got well enough to walk. Who knows, we could bash each other back and forth until we were both double amputees. Retribution definitely was required. But against whom?

Gus Baboo called after that to apologize for blowing the cop interview.

"I changed my story and said my mom was also named Princess and she was the Sagittarius. Did he buy it?"

"Apparently not, Gus. But that's OK. You did your best."

I told him about my broken leg and said I would have to send him a check for the second $500 because I couldn't drive. He said he'd drive me anywhere I wanted to go, and I could pay him the $500 at the rate of 20 bucks an hour for his time. I told him I'd keep his offer in mind.

I snoozed for about ten minutes, and then Claudia entered with her passkey with a nice boxed lunch for the invalid. That gal is so thoughtful. She must be older than I first thought. She confessed to having a 30-year obsession with David Cassidy, the former "Partridge Family" star. She knows every detail of his personal life and believes she owns the world's largest collection of David Cassidy photos, magazine clippings, commemorative plates, and other memorabilia. She told me how David had broken his own manly leg once and how long to the day he'd been on crutches. I decided she would be a valuable resource for Mr. Invisible should David find himself at the center of some photo-worthy media storm.

While Claudia was playing with Bob, Rachel called to tell me she had taken off from work again to hand in the signed divorce forms. I tried not to take it personally, reminding myself that she'd always been an organized and efficient person. Still, a little less zealousness would have been appreciated. Since she had submitted the original petition two months before, our divorce would become final in four months.

"Oh, I thought it would take effect right away," I said.

"No, the state imposes a delay. I suppose that's in case the parties change their minds. Is that a woman I hear in the background?"

Time to plant those green seeds of jealousy.

"No, that's the TV."

"Someone on TV is calling a dog named Bob?"

"Yep, strange coincidence, huh?"

"I don't recall seeing a TV in your apartment, Axel."

"Got to go, Rach. Keep in touch. 'Bye!"

So far, I'd have to rate that as the most satisfying phone conversation of the day.

I have four months to win back the love of my wife.

The gorilla chop to the leg was no picnic, but I think it helped get the ball rolling reconciliation-wise. After all, my wife *is* a nurse. She likes nothing better than to nurse people through life-threatening illnesses. What I need now is a serious disease–like a light case of bubonic plague.

Late bulletin: Myron came through with Desma's gun. Our date is on for Friday night!

# Chapter 10

Desma wasn't willing to give me her actual address, so I agreed to pick her up in Venice at the corner of Lincoln and Amoroso. I liked the thought of dating a woman who possibly lived on Amoroso Place. It seemed somehow romantically promising.

I phoned Gus to take him up on his offer to serve as my driver. I warned him, however, that I expected him to act like a professional chauffeur. He was to dress in his Sunday best, address me as "sir" and my date as "miss," and speak only when spoken to. I emphasized that as my employee he was *not* to join in our conversations and was to treat anything he overheard as confidential. Nor was he to gossip about my activities with his dog-park pals.

"God, Axel," he said. "You sound like some kind of paranoid Republican."

"Just get here on time. I'm counting on you."

"Is she cute?"

"Don't you worry about that. And shine your shoes."

"Can she bring along a friend for me?"

"This is *not* a double date, Gus. You are my driver. That's all!"

"OK, Axel. I hope you get laid."

"*That* is not your concern!"

I also warned Desma that she was not to mention the word "invisible" within hearing of my driver.

"Well, won't you be invisible?"

"Not at all. How can I take you to dinner in a classy place if I'm invisible? How would you explain to the waiter why food was rising up from the plate and disappearing?"

"Yeah, that could be awkward. Let's go someplace dark, Axel, in case you're really disfigured or heinous."

"I am not heinous, Desma, in any sense of the word. If you wish to discuss anything relating to invisibility, you can substitute the phrase 'Mr. I'."

"Mr. I. OK, I gotcha. Mr. I, that's cute."

"We'll pick you up at 7:30. Don't be late."

"OK, Axel. But just remember: I'll be armed and dangerous."

"Right, darling. I'll keep that in mind."

"And locked and loaded."

"Fine. I'll wear my bulletproof vest."

Had I not been Crippled on Pico, I would have gone to Beverly Hills for a snappier wardrobe for my date with Desma. Some of their fancier men's stores require to you make an appointment in advance–just to shop. What a racket. So I wore the outfit I'd gotten married in: tweed jacket, wool slacks, dress shirt, and knit tie. Kind of warm for L.A. summer wear. The jacket I bought years ago on sale in a thrift store for $3. The label inside read: "Finkelsteins, Omaha." I liked to imagine this was Nebraska's most elite men's shop. OK, I didn't look like some Hollywood hotshot, but to my credit, I had trimmed eight pounds off my beer gut. A total slob I was not.

Gus rolled up in his retired and repainted postal van with a few minutes to spare. He was wearing a blue suit that looked to have been swiped off a 12-year-old. The jacket was way tight and he was exposing about three inches of shirt cuffs and stark white socks. His bright red tie matched the bow on Princess's head.

"How come you brought your dog?" I demanded.

"She *always* goes where I go, Axel. You know that."

"Well, we'll have to leave her here with Bob."

"No problem. I'm sure your neighbors won't mind hours of non-stop Rottweiler barking."

So Princess came along. She rode in the front seat of my car with Gus. I suffered fresh agonies climbing into the back seat with my stiff cast-encumbered leg. I had learned a valuable lesson: people with violent enemies should never buy a car with only two doors.

Waiting on that busy Venice corner, Desma was clearly annoyed. We checked each other out as Gus held open the door and she clambered into the back seat. She looked extraordinarily glamorous in a slinky black velvet and animal-print dress.

"God, Axel, do I look like a prostitute? This is the fifth car that stopped in the last two minutes."

Exuding aromas of pricey toiletries, she smelled just as wonderful as she looked.

"You *are* Axel, I hope!"

"It's me, Desma. You look quite beautiful, darling."

"Let me see the other side of your face."

I turned to face her straight on.

"Not horribly disfigured except for your leg, but dressed like a screenwriter. My agent wasn't too impressed with your script."

"Yeah, me neither. I'll do better on the next one. I'll write a juicy part just for you."

"You better. Geez, I never went on a date with two guys and a Rottweiler before."

"Princess is my guard dog, Desma. As you can see, I'm very concerned about your welfare."

Princess emitted a menacing growl.

"What's the dog's problem, Gustavo?" I asked.

"Princess kinda doesn't like strange new chicks, boss. But it may be the perfume too. Quiet, girl!"

Princess shifted to a low whine.

I took Desma's hand and smiled at her. She studied my cast.

"I admire your courage, Axel."

"Oh, the pain is mostly tolerable, darling."

"If I had something wrecking the lines of my pants that bad, I'd never be able to leave the house."

Since the forecast called for a pleasantly warm evening, I had reserved an outside dockside table at The Chandlery in Marina del Rey. I tried for a table aboard the restored schooner that was berthed adjoining the restaurant. The story was that Errol Flynn had deflowered countless virgins on that very boat. The maitre d' asked my name, then declined my request. You had to be someone to get a table on their boat.

Gus parked the car, then joined us as Desma strolled and I hobbled toward the restaurant.

"Gustavo," I said, "you can wait with the car."

"But, boss, I'm hungry."

"Oh, all right."

I slipped the maitre d' a ten-spot, and he graciously found Gus a dining spot at the long nautical bar. I told him to add Gus's tab to my bill. Then Desma whispered something to him, and we found ourselves being led up the gangplank to a choice table on the bay side of the schooner's deck. After a waiter dressed in a starched white steward's uniform took our cocktail orders, I asked Desma what she had said to the maitre d'.

"I said we needed a table for three because George Clooney would be joining us later."

"I'll have to remember that."

"It wouldn't work for you, Axel. You have to look like someone that George might conceivably be meeting. For example, I'm wearing a Michael Kors design that any clerk at K-Mart could tell cost over $5,000."

"And did you pay that much for it, darling?"

"Me personally? No. But I am giving the designer some

excellent exposure by wearing his dress in this premier location. God, Axel, can't you stick that cast under the table?"

I grimaced as I struggled to conceal my gauche infirmity from public view.

Our cocktails arrived and soon the alcohol began to dull the pain from my pinched position. I figured I had a medical excuse for going off the wagon.

"You're not wearing your pin tonight, sweetheart," I pointed out.

"Naturally. It wouldn't go with my gold belt and bangles. I could have worn it with my new Louis Vuitton number, but I really need the matching earrings."

I chose not to interpret that as a hint.

"God, Axel, did you really buy that jacket in Omaha?"

I hastily re-buttoned my coat.

"Some very fine designers are relocating to Omaha, Desma. They do it for Nebraska wool. It's the finest in the world."

"Well, you couldn't prove it by me. I'm glad you're not ugly though. In fact, you're kinda cute."

"Thanks. And how is your new gun working out?"

"Great. It's right here in my bag. So don't make any sudden moves."

We sipped our cocktails and watched the yachts motor by in the setting sun.

I was feeling hardly any pain when our food finally arrived. Desma had the grilled prawns; I stuck with a steak. I figured I might need the protein for later. I asked my date how her commercial had gone.

"It's over, thank God. Geez, what a pain. Now when you do a movie, you might once in a while do a dozen takes of a scene. That's only if an actor is drunk or the director is being an ass. But you do a commercial, these guys have rented the studio for the whole day. They're happy as a clam doing 300 takes. They don't care if it drives the actor insane."

"You do it for the money?"

"And the exposure. Diane Keaton got her start doing a deodorant commercial. And lots of other stars did them too."

Desma flashed a warm smile at a couple walking by. The fellow I recognized as an actor on TV.

"Someone you know?" I asked.

"No, but it doesn't hurt to make a positive impression."

I told Desma about my lucrative new career as a deep-cover photographer of the stars. She was impressed that I'd had the stomach to observe Teresany give birth.

"How was it?"

"Not quite as gross as pork belly processing in a packing plant. Do you want children, Desma?"

"I suppose. I'll be happy to provide the egg."

"Provide the egg?"

"Yes, of course. You know–for the surrogate mother. Nobody who's anybody gives birth to their own kid these days. It's all done in a test tube and hired out."

Listed on the enormous bill were eight margaritas and a prime rib dinner consumed at the bar. I paid with cash, peeling the bills off my impressive roll. Gus was too drunk to drive, so he and Princess moved to the back seat, and I turned the keys over to my date. She got us back to my place alive but traumatized. I made Gus give me his keys; he was OK crashing with Princess in the bed in the back of his postal van.

When I opened the door to my apartment, Desma exclaimed, "Oh, no, Axel! Someone's stolen all your furniture!"

I kissed her anyway as Bob hopped around and sniffed my date's $1300 shoes. She retired to the powder room, while I stripped off my sweaty jacket and shirt, exposing my steak-infused paunch. I hastily ditched the rest of my clothes and slipped on a robe. I re-fastened my cast and hobbled over to the bed. Desma pranced out of the bathroom in one of my expensive new towels.

She leaped onto the bed and kissed the end of my nose.

"How come you have a picture of David Cassidy in your bathroom?"

"I have no such thing."

"Want to bet?"

I got out of bed, ordered Bob from the room (he ignored me), I chased him out (he was afraid of my crutch), closed the bedroom door, and checked out the bathroom. As I pissed into the bowl, David Cassidy winked back at me in full color from his place of honor over the toilet. I could see I would have to place some limits on Claudia's use of her passkey.

I returned to the bedroom and the business at hand.

"Are you a closet Partridge Family fanatic?" Desma inquired.

"Must have been left by some previous tenant," I lied. "I never noticed it before."

Desma smiled and flung away her towel. As I had suspected, her body could only be classified as a supreme Playland of the Gods.

Since meeting Desma, I had devoted much mental effort to speculations of an erotic nature concerning her. She was alluring in the extreme, and I had gone without for a very long time. As someone said: sex was like water; you only miss it when you're not getting any. But I was cursed with the monogamy gene. For over eight years I had not looked at any woman except Rachel. And suddenly I was in bed with someone who wasn't my wife. Someone who looked different and smelled different. Who acted and sounded not at all like her. Extensive inner gear-shifting was required as I embraced this new object of desire. Plus, I had five pounds of engineered plastic clamped to my broken leg. My leg hurt with every movement, and I was as nervous as a 14-year-old in the sack with the babysitter.

All of which is not to say that we didn't get it on like two bunnies in heat. It just took a little longer than usual. And Desma had to do most of the work as I lay on my back and tried not to get jostled so much that the pain distracted from the pleasure. We used the condom she thoughtfully provided. Desma said she always used that brand because it was proven to stay on and never broke. I liked that she was a gal who watched out for such things. She would be totally credible as a spokesperson in a condom commercial.

Desma gave every indication of having had a satisfactory time. She snuggled against me and ran her long fingers through my chest hair.

"If you promise not to look at me in the morning, Axel, I'll go remove my eyelashes and wash off my make up."

"I promise. Shall I remove my toupee?"

She chuckled and tugged at my hair.

"You better have all your hair!"

Her ablutions were delayed by further exertions with a fresh condom. My enraged wife did not burst into the room and whack us with her bat. Eventually, all preparations for bedtime were made, and we settled into the peaceful sleep of the sexually satiated.

# Chapter 11

Next morning I was jarred awake by a woman's piercing screams. The woman was close at hand and she was screaming right into my ear. The problem was I couldn't see her. Nor, I soon realized, could I see myself.

I clutched a warm body. Scoping out its geometry, I placed a hand over what I gauged to be Desma's mouth. She bit me and resumed her screaming.

"Desma, Desma! It's OK! Don't panic! It's OK!"

"Damn you, Axel! You did this to me!"

"I can fix it! I can fix it! It's all a mistake! Calm down!"

She went limp in my arms.

"Just relax, for a goddam minute. Jesus, what a way to wake up."

"What are you trying to do to me, Axel?"

"Not a thing, darling. I must have said the words in my sleep. Now, hold on tight, and I'll switch us back."

I said the words and saw the now-familiar magenta stars flash before my eyes. I felt myself return to the visible sphere.

Oops, my bed companion had not transmogrified with me.

I felt Desma tear herself away from me. The bed covers flew back and two seconds later I was staring into the barrel of a small silver revolver floating shakily in the air a few feet from my head. At that distance I could make out the coppery gleam of the bullet in the chamber.

"You will change me back right now, Axel Weston. I will not be your invisible sex slave."

"Be careful with that gun, darling. Shooting me now would not be helpful to your situation. I guess you'll have to say the words yourself. Put the gun down and I'll teach them to you."

"I'll put the gun down, wise guy, when I'm visible again."

I sighed.

"I need a pen and a piece of paper."

"Don't try anything, buster," she warned, opening her purse and removing a gold Montblanc pen and a small notebook. These she tossed over to me while keeping her revolver trained on my head.

I wrote down the words and had her say them. It took several attempts before she got the inflection right, and she returned to the world in all of her glorious nudity.

She was relieved, but not that grateful. Nor did she put down her gun. She stomped around the room and dressed hastily, while I sat in the bed with my hands in the air. In less than three minutes she was ready to leave.

"Desma, darling. I'm sorry. It won't happen again."

"You bet your life it won't. I'm outta here for good. I should have trusted my instincts in that dressing room. I should have run screaming for my life."

"Desma, you can't mean that. I like you. I want to see you again."

"Not on your life, buster. I don't go in for this kinky stuff. I'm not that kind of girl. You can get yourself another patsy for your depravities. And don't try phoning me. I know important people in Westwood. I'll have Myron get a restraining order against you."

"Be reasonable, Desma. Why would I want you to be invisible? You're beautiful. You've got a gorgeous body. Making you invisible would be a crime against nature."

She grabbed her purse from the floor beside the bed. "Don't sweet talk me, you pervert. And keep your hands up!"

"Desma, honey, stay for a cup of coffee. We can discuss things like adults. Don't leave me like this."

But she turned and fled from my apartment.

Damn. What a way to spoil a beautiful budding relationship.

All that I had to remember her by were a pair of false eyelashes and two well-used condoms.

Gus showed up with his dog about an hour later. His tiny suit was now wrinkled and matted with Rottweiler hair. He said "your girlfriend" had kicked him awake and made him drive her back to Venice. He used the spare van key he hides under the bed.

"She seemed kind of pissed, boss. You guys have some problems in the sack?"

"No, we had a disagreement over another matter. Did she say anything to you about what happened?"

"Nope, she was as frosty as a popsicle the whole trip. You want me walk the Bobster?"

"Sure. I'd appreciate it."

Gus used my bathroom, gulped some aspirin for his pounding head, then left with the two dogs. He promised to return with donuts and coffee.

Claudia lumbered in while I was getting out of the shower. I clutched my towel tighter and inquired about the unexpected artwork.

"Your apartment's so bare, Axel," she said, averting her eyes. "I love helping my tenants decorate."

"I appreciate that, Claudia. But Mr. Cassidy is your thing, not mine. And it might be helpful if you knocked before entering."

"I did knock, but I guess you were in the shower. I noticed quite an attractive lady exiting your premises earlier. She was not dressed for daytime."

"No, she wasn't."

"She looked kind of like that gal in the mop commercial."

Too bad Desma missed that comment. I know she would have appreciated being recognized by her public.

Claudia stayed to help out on the dozen donuts Gus brought back. I made the introductions, and they had a lively conversation about Rottweilers, dogs in general, and David Cassidy. David, it turns out, is not a Sagittarius, but Susan Dey (Laurie Partridge)–who, Claudia claimed, David once slept with–is.

I felt rotten about Desma, but at least my leg was better. The swelling had subsided and the ghastly bruise was beginning to fade. Something seemed to have speeded up the healing. I figured it was either the spectacular sex or waking up invisible.

Gus got his money and went back to Glendale. I practiced walking with my crutches, then sat on the futon and stared at the four walls. Life as a house-bound gimp was beginning to pale. It was the middle of the morning and I needed a drink. True, I had gone off the wagon with those three cocktails at The Chandlery, but to my credit I had ordered Campari on the rocks, which I loathe. Want to mix socially, but not go off on a bender? Stick to the drink you detest.

The cable man finally arrived and hooked up my WiFi. Now, if I got too bored, I could watch Broderick Crawford in old episodes of "Highway Patrol" on my laptop. I identified with a TV hero who had a bigger gut than I did.

Waiting in my inbox was another terse email from Rachel. Peter, the adulterous film editor, was pleading innocent on the husband-bashing charge. Rachel reports he "sounded offended" at the mere suggestion he could have been involved. Oh yeah? I know some cops back home who could get a confession out of that guy in 15 minutes and not leave a mark on him. He was fortunate the damn crutches limited my ability to prowl unseen.

All that gear-shifting last night had muddled my feelings about my exiting wife. Plus, I was tired of my brain torturing me with endless replays of her nude bedroom grapplings with the Sexy Gimp. I was beginning to wonder if I really wanted her back.

I nuked another Stouffers brick for lunch, then watched the Youtube video of the mystery Pasadena bank robbery. It had accumulated over 100,000 viewings and lots of speculative comments about how the cash had been contrived to levitate and disappear. Many people thought the video had been faked, some believed Jesus was involved, others suggested sleight-of-hand machinations by the bank teller. One comment read simply: "Bad use of the power."

"Bad use of the power." What the hell did that mean?

All that tedium made me tired, so I went to bed early. I said the words before retiring and went to sleep as Mr. Invisible. I slept like Briny X in his box, and didn't wake until I heard Claudia enter the next morning with her passkey. She greeted Bob, then proceeded to knock on my bedroom door, a half-second prior to opening it. That's when I remembered I was invisible and dived under the covers.

"Good morning, Axel. Are you OK?"

"I'm fine, Claudia. Can I help you?"

"Did you want me to continue walking your dog?"

"Yes, please."

"Do you need anything?"

"No, thank you."

"Can you breathe under there?"

"With increasing difficulty."

"Even if you're naked, Axel, you don't have to hide your head. I'm not offended by a guy who needs a shave and may have morning breath."

"That's nice to hear."

"I don't care either if you have a woman in your room. This is the 21st century after all."

"I don't have a woman under here."

"I didn't think so. I mean I'm not spying, but there appears to be only one person in your bed."

"Claudia."

"Yes, Axel?"

"I believe Bob has to pee."

"Oh, right. I'll get right on it. We aim to please. Well, have a nice day."

"You too."

When she finally extracted her perfumed bulk from my room, I said the words, and hopped into the shower. Even without the cast, I felt barely a twinge of pain in my leg. The swelling had disappeared and the bruise was the palest of purples. So it wasn't Desma's healing touch that had reknit my torn flesh. It was being invisible.

As previously arranged, Gus and Princess showed up to take me to my follow-up visit with the Presbyterians. The doctor was amazed when I walked in and handed over my crutches. I said I thought I might need to keep the walker cast for a few more days. He sent me straight down the hall to the X-ray room. A half-hour later he and his colleagues were clucking in wonder over my startling close-ups. My bashed-in leg was nearly back to normal.

"Vigorous sex with a beautiful woman," I announced. "That's my treatment regimen. Got to keep that leg moving in primeval rhythms!"

On my way out I had to drop by the billing office to settle up my final monumental bill. They charged me Cadillac rates for everything except the air I breathed. The markups were so breathtaking, I was surprised the Mafia hadn't started muscling in on the hospital racket.

Or had they?

# Chapter 12

After another night as Mr. Invisible I was nearly back to normal. I wasn't ready for the football World Cup, but I could walk without the cast. I did feel a bit of a twinge when I put my full weight on the leg going up or down stairs. The improvement was so dramatic, I excused my intrusive landlady from further dog-walking duties; she refused the $50 in cash I offered in payment.

"No tipping required," said Claudia. "It's a pleasure walking that little sweetie. Would you like me to take Bob to the dog park with Gus on my day off?"

"Uh, sure. Be my guest."

Could Gus be dating my landlady? Would Princess tolerate such a thing?

I was watching my man Broderick Crawford roust some marijuana traffickers driving a sharp 1955 Desoto when my cell phone buzzed. It was long-lost Desma in a total panic.

"Axel, you've got to help me!"

"Hi, Desma. I thought you were out of my life."

"Axel, it's not working!"

"What? Our relationship? You hardly gave it a chance."

"The words aren't working! I'm still invisible!"

"You were extremely visible that last time I saw you. What happened?"

"Well, I, uh . . ."

"You went back for the earrings, didn't you?"

"Well, what if I did? I mean, what good is the pin without the matching earrings? They're a set, Axel!"

"Did you get them?"

"Of course. What do you take me for–an amateur? Help me with the words. I'm doing something wrong."

So she repeated the magic phrase several times.

"It sounds correct to me, Desma. I can't really tell. Your phone is breaking up."

"Axel! You've got to come here and help me!"

"Not a chance, darling. The last time I was in your delightful company you had a gun pointed at my head."

"Axel! I'm parked here in a tow-away zone! At 4:00 they're going to tow me away!"

Eventually, she resorted to tears, which aren't really fair to employ against an emotionally vulnerable recovering boozer who very much wanted to have sex with her again. I sighed, got her fucking location, got a description of her fucking car, and said I would be there as soon as I damn well could. I looked at the fucking time on my fucking laptop. It was 3:37 pm.

I got there just as the tow truck was maneuvering into position in front of Desma's 10-year-old Miata. I waved the driver off, and–as arranged–tapped on the trunk. The passenger window rolled down two inches, and Desma's little silver gun emerged through the space and dropped to the pavement. I pocketed it, entered the car, started the engine, and drove down Olympic until I found a quiet place to park. Naturally, her car had a stiff clutch pedal that hurt like hell to press. I had overdone it on the frantic running around to assist her.

When I stopped the Miata and killed the engine, someone invisible embraced me and kissed me on the cheek.

"Axel, honey, you saved my life."

"OK, Desma, before we do anything else you're going to listen to me. Do I have your full attention?"

"Of course, Axel. I'm right here beside you."

"OK, so listen. I don't have any magical powers. I am not a witch."

"You'd be a warlock. A male witch is a warlock."

"OK, I'm not that either. I'm just a normal, everyday guy. I stumbled upon those words–by accident. I was in a bad way financially at the time, so I used them to make a little money. I don't know any more about this invisibility stuff than you do. Desma, do you understand what I'm saying?"

"Sure. If you say so, Axel."

"So, I wasn't trying to make you my sex slave. I'm not trying to ruin your life by making you invisible."

"But I wouldn't be invisible now, Axel, if it wasn't for you."

"You mean if it wasn't for your being so damn greedy."

"A girl on her own has to look out for herself, Axel. Now, help me say the words."

She said the words again and again and again.

There was no change.

Lovely Desma was still invisible.

I could think of nothing else to do except drive back to my apartment. I could hear Desma weeping in the seat beside me. The presence of a distraught invisible person spooked Bob so much I had to lock him in the bathroom.

We sat on the futon and continued our efforts to get the words to do their magic. Every ten minutes Desma would ask me the time.

"Do you have some previous engagement?" I asked.

"Of course I do. Steve has tickets to see Paul McCartney tonight at the Hollywood Bowl."

"Wow, those must have cost a fortune. Well, you'll just have to call him and cancel."

"I can't do that!"

"Why not?"

"That would be a disaster, Axel. I know the rat would wind up taking his wife."

"Well, sometimes we all have to make sacrifices."

While Desma was busy with her cell phone, I excused myself by saying I had to go put my laundry in the dryer. I did go down to the building's laundry room, but it was to hide Desma's revolver behind a large hot-water boiler. I didn't feel safe being in the same room with that gun and an invisible Desma.

When I returned, she was continuing her endless variations on that recalcitrant phrase. She said it was like being trapped in a studio and recording endless takes of the commercial from hell.

Finally, I suggested we take a break and have some dinner. No way I could face another nuked frozen-food brick after that ordeal.

"How about I call up and have a pizza delivered, Desma? That sounds good, huh? What would you like on it?"

"Arsenic and cyanide."

Instead, I ordered a large mushroom-pepperoni pizza and the grande caesar salad. As promised, it was delivered in less than 20 minutes. The salad came in a paper bucket you could bathe a toddler in. I still had no plates, but Rachel had thoughtfully left behind her plastic forks. I asked Desma what she wanted to drink.

"I'll have a large Bailey's straight."

"Sorry, no have."

"OK, make it a double bourbon."

"Sorry, I'm on the wagon, darling. I can offer you tap water or orange juice."

We both settled for tap water. We ate picnic-style on the futon. Bob had settled down, so I let him out of the bathroom to snare the scraps that fell from Desma's fork. My guest seemed distracted throughout the meal.

"You know, Axel, I always thanked God I wasn't born ugly. I always thought what a nightmare that would be. You know, not being attractive. Not having guys give you a second look. Having pretty girls shoot you down with those awful, dismissive glances. Being snubbed by the popular, good-looking crowd."

"Not much chance of that in your case, Desma. You're a knockout."

"Yeah, well, now I wish I was ugly. I wish I was hideous and deformed. Then I might not mind being invisible. I might even like it."

"Desma, don't worry, darling. We're going to figure this out. I tell you, it's only temporary."

"Axel, promise you won't abandon me. I don't know what I'd do if you did."

I pushed the pizza box aside and embraced her. "Of course, I won't abandon you, darling. We're going to work this out together."

I could see why Desma was so upset. Her appearance was all-important to her. And she was an actor. Actors live to engender a response from their audiences. They accomplish that in large part through facial gestures, movements of the body, and their physical presence. Invisibility was a challenge to Desma's entire way of life. Not to mention a scary impediment to wannabe boyfriends.

When I returned from walking Bob, the apartment was entirely dark. Desma had drawn the drapes and switched off all the lights.

"Where are you, darling?" I called.

"In bed. I don't feel so invisible in the dark."

"Right. Er, I'll sleep out here on the futon."

"No, Axel. I need you beside me."

I gave Bob his good-night biscuit, did my business in the bathroom, and joined Desma in my king-size bed. She kissed me and peeled off my pajamas.

"I slept with you once, Axel, and woke up invisible. Perhaps if we do it again, things will be reversed."

I said I thought it was worth a try. Besides, I liked very much what she was doing with her warm hand.

We made love slowly, savoring the full-body physical contact. I tried to embrace her as fully as possible, caressing every part of her body. I wanted her to feel fully there, fully alive and real. She responded with an almost compulsive urgency. I came–finally–with an intensity I had never before experienced.

Later, drifting off to sleep, it occurred to me that she had become my de facto invisible sex slave. I hoped very much that the same thought wasn't crossing her mind.

# Chapter 13

When I opened my eyes, I could tell the person next to me wasn't asleep. I could feel the tension she radiated across space. The hoped-for overnight change hadn't occurred.

"That dog of yours is scratching at the door."

"Yeah, he does that. I'm sorry it didn't work."

"I didn't really think it would. What am I going to do?"

"We'll just have to keep trying."

"I had a life, Axel. It wasn't totally great, but it was a life."

Jesus, I felt bad for her. I knew in her heart she blamed me. It's quite a formidable burden, having wrecked someone's life. It's like those tearful DUI drunks I used to interview in jail–the guys who ran down pedestrians in crosswalks and left them paralyzed for life. They wanted to crawl into a hole and die. And now I felt like crawling in after them.

"I'll need some clothes, Axel."

"You're welcome to anything in my closet. And we can make a run over to your place today."

"Hold me."

I embraced her warm nakedness. I held her for a long time–while Bob scratched at the door and the commuters inched by on I-405.

After we showered and dressed, Desma checked out my kitchen.

"You know why I go out with married men?"

"Why, Desma?"

"Because bachelors never have anything in their refrigerators."

"OK, make me a list and I'll go to Vons right now."

I watched her Montblanc pen move eerily by itself over a sheet of paper, then drove her Mazda to the market. I would have to call Gus to help me retrieve my car from Beverly Hills–assuming it hadn't been towed. The old red Miata was the classic chick's car: glovebox stuffed with unpaid parking tickets, a tube of lipstick clipped to the sun visor, and hardly a drop of gas in the tank. Despite making an emergency fuel stop on the way to the market, I was back with the groceries and other items in under an hour.

"Some giant woman came in while you were gone."

"Oh, right. That would be Claudia, the apartment manager."

"She was snooping around. She looked in the bedroom and under the bed. She looked in my purse!"

"Yeah, that gal has boundary issues. I'll talk to her."

"She's lucky I didn't have my gun. We would have a very large body to dispose of."

"You were quiet, right?"

"I was quiet, Axel. It was a struggle, but I was quiet."

Desma turned out to be a much better cook than Rachel. She made a terrific vegetarian and cheese omelet. We dined in style on our new melmac plates using our new stainless steel flatwear. Over second cups of coffee I told her how being invisible had sped up the healing of my leg. I asked her how she was feeling physically.

"Surprisingly good, I guess. I don't know, kind of upbeat even. Like I had about six cups of coffee instead of two. Damn, I should have had you pick up some more condoms."

We returned to the bedroom, locked the door, and blew through her last two in the most spectacular way imaginable. By the end of that strenuous session, I was beginning to suspect that the sex slave label had been applied to the wrong party.

While Desma napped in the locked bedroom, I went with Gus to pick up my car. It was still where I had left it, but had accumulated four parking tickets. Like everything else in Beverly Hills, parking infractions make a serious dent in the wallet. Even the rich and famous blanch noticeably when they read the schedule of fines. Just imagine multiplying that bad news times four.

Desma and I had just finished lunch when we heard a knock on the door. It was West L.A.'s largest apartment manager.

"Hi, Axel, Gus said you wanted to see me."

"Uh-huh."

I motioned for her to enter.

"Claudia, I can't keep having you coming into my apartment when I'm not here. That is an inexcusable breach of my privacy."

"Oh, sorry."

"If you do it again, I'll have to bring it to the attention of the management."

"Please don't do that, Axel. I know I've been a bad girl. I know it's kind of silly, but you do look a little like David around the eyes. And I'm really impressed that you're going out with Diane Phillips."

Something dropped to the floor in the kitchen.

"What was that, Axel?"

"Uh, just Bob."

"I mean I was way out of line checking her I.D. in her purse. Still, I am responsible for the safety of the residents of my building. I mean what if there was a fire and I was called in to identify some charred body."

Another crash in the kitchen.

"Wow," said Claudia, "that little sweetie Bob must be getting rowdy. Please don't be mad at me, Axel. I just loved Diane in 'Highway to Hell in 3-D.' It's such a shame she had to be brutally slain so early in the film."

"Well, I know she'd appreciate hearing that."

"And she was marvelous in 'Nightmare in Pismo.' Do you know if they dubbed in that scream or was it really her?"

"Uh, not sure on that one. So, you'll stay out of my apartment—right?"

"You got my word on that, Axel. Say, would you and Diane like to double date with me and Gus? That would be awesome!"

"Uh, well, I think she's leaving on a shoot. I'll have to get back to you someday on that."

After Claudia left, someone poked me hard in the stomach.

I grabbed at thin air and wrapped my arms around an enticing, lovely-scented form.

"So was that scream dubbed in?" I asked.

"Just hope you never find out what kind of noise I'm capable of."


We waited until after dark to make a visit to Desma's apartment. She lived in a tiny place that looked like it had been plopped down as an afterthought on the roof of a four-plex one block over from Amoroso Place. Access was via an exterior metal fire escape that went up to the roof from the parking lot in the rear.

"How much do they clip you for this shoe box?" I asked, looking around as Desma packed a black carry-on and duffle bag. The place had a low roof and the dimensions of a shipping container. Hell, it might have started out as a shipping container.

"$1500. That's not bad for the west side. I can bike to the beach. And it's very private up here."

"I pegged you as the type to have a roommate."

"I've had them in the past. They all say I'm impossible to live with."

"Oh, yeah? Ever lived with a guy before?"

"That's for me to know and you to wonder about."

"Will anyone worry that you've gone missing?"

"I'll have to phone a few friends. Now lug these bags down to the car while I check my phone messages."

"Expecting some urgent calls from lovesick beaus?"

"You got that right. Now get out of here."

We stopped at a drugstore on the drive back; Desma insisted on going in with me. I bought their entire stock of Desma's reliable brand and a few requested fashion magazines. She admitted to walking out with a box of tampons and two pints of bourbon. I made a mental note never to take her to any store that had a firearms department.

As I drove up Lincoln she took a swig of bourbon and offered the bottle to me. I shook my head.

"You know, Desma, other drivers might wonder why a whiskey bottle is floating in the air in my car."

"Oh, all right."

I saw the bottle drift down into her purse.

"I've got a problem with alcohol," I admitted. "Do you?"

"Get off my back, Axel! I'm fucking invisible! You're lucky I'm holding myself together at all!"

"I think you're doing remarkably well."

"Yeah, well, back off. I may be invisible, but I need my space."

She said the words all the way back to my place, but the gods of visibility still weren't listening.

The tampons evidently were purloined for some future need. We hit the sack and went at it like Adam and Eve discovering sex for the very first time.

While Desma was showering the next morning, I checked the level of bourbon in that bottle. It hadn't gone down. I came from a long and undistinguished line of boozers and I knew alcoholics tended to hook up with their own kind. It has something to do with wanting to relive the dramas of our childhood, or so the "experts" theorize. I had lucked out with Rachel, who thought anything with alcohol in it tasted like dirty socks. (I should have taste buds that deformed.) Closet drinkers really scared me, and I hated to think dear Desma might be one.

At breakfast Desma dropped her first bomb of the day.

"Axel, I can't live with a dog. I really don't like them. They slobber too much, they're way unsanitary, and their hair gets all over my clothes."

Bob and I exchanged incredulous glances.

"Desma, I raised Bob from a puppy. There's kind of a bonding process that goes on."

"He's not your kid, Axel. He's just a dog."

"That may be. But I love the little guy."

"I'm not saying you have to get rid of him. Can't he go live with that wife of yours? You could have, you know, visiting rights. Joint custody–all that stuff that divorced people do."

"Well, OK. I could talk to her. But she works long hours at the hospital."

"So she could get him a litter box."

"Litter boxes are for cats, Desma."

"Dogs can use them too. Or put newspapers down on the floor. I can't live with a dog, Axel. I just can't."

Damn.

"You have to show some flexibility here, Axel. I know you old guys get set in your ways."

"I'm only 37, Desma. My decrepitude is still a few months off."

Violent pangs of male insecurity.

"Desma, on the Tommy, Steve, Myron, and God-knows-who-else continuum, where am I ranking with you these days?"

"Pretty high, Axel."

"That's good to hear."

"You make me visible again, and I can just about guarantee you my very highest rating."

I looked over at Bob. He was a sweet dog, but he didn't smell enticing and have lovely firm breasts.

While Desma had an animated cell-phone conversation with her agent, I checked her driver's license in her purse. She was *not* 25; she was a well-preserved 28. So I was not robbing the cradle quite as acutely as she had implied.

More grief came my way when she got off the phone. The stain-remover idiots had revised the script. They wanted her again for a half day of reshoots. Her agent went ballistic when she told him she couldn't do it.

"He said who did I think I was–Barbra Streisand?"

"Sorry, darling. What did you say?"

"I told him I thought I was done with that commercial, so I got some work done around my eyes. I told him I had two black eyes and looked like a raccoon!"

"Good work, Desma. That was fast thinking."

"Yeah, plastic surgery is the one excuse that agents understand."


I was getting ready to phone Rachel when the doorbell rang. There she was, shockingly visible, right in front of me. (I'd sort of gotten used to the chicks in my life being heard but not seen.) Not just visible, she was smiling warmly and dressed attractively.

"Hi, Axel. Your doctor alerted me to your miracle progress, so I came to check it out. Drop those pants!"

Only a few days before, I would have complied happily and doubtless tried to remove hers as well. Now I modestly rolled up my pant leg and peeled down my sock.

Rachel whistled in professional amazement. "That's incredible, Axel. Just, uh, unbelievable. I'd have thought you'd be on crutches for at least a couple of months."

"Yeah, well, don't tell your boyfriend, or he'll send that thug to bash my other leg."

I gave a start as someone stuck their tongue in my ear.

"I'm not seeing Peter any more, Axel. He told me he

was separated, but I figured out the only thing separating him from his wife was the length of their breakfast table."

"I'm sorry it didn't work out," I lied, not even simulating sincerity.

"What's that odor? It smells like Étrangler in here."

Desma was being naughty. She was squeezing her breasts against my neck.

"What's that?" I croaked.

"A very expensive French perfume. Sorry, Axel, am I interrupting something?"

"Not at all. Must have been my landlady's perfume. She was just here collecting the rent. Rachel, can Bob come live with you?"

"But that dog's like a son to you, Axel."

I got up abruptly and moved to another part of the room.

"True, but I'll have to travel a lot for my job. How about it, Rach?"

Someone goosed me in the ass. I took a defensive posture against a wall.

"So what do you do, anyway? Don't lie, Axel. I can see right through you."

"I've joined the paparazzi, Rach. You know those pictures of Teresany and her baby?"

A sharp poke to the crotch. Damn. I moved again.

"How could I not? They're everywhere."

"Well, I took them."

"You did? And they pay money for that?"

"Quite a bit, actually."

Another poke. I broke into a jog.

"Axel, what are you doing?"

"Uh, exercising my leg. Got to keep moving. Can you take Bob?"

"Of course not, Axel. They don't permit dogs in my building. Anyway, I work really long hours. I'm off on Saturday. Would you like to do something?"

Damn! Rachel was inviting me on a date!

"Love to, Rach," I called, picking up the pace of my jog. "But I have a photo assignment. I'll call you real soon. OK?"

"Sure, uh, you do that. Is everything OK with you, Axel? Are you drinking again?"

"On the wagon for good, Rach! Haven't touched a drop! Thanks for dropping by! See you soon!"

My wife looked at me wonderingly, shook her head, and left. I stopped, listened for telltale footsteps, and began advancing toward my invisible tormenter.

"You can't get away, Desma. You're going to pay. You're going to pay big time!"

"Axel's going on a date with his wife," she taunted. "Can I watch?"

I finally cornered her in the bedroom, where I exacted a very satisfying revenge.

To counteract cabin fever and to reassure Desma that I wasn't going to abandon her to get back with my "pretty wife," we put the top down on her Miata and went for a long drive. We stopped for picnic supplies in Malibu and found a secluded beach south of Oxnard. We spread a blanket on the sand and stretched out in the sun.

"Axel, do you think I need to put on sun block?"

There's a question for you: do invisible people burn in the sun? I told her she should probably grease up just to be safe. I watched as her garments accumulated in a neat pile at the foot of the blanket.

"Take off your clothes, Axel. Don't be shy."

"I don't know, darling. There are houses up there on that ridge. People could be watching through a telescope."

"So show them your dick. It would make their day."

"Or make them call the sheriff."

"Your dick's not that sensational, Axel."

I took off my shirt, but kept my pants resolutely on. Desma paraded her invisible nudity and called me a prude.

I watched the bourbon bottle as Desma took a swig. It

appeared to be her first drink since the other night.

"You know, Desma, there are two sets of footprints in the sand leading to this blanket, but only one person on it."

"And there are the victim's clothes. You're looking very suspicious, Axel. Obviously, you have resorted to cannibalism. That's the only logical explanation."

"Damn, you're right. I must have been awfully hungry too. What a fiend!"

"That reminds me, let's eat."

Five minutes later I knocked a baguette out of her hand as two tanned fellows strolled around a rock in the buff. I nodded in greeting as they passed.

"Why are all the beautiful men gay?" whispered my companion.

"Don't stare, Desma. People can sense they're being looked at."

"They'll just assume it's you, longing to make it a threesome. And give me your baguette! You got sand on mine."

I handed her my pristine roll.

"They've got much nicer asses than you do, Axel. Your ass looks like something you'd find on a Polish coal miner. It's all white and lumpy."

"And how does it compare to Myron's?" I asked.

"God, Axel, don't make me think about any part of Myron's body while I'm eating."

"Desma, have you ever been in love?"

"I don't know. I don't think love is helpful to a girl's career. You love that wife of yours, I can tell."

"I used to. I could love you, if you let me in."

"Hey, I'm constantly letting you in. That's about all we do."

"Into your heart, baby. That's where I really want to go."

"Why? So we can break up six months later and make each other truly miserable?"

"It doesn't have to end that way."

"Doesn't it, Axel? How's that divorce of yours coming along?"

Desma wanted to continue on up the coast, but I re-minded her that we had to get back to feed and walk Bob.

"That damn dog again," she sighed. "He's got to go!"

"And what if he were our human baby," I pointed out. "What would you do then?"

"We'd drive up to Santa Barbara, visit some nice shops, check into a five-star hotel, soak in their giant tub, phone room service for dinner, and let the nanny take care of the little bastard."

"Bad news for you, Desma. The hormones take over. Parents bond with their babies. It's nature's way. Mothers take care of their children. They worry about them."

"God, Axel, I thought you used to be a reporter. How come you're living in such a fuzzy, pink world with all the hearts and the bunnies?"

# Chapter 14

The next morning while Desma was showering, I checked out my ass in the bathroom mirror. OK, it was certainly white, but I couldn't see any lumps. It was pretty damn smooth if you ask me. A bit hairy, but smooth. Not something that would attract a crowd of admirers on a gay nude beach, but a fairly decent ass for a guy who worked 13 years at a sedentary occupation.

After breakfast I trooped down to the office and asked Claudia if she wanted a dog.

"You want to get rid of that little sweetie Bob?" she asked, incredulous.

"Well, uh, my work keeps me away a lot."

"Really? I hadn't noticed. So, Diane doesn't like him, huh?"

"Uh, well, she hasn't warmed up to him that much."

"You know, Axel, people are always wondering about Elizabeth Taylor."

"Does she have dogs?" I asked.

Claudia I knew was a person who could veer off on tangents.

"I think so. She's a real animal lover. But people wonder which of her many husbands she loved the most."

"Right."

"But the love of Elizabeth Taylor's life is clearly Elizabeth Taylor. That's often the case with actresses."

"I suppose so. But I really need to find a home for Bob."

"I'd love to have him, Axel. He could keep me company in the office. But it would have to be a one-way trip."

"Meaning?"

"If I took him, you couldn't have him back. He would be my dog. You know–forever."

"Right, Claudia. I understand. I'll bring down his food and his toys."

"Great. And I'll need his medical records too if you have them."

"Oh, sure."

"You don't want to think about it some more, Axel?"

"No. I think he'd be happier with you."

"OK, if that's what you want. Do you mind if I change his name?"

"Of course not. He's your dog now."

"I think I'll name him Bruce. That's not too much of a leap from Bob."

"Bruce?"

"Yeah. That's David's middle name. His initials are D.B.C. Isn't that perfect?"

I packed all of Bob's possessions into a shopping bag, and took him and his stuff down to Claudia's office. I'm not sure if he knew he'd been officially abandoned, but he settled into the bed she made for him under the copy machine and went to work on a new nylon chew bone. I shook her hand in thanks, she gave me a hug, I waved good-bye to Bruce, and was out the door.

I got another hug when I returned to my apartment.

"You made a sacrifice for me," announced Desma, "so I am going to make one for you."

I followed her footsteps into the bedroom. I was bummed about my dog, but something kinky under the sheets might perk me up. Desma had something else in mind. She retrieved the purloined earrings from her duffle bag and placed them in my hand.

"You're giving me these earrings, Desma? Uh, I don't have pierced ears."

"I need to make a sacrifice, Axel. These earrings have caused me nothing but trouble. Perhaps they are in some way responsible for my not becoming visible. I want you to flush them down the toilet."

"Really?"

I checked the price tag that was still attached.

"Desma, you want me to flush $48,500 worth of rare yellow diamonds down the toilet?"

"Set in genuine platinum, don't forget. Yes, they have to go."

"Wow. You sure?"

"Do it, Axel! Do it before I change my mind!"

They made an expensive-sounding plop into the water. My hand hovered over the toilet handle.

"Flush, Axel! Send them out of my life!"

I flushed.

The water cascaded down, the diamonds sparkled as they whirled around, gravity did its thing, and they were gone.

"I feel like a great weight has been lifted from my shoulders," said Desma.

She gripped my arm and said the words.

Alas, the gods had not been appeased.

She was still invisible.

Desma made rigatoni with clams in a white-wine sauce for lunch. As I was chewing that first savory bite, she dropped another bomb on me.

"Axel, I got a bladder infection."

I swallowed.

"Really? Uh, how do you know?"

"Believe me I know."

"What causes that?"

"What do you think? I need you to get me the pills."

"Pills?"

"Yes. They require a prescription. You'll have to get them from your wife."

"My wife!"

"Yes, your wife the nurse. After lunch I need you to drive to Burbank and see your wife. It's not good for me to delay. Plus, it's as annoying as hell."

"She'll know what I need?"

"Of course. Your wife is a woman. She sleeps with men. I'm sure she's had a bladder infection."

Damn. The tasty clams had begun to pall.

All the freeways to Burbank were remarkably unclogged. I sailed on to my doom as if God were clearing the lanes ahead of me. Besides groveling, I knew baksheesh would be required. I stopped at the hospital gift shop and bought a box of chocolate truffles.

Rachel received my gift with wary skepticism. Very little eye contact was made as I explained my problem.

"Why doesn't this friend of yours go to a doctor?"

"Believe me, Rachel, she would if she could. But she can't."

"Oh, my God! She's under-age! My God, Axel! You're balling a 14-year-old!"

The other nurses at the station looked up with interest.

"Don't be ridiculous, Rachel!" I hissed, motioning for her to lower her voice.

"They're cracking down these days, Axel. Even if she's 16, you're playing with fire. You could go to prison for a long time!"

"Desma is 28! She's not a child!"

"So you say. Twenty-eight, huh? That's practically a child."

Rachel had always been sensitive to the fact that she was 11 months older than me.

"So why can't your young and sexy 28-year-old girlfriend go to a doctor like the rest of us peons?"

"Believe me, Rachel, no doctor in the world could help her."

"What's that supposed to mean?"

"I can't explain any more, but I'm desperate. Please help me!"

I had gone beyond begging and pleading to the crawling-on-your-belly stage. My wife studied me with evident distaste.

"What does she want? Sulfamethoxazole?"

"Uh, if that's what does the job."

"It requires a prescription, Axel."

"You have friends in the pharmacy, Rach. If you say it's for you, they'll pack you up a bottle."

"But I haven't been fucking my brains out."

"Please, Rachel. I'm throwing myself on your mercy."

"Chocolates, huh? Your girlfriend gets expensive French perfume and I get a crummy box of hospital chocolates."

I had never known Rachel to be so mercenary.

"I didn't buy her the perfume, Rach. But if you do this one thing for me, I'll get you the biggest bottle of Étrangle they sell."

"You got yourself a deal, asshole. And make sure it's the perfume, not the cologne."

"Fine. Whatever you want! Can you get on it right away? I'm double-parked."

Rachel looked at me like I had just been tracked in on her shoe.

"God, I'm glad you're getting out of my life."

As requested, I also stopped at a market and got a bottle of cranberry juice for Desma. I didn't inquire if she intended to drink it or apply it topically. While there, I spent a few minutes in the magazine aisle boning up on the latest celebrity gossip. A guy in my profession needs to know who's hot and who's not.

Desma was grateful for the medications. She's certainly making a lot of trips to the bathroom. I hope she's not in there fishing an invisible arm up the toilet in hopes of recovering those flushed diamonds.

Bedtime came, but sex was definitely off the menu. So we held each other for a long time in what a guy living in a fuzzy, pink world might term a snuggle. For a gal who thought love was a bad career move, Desma seemed to require a great deal of close bodily contact.

I filled her in on my younger days and my lackluster family. She told me about growing up in Connecticut. Her father was a big-shot at an insurance company in Hartford. He loved to fly and had his own twin-engine plane. When Desma was in college, he took her mom and two younger brothers on a ski trip to Vermont, and flew the whole lot of them into a New Hampshire mountain peak. His insurance paid for the rest of her education, but she's been on her own ever since.

I expressed my sympathy and said it must have been a horrible ordeal to go through.

"Yeah. It was a phone call out of the blue. One call and my whole family was gone. All in less than a minute."

"That's terrible. What a shock to deal with at that age."

"Yeah. I can barely remember how I was before. I think I was nicer. You probably would have liked that girl."

"I like you, Desma."

"Yeah? Prove it."

"How?"

"Make me visible again and I'll marry you."

The idea came to me in a dream. It seemed fairly obvious, but it was one thing we hadn't tried. When the bedclothes stirred beside me and invisible lips whispered, "Good morning, Axel," I suggested the idea. So, face-to-face in a full naked embrace, we said the words together. I felt the icy bar goose my insides as I disappeared from view. Just as quickly, Desma rematerialized in my arms. I'd almost forgotten how beautiful she was.

She leaped from the bed and, shrieking with joy, ran to the bathroom to inspect her visage in the mirror.

"It worked, Axel! It worked! I'm back! Oh, my God, I'm back!"

I lay on my back and watched with pleasure as she danced about the room in her glorious and visible nakedness.

"Get up, Axel! Get up! I'm taking you out to breakfast! Where would you like to go? How about Algernon's?"

Algernon's was Beverly Hills' poshest breakfast spot. A mere onion bagel there cost as much as breakfast for two at Denny's.

"Great," I replied. "Let's go there."

Many a loving couple had celebrated their engagements over breakfast at Algernon's.

Desma hopped into the shower, and I said the words.

Nothing happened.

I said the words again.

Still nothing.

I was still repeating the words when Desma, clutching a towel and looking stricken, edged out from the bathroom.

"Oh, damn," she whispered.

I said the words with every inflection and cadence I could think of as lovely Desma hastily packed her bags. In under ten minutes she was fully dressed and ready to leave.

"Are you going for good?" I asked.

"Don't ask me to stay, Axel. I can't. It's too dangerous. I don't want that to happen to me again."

"Can I call you?"

"Let me know if the words work. Please don't come to my apartment or try to find me. I gotta go."

"Bye, darling."

"Good-bye, Axel. I wish you the best."

She left.

I turned the place upside down hunting for her bourbon pints, but she must have taken them with her.

Then I remembered. I still had her little gun.

# Chapter 15

I retrieved the gun, but found I lacked the courage to pull the trigger. I'm amazed that anyone can deliver such a bloody assault to their own flesh, although I suppose it must be easier than stepping out of a high window. Checking out that way really takes some guts. A bullet is quick, probably not that painful, and you're not obliged to ponder the rapidly approaching pavement as you have those inevitable second thoughts.

Lacking booze and the will to kill myself, I showered, got dressed, made breakfast, and read the *Los Angeles Times*. I read every word in every section. Then I felt like taking Bob for a long walk, but I remembered I was alone.

Alone and invisible.

That's about as alone as alone gets.

Curiously, this invisibility business does have a weird energizing effect on the brain. Being invisible had its drawbacks, but it also afforded one a power that many would envy. I could sneak and snoop and spy and pry. I could invade just about any uncarpeted space. The peeping tom opportunities were legion. I could tickle starlets as they serviced producers on their knees. I could expose the evil that lurked behind closed doors. I could be the first investigative journalist to win a Pulitzer anonymously. I could comfort the afflicted and afflict the comfortable. I could sneak into his studio and stuff a sock into Rush Limbaugh's big mouth. I could make a difference in this world.

I suppose, but what I really wanted to do was find a way out of this mess.

Like any modern person in a desperate pickle, I checked my email. Sparse pickings as usual. Rachel wrote that she hoped "my friend" was better and to forget about the perfume. I couldn't decide if my wife's one-sentence message was conciliatory or dismissive. I wrote back that "my friend" had departed, had turned out to be 43, had a boyfriend in San Quentin, and three children out of wedlock. Don't ask me what those lies were supposed to accomplish.

I did some web searches on invisibility, but all I got were a hodgepodge of topics and ads for invisible mending. I needed invisible mending all right, but not the kind being advertised.

Time to review my recent history: Boozer Axel Weston, penniless and despondent, stumbles upon means of becoming invisible. Finds it fairly useful. Reliably goes back and forth at will. Accidentally transfers invisibility to girlfriend, so obliged to disclose method. She uses it on her own and develops virulent form that does not respond to usual command. Axel has stupid dream, and discovers way to transfer virulent form to himself while enabling girlfriend to regain visibility.

A glimmer of hope. This transfer technique might work between me and someone else.

All I needed to do was find somebody with a strong desire to be invisible–on a possibly permanent basis.

Now there was that recent case in Germany of the fellow who advertised for victims who wished to be eaten. He got at least five valid responses and ate the lucky fellow he selected.

It seems to me that being rendered invisible is considerably more appealing than being murdered and eaten by a cannibal. My task did not appear to be hopeless.

I knew my search would have to be discrete. I couldn't do anything so public as advertise on Craigslist. Such a notice might be seen by the FBI investigators still puzzling over that Pasadena bank robbery.

Jeremy the Brit called to check up on my bum leg. He was thrilled to hear it was 99 percent back to normal.

I asked Jeremy if he had any interest in the wedding.

The big news locally was the upcoming wedding of Tara, the fast-rising comedienne, and Richard, the intense method-actor whose mantel was symmetrically balanced with two Best Actor Oscars.

"Don't tease me," said Jeremy. "Nobody can get in except the invited guests. It's impossible."

I had read about Richard and Tara's elaborate security precautions in the *Times*. The site of the wedding was an ocean-front estate in Malibu. It occupied a promontory extending out into the Pacific. On three sides were sheer cliffs dropping nearly a hundred feet to the seething waves below. The narrow sliver of land connecting the property to the mainland was protected by a high fence. Armed guards would be manning the only access gate. All the help were to be strip-searched to prevent them from smuggling in cameras. The ceremony would take place in a large tent, erected to foil paparazzi in helicopters.

"Absolutely no photography will be permitted," continued Jeremy. "They're not even having photos taken for themselves. Of course, it's her second wedding and his fifth. How many wedding albums do people really need?"

"Would you like some video of the event, Jeremy?"

"Please, Axel, don't be cruel. Don't tease me."

"How about high-definition, optically stabilized video with Dolby stereo sound?"

"720 or 1080 lines?"

"1080p for you, Jeremy. Only the best."

"Are you serious, Axel?"

"Piece of cake, Jeremy. Just tell me you want it."

Jeremy squealed and said he nearly wet his pants. He

seemed to be a guy with bladder control issues.

I needed to make more money. If I were going to pass my invisibility racket on to some other lucky stiff, I had to put Mr. Invisible to work now to build up my bank balance. Jeremy said he got a "golden flush all over" just contemplating what he could command for an actual video of Richard and Tara tying the knot.

The Japanese never sleep. I'd been reading on Gizmodo about their latest video-capable camera that was even thinner and lighter than my present model. I called around and found a store in Hollywood that had just got some in stock. They also had a pro-quality camera head-strap, such as employed by mountain bikers and adventure skiers to record those final scary moments as they hurtled off into eternity. The salesman totaled the price for both, plus extra camera batteries; I said I would send my man around with the cash.

Yeah, I intended to pay for them. Shoplifting has proven way too stressful to my nerves. And besides, I could use the receipt for a tax deduction.

Gus answered his cell phone at the dog park, where he was observing Princess and Bruce at play. I asked him how my former dog was coping with his abandonment.

"He seems fine, boss. He's getting in way more dog-park time now. He'd been kind of bored just hanging out at your place."

Damn. I wonder if Desma is coping just as well without me?

"Gus, I need you to run an errand for me. How soon can you get here?"

"I'm practically there now, boss."

"Good. Oh, and I need you to reserve Sunday for me. We'll be taking a drive to Malibu."

"OK, boss. Should I bring my bathing suit?"

"Uh, sure. Why not? Oh, and when you come to my apartment, don't bring any dogs–ever! I can't stress that enough.

Desma has a thing about dog hair."

"OK, boss," he sighed. "I hope the pussy's worth it for you."

The freeways must have been clogged. Gus arrived nearly an hour later. He did as I said and left the dogs in his van. The last thing I needed was to have them jumping and barking at my invisible form. I'd left a note on my door saying I'd been called away and for Gus to come in and look on the kitchen counter. He did so and found the pile of cash and directions to the camera store. I wrote out everything plainly and in detail for a guy of his I.Q. He pocketed the cash, studied the note for a full four minutes by the clock on the stove, looked in the refrigerator, and muttered, "Damn, no beer. What a cheapskate!"

It was Friday rush hour by then, so Gus didn't make it back until after 7:00. I left a follow-up note on my door telling him to put the items on the kitchen counter. He did so and picked up the $200 I'd left there for him. He counted the cash, exclaimed, "Yes!" and peeked again in my refrigerator. Still no beer. Disappointed, he looked around the apartment.

"Hells bells," said Gus. "No TV or nothing. Guess they spend all their time screwing."

Gus had a very long and vigorous piss into my toilet, flushed, didn't wash his hands, and left. So far, this peeping tom business was proving less than titillating.

I spent the rest of the evening getting to know my new camera and acutely missing Desma. My apartment was still redolent with her French perfume–waging a war of scents with Bob's lingering odor. I wondered if her bladder was recovering and hoped she wasn't risking a relapse by getting it on with Steve or Myron or other unknown beaus.

I wanted to climb into bed and hold her.

Yes, I admit it. I desperately needed a snuggle.

Being invisible has its inconveniences, but it's a sure cure for insomnia. Sleep had never before been this blissful, uninterrupted, and refreshing. As a reporter I've always tried to be precise in my use of language. And I'm not exaggerating when I say Mr. Invisible passed the night in a sleep that was positively delicious.

My breakfast–without Desma at the helm–was less delicious. As I chewed my stale bagel and read the newspaper, my cell phone rang.

"Axel!" exclaimed a familiar voice. "Did you see the paper!"

"I'm reading the article in question now, Desma darling."

The *Times* reported that a valuable yellow-diamond earring had been extracted from a filter screen at the Hyperion sewage treatment plant. It had been identified by a representative of Harry Weinstock as part of a set stolen from their Beverly Hills store. Sewage workers were now searching other filters for the companion earring and matching pin.

"Axel, did you see? They published a big photo of my pin!"

"I see it, darling. In full color too. On the front page of the Metro section."

"Axel, lots of people saw me wearing that pin. And Harry Weinstock is offering a $10,000 reward for its recovery!"

"Did you tell anyone it was yellow diamonds?"

"No, I just let them assume it was citrines."

"So, if anybody mentions it, you just say your pin is a cheap knockoff."

"You think?"

"Sure. Did you flush it down the toilet?"

"Of course not. But I hid it really well. What should I say if the cops show up?"

"Just deny everything. Without the pin, they have no evidence against you."

"But what if they want to see my cheap copy?"

"Say your purse was stolen. Just stay calm and cool. Remember, you're an actor."

"Right. That's good advice, Axel. Are you still. . .you know?"

"Yeah, but I'm working on it."

I told her about my plan to transfer my problem to someone new.

"You know anybody who needs to disappear in a big way, Desma?"

"No. But I'll keep my eyes peeled."

"Good. So how's your bladder?"

"Better, if you must know. Say, how come you didn't call me?"

"I believe you instructed me not to, darling."

"Did I?"

"Uh-huh. Desma, I miss you in a very big way."

"Yeah, I kind of miss your lumpy butt too."

"I've checked, Desma. My ass is not lumpy. It's remarkably smooth for a man of my age. You must be thinking of someone else."

"You think? Maybe it's Steve's. No, I know—it's his wife's! Man, you've never seen such cellulite. Like a relief map of the Sierras. And she's married to a plastic surgeon too."

Call me paranoid, but I decided I needed to start protecting my assets. I got an online account at a Cayman Islands bank and transferred all but $5,000 of my local bank balance into it. I also called Jeremy, gave him the details of my new account, and told him to wire all future payments there. I told him if he ever got any inquiries about me from the cops, he was to give out as little information as possible and to alert me afterwards. He was thrilled, as usual, and said he got "goose flesh all over" every time we spoke.

I decided to test my new camera and Gus control system by making a test run to a market for groceries. As arranged, Gus arrived at my place and located the new device

I said I was testing for a major motion-picture studio.

"Hello, Gus," I said. "It's nice to see you. My voice is coming from the box on the kitchen counter. Do you see it?"

"Yeah, it looks like a shoe box somebody taped up."

"Yes, we have disguised it to look like that. Can you hear me OK?"

"Sure, it sounds like you're standing right next to me."

"No, I'm at my office in Hollywood. I can see you through the lens in the box."

I had cut a hole in the box and affixed my old camera to the inside.

"Oh yeah, I see it."

"Put the cash, the grocery list, and my car keys in your pocket and pick up the box. Whatever you do, don't drop it. It is a $2 million device."

"Wow, that's impressive."

"Now take the box down to my car and drive to the store."

"OK, boss. You got it."

Treading as quietly as possible, I followed Gus down to the parking lot.

"Gus, open the car door and place the box in the center of the rear seat. Then leave the door open and stand back until I tell you to close it."

"OK, boss."

"I will now have the box generate a protective force field that will depress the seat next to it."

Mr. Invisible climbed into the back seat.

"Wow," exclaimed Gus. "That's amazing!"

"You may now get in, close the door, and drive to the market."

"Can I bring Princess? I left her in Claudia's office."

"Sorry. No dogs, Gus. Never. Dogs overload the delicate technology."

As we drove to the market I asked how things were going with him and my landlady.

"Not bad, boss. She's kind of a fun chick. We get along OK. We take turns talking."

"How so?"

"Well, I talk about Rottweilers for a while. Then she rattles on about David Cassidy. You think I should be jealous of that guy?"

"I wouldn't be, Gus. He's just a hobby for Claudia–like stamp collecting or dog breeding."

"We also talk about your girlfriend. Claudia's very impressed that you're going out with a movie star–even if she did make you ditch your dog."

"A major film personality cannot be seen in public with dog hair on her dress, Gus. Her studio contract forbids it."

"I guess Claudia's right. She says you have to sacrifice a lot for stardom. That's why she went into property management instead."

I reversed the procedure to exit the car at the market. Mr. Invisible then switched on my new camera  (strapped securely to my head) and followed Gus with the box into the store. I shot test video under various lighting conditions as Gus shopped for groceries in the meat department, frozen brick aisle, etc. He brought the cart to a halt beside the chilled beer display.

"You're all out of beer, boss."

"I'm on the wagon, Gus."

"They got Negra Modelo on sale. I know you like that beer."

"I can't drink, Gus. Uh, Desma doesn't like it."

"Pussy-whipped." muttered Gus. "The guy is pussy-whipped."

"I heard that, Gus. The microphone in the box is extremely sensitive."

"Sorry. Just my personal opinion."

I did let Gus select a dozen of his favorites from the donut case. At the register, the cashier eyed Gus's box suspiciously.

"What's in that box?" she asked.

"Don't worry," he replied. "It's not a bomb or nothin'."

"Are you taking pictures? That looks like some kind of spy camera. Taking photos is strictly forbidden in this store."

Right, like we're trying to steal your top-secret method of arraying onions. It looked like she was going to call the security guard, so I knocked over a magazine rack as a diversion. Gus paid the bill and we walked out without being stopped.

Now I've got groceries for a week. And my test videos came out great. The auto focus genie honed right in on faces, while correcting for accurate color balance. And the new camera used the same kind of memory cards as my old one, giving me the capacity to shoot several hours of Richard and Tara's gala celebrity-packed nuptials.

# Chapter 16

Neither the *Sunday Times* or the *Times* website had any more news about the Harry Weinstock heist. The other earring must not have been found. Considering the tidal wave of muck descending every minute on the sewage plant, it was pretty amazing they'd fished out the first one. As usual, I scanned the paper for newsmakers who might have a pressing need to become invisible. Two actors were in trouble on domestic violence raps, but those guys have expensive lawyers to get them out of such jams. Ideally, what I needed was an ugly older guy with financial problems, a bad marriage, obnoxious relatives, poor self-esteem, and Mafia hitmen hot on his trail. I knew they were out there; it was just a matter of finding them.

I checked in with Desma, who claimed she was home and alone. She said she had spent yesterday phoning everyone she knew and "laughing casually" about her cheap costume-jewelry imitation of that famous Harry Weinstock pin.

"Did they buy it?"

"I think so. Half the jerks claimed they hadn't noticed my pin. Can you believe that? Glittering flawless stones that could blind people a half block away. Set in solid platinum. Damn, Axel, sometimes I wonder why I even bother to try to look nice."

"Well, Desma, it was pinned to your breast. Some people's eyes never get past your tits."

"Thanks. I'll take that as a compliment. Are you still saying the words?"

"Every ten minutes."

"Any results?"

"None. But I feel good and sleep like a baby."

"Yeah, I did too. And it's really great for the complexion."

"Makes a guy kind of horny though."

"Yeah, I noticed that too. Watch you don't get a bladder infection."

"Not much chance of that."

We sighed and moved on. Desma was extremely envious that I would be attending today's "wedding of the decade."

"God, Axel, there are people in this town who would kill for an invitation. I hear the A-listers who were excluded are really pissed. They all had to leave town on important business."

"You can come with me, Desma. Say the words and we'll sneak in together."

"Not on your life, Axel. I learned my lesson. Invisibility is not a look I'm trying to achieve."

Gus was 15 minutes late. I was about to panic when an old lady–about four and a half feet tall–burst into my apartment, grabbed the shoe box, and headed toward the door. I screamed, "Halt!" and slammed the door in front of her. She skidded to a stop and looked wonderingly at the box.

"Hey, did you do that?" she asked the box.

"I did. Who the hell are you?"

"I'm Gus's mother. I thought you wanted to go to Malibu."

"I do. Where's Gus?"

"He got called to work. A dust storm blew in from Lancaster last night and the car wash is swamped. Are you really inside this box?"

"Of course not. I'm speaking to you from Hollywood, California. You have to do exactly as I say."

"Yeah. I got the story already. Gus said you could be a major pill. So, you wanna chat or you wanna roll?"

I followed her down to the parking lot. She was dressed in a thrift-store bouffant wig, a house dress featuring a garish print designed to overstress the human retina, and flip-flops. She refused to drive my car and tossed the box into the front seat of her 1960s Rambler station wagon—even though I instructed her to place it carefully into the back seat. It took three requests—the last one bellowed at the top of my lungs—to get her to open the passenger door and stand back.

"I am now activating the protective force field, causing a depression in the front seat."

"Yeah, get on with it before you cause a depression in my life."

She slammed the door behind me, hopped in, fired up the aging six-cylinder motor, and headed out into L.A. traffic—some of the fiercest in the world. She sat so low in the seat, I was amazed she could see where she was going.

"Get on the Santa Monica freeway," I commanded.

"No way, Adolph, the freeway's a parking lot. We'll go down Olympic."

She was right. Olympic was faster.

"That's not my name, Mrs. Baboo."

"Whatever. Call me Babs. So, you know the traffic's going to be a mess out in Malibu from that stupid wedding."

"Right. We have to get as close as possible. I'm invited."

"They invited a box to a wedding? What are you a gift from Tiffanys? I'd say your wrapping leaves something to be desired."

"This box represents over $2 million of advanced technology."

"And what good are you? Taking an old lady away from her Sunday potroast so you can watch a couple of nitwits show off their money?"

"I'm paying you well for your time."

"So I can do what–line my casket with it? And how come you gave all that beer to my son? So you can both be drunkards?"

"I'm sorry for that, Mrs. Baboo. I was just trying to be sociable."

"And then you introduced him to that giant girl. You think he can keep her in groceries on what he makes?"

"Claudia has a very good job, Mrs. Baboo. She's nice too. And she loves animals."

"I already had a nice girl picked out for him in Burbank. A very nice and pretty nurse who helped me when I got my hip replaced. She was dumping her bum of a husband."

"Really? Her name wasn't by any chance Rachel, was it?"

"How did you know?"

Damn. I hope Rachel hadn't been denigrating me to all of her patients.

After an hour of increasingly slow traffic on the Pacific Coast Highway we had inched within a quarter mile of my destination. That would have to do. I instructed my driver to pull over.

"Mrs. Baboo, give me your cell-phone number. I'll call you when I want you to pick me up."

"Do I look like a person with a cell phone? In my day we were happy to make do with a party-line phone!"

"You don't have a cell phone!"

"Sorry, I have enough trouble with my hearing aid and my stupid microwave."

"Uh, OK, go back to the gas station we just passed and wait for me there."

"So how long am I going to be waiting, Adolph? Time is running short for a person of my age."

"I shouldn't be more than a couple of hours. Have some lunch at the restaurant next door. Save the receipt and I'll reimburse you. Please open the passenger door now so that I can deactivate the protective force field."

Babs Baboo sighed and did as I requested. Mr. Invisible got out of the car and told her to close the door.

"Oh dear, Mrs. Baboo, I have detected a fault in the circuitry. Please take the box with you back to the gas station. I will work on the problem at my end and re-activate the box when it is corrected. I am now signing off."

"Hah! Technical problems!" she exclaimed. "You guys only want to fool around all day with your tubes and transistors so you don't have to face us women."

Police barricades had been set up, and sheriffs deputies were controlling traffic around the estate. A large and lively crowd, dressed mostly in beach wear, had gathered behind the barricades to watch the arriving limos. Paparazzi, sporting their longest lenses, were leaning far over the barricades and clicking away as each group of wedding guests made its way past a gauntlet of private security guards. There were no helicopters buzzing overhead. Phone calls had been made–reportedly to the White House–and the FAA had declared that section of the coast a "no fly zone" for the day.

Mr. Invisible scooted up on the trunk of a waiting limo and rode in past the barricades. I slid off when it stopped, ducked behind the line of guards, made my way toward the final checkpoint at the gate, and accidentally stepped on the back of someone's shoe. That person turned around and I found myself staring at Jay Leno's famous chin.

"Excuse me," he said to Meg Ryan.

"Don't mention it," replied Meg.

Mr. Invisible went through the gate between them. I was past the final hurdle and safely inside. I switched on the camera and strolled around, endeavoring to record as many famous faces as possible. The grand estate, bedecked with more flowers than a Rose Bowl Parade, was teeming with celebrities. Lots of actors, but even more comedians, including quite a few I had somehow assumed were deceased. Waiters, garbed in formal tuxes of a blindingly orange hue, were circulating among the guests with trays of champagne and hors d'oeuvres. Everywhere you looked were little six-year-old girls dressed as 1940s gas station attendants: crisp white shirt, snappy red bow-tie, blue pants with stripe down the side, black patent leather shoes, and jaunty cap that flashed "super service" in red LEDs. Each girl had a yellow silk "rag" in her back right pocket and a little spray bottle in her left pocket. Embroidered on each shirt was a name such as Mack, Butch, Lloyd, Vern, Smitty, etc. Unquestionably adorable, but rather puzzling.

I looked in the house for the bride and groom, but got only shots of harried cooks preparing for the lavish post-nuptials banquet. I spotted America's TV sweetheart and her husband chatting with Chris Rock. Her blackened eye had healed nicely. Then the tiny gas jockeys started clapping their hands and calling for all the guests to take their seats in the tent. So that was their purpose: they were ushers.

I went out through the terrace and got the magnificent view straight on: sweep of green lawn above high cliffs, embraced on all sides by the blue Pacific. In the center of the lawn was a massive red and white tent, topped with decorative banners flapping in the warm breeze. A rope barrier had been strung along the cliffs to keep guests and six-year-olds from toppling into the sea. Weeks of preparations had nicely trampled the grass, so Mr. Invisible could follow the guests into the tent with little fear of detection.

The bride and groom were seated on pillows on a flower-strewn elevated platform at the far end of the tent. They smiled and waved at the arriving throngs. She was in a frilly dress and hat that looked like something Mary Pickford's grandmother got married in. He was in the dress uniform of a Canadian Mountie–complete with flat-brimmed felt hat, scarlet tunic, shoulder and collar badges, lanyard, cross-strap and belt, pistol holder, handcuff pouch, double magazine holder, appointment and qualifying badges, gloves, black breeches, long Strathcona boots, and spurs with tabs.

Mr. Invisible waited beside the stage until everyone had been seated, then claimed a prime spot for videoing right in the center of the aisle. The little gas jockeys blew silver whistles until even the richest and most famous shut up. Then Sting and Linda Rondstat, accompanied by Lyle Lovett and his band, sang "Indian Love Call." Now I got it. Tara was dressed like Jeanette MacDonald in "Rose Marie;" Richard was impersonating that swinging swain Nelson Eddy.

Next, three of Richard's four ex-wives got up and sang "Thanks for the Memories" with cleverly altered lyrics. As Tara was younger than me and Richard had to be pushing 70, the reformulated stanzas rhymed "Niagara" with "Viagra" and "dimpled nymph" with "impotence." Not exactly Lorenz Hart, but vastly amusing to the crowd.

Then Tara stood up and did ten minutes of shtick on her husband-to-be and his famous ego, his perfectionist compulsions, his heart pacemaker, and his legal wrangles with his most recent ex-wife, very conspicuous by her absence. Big guffaws from the audience, but only scant chuckling from the groom. Then Richard sang "You Are My Sunshine," accompanying himself on the ukelele. When he finished, massed sirens could be heard, and the gas jockeys entered driving a long line of miniature black and white 1949 Ford convertible police cars, which must have been battery powered because otherwise everyone in the tent would have been asphyxiated. Riding in the back of each car was a full-size woman dressed in a colorfully embroidered dirndl. Mr. Invisible jumped out of the way as the cars motored by–sirens blaring and lights flashing. The cars stopped in a neat formation around the stage, then the sirens mercifully were switched off. Those girls were young, but they sure could drive. The peasant ladies climbed out, sorted themselves out by height, and burst into song in the manner of Bulgarian throat singers (which indeed they were).

The tune was quite lively, and soon everyone in the tent was singing along in improvised Bulgarian–Mr. Invisible included. I did see some flashes of magenta, but I must have attributed them to the lights on the little cars. Anyway, just as the ladies were starting their second song, Tara stood up and screamed, "Who the fuck is that?!"

Immediate silence in the tent. Everyone turned to look where the bride was pointing.

To my dawning horror, I realized she was pointing directly at Mr. Invisible, whose improvised Bulgarian must have included those special words.

I looked down. Mr. Invisible was no longer invisible.

"Get that bloody bastard!" shouted the groom.

In retrospect I should have allowed myself to be captured, possibly Tasered or otherwise forcibly subdued, had my camera confiscated, and been tossed–bruised but visible–out on the street. But in the panic of the moment, I acted on my first impulse. I ran.

I dodged guards, angry six-year-olds, surprised Bulgarians, Tara's enraged mother, Hugh Hefner, several of his girlfriends, Barbra Streisand herself, and a blur of other lunging figures. I might have had a chance had I headed toward the house, but I went the other way. Looming ahead of me was the end of lawn and the beginning of empty air many dizzying feet above jagged rocks and crashing waves. I ducked under the rope, rolled toward the precipice, and said the words. Mr. Invisible scrambled away from the cliff and edged away from the crowd now gathering at the rope.

"My God!" cried Richard. "The fellow's gone over the cliff!"

"Good!" screamed his bride-to-be, "I hope the bastard drowns!"

More guards arrived, and one of them radioed back to his commander to call the Coast Guard.

Tara was all for resuming the program, but Richard thought they should wait until my fate had been determined. At that point several of the gas jockeys began to cry because their tap dance–scheduled to follow the Bulgarians–had been postponed.

I lingered as long as I dared to video the aftermath, but it was clear the party mood had been spoiled. Guests gathered in small dispirited groups to peer over the edge in hopes of spotting my wave-tossed corpse. Waiters circulated with more champagne, quite a bit of which went into the disconsolate bride. Many comedians could be heard cracking jokes and chortling inappropriately.

Eventually the champagne took effect and some of the rowdier guests started playing bumper cars with the little Fords, causing the gas jockeys to become even more upset. Several cars were run off the cliff, a la the "chicken game" in "Rebel without a Cause," but the drivers bailed out safely. Many of the gas jockeys then had to be taken home in tears. They had been promised the little cars in payment for their services.

I left after the bride spit up on her Jeanette McDonald gown and had to be assisted from the scene. It was apparent that no one would be getting married that day after all. Too bad. It might have been one of the more memorable Hollywood weddings.

I found Babs Baboo asleep in the back of her station wagon. My shoe box had been ripped open and its contents (camera and several large rocks for weight) scattered about the car. I rudely shouted for her to wake up.

"Who are you?" she demanded, looking around suspiciously. "And *where* are you?"

"I am speaking to you from the largest of the rocks, Mrs. Baboo. All the secret technology is contained within the rock. The box, which you were not authorized to open, is merely a ruse. Now place the rock in the center of the front seat and open the passenger door."

"OK, Adolph, whatever you say. And how was the wedding?"

"A very curious affair, Mrs. Baboo. Very curious indeed."

# Chapter 17

I was hoping my problem with the words had been corrected, but that was not the case. I was stuck again as Mr. Invisible. I even tried singing the words while a Youtube video of the Bulgarian ladies played on my laptop. No go. Perhaps it only worked when they were there warbling in the flesh. How much do you suppose it costs to rent the whole troupe for the day?

I transferred the wedding video to my laptop and checked it out. God, I love those Japanese camera wizards. As each sensational minute of video played back, the jingle of cash registers grew to a crescendo in my mind. The realization dawned that I was set financially for life. I would never have to work again! Hell, I could hire a Bulgarian lady singer to live in full-time. One of the cute younger ones without the mustache.

The video files were too large to email, so I uploaded them to my Google file storage and emailed the link to Jeremy. A cold beer to celebrate would have felt good, but instead I nuked a brick, ate a lonely dinner, and went to bed.

I drifted off to sleep thinking about '49 Fords. I'd always liked those cars. The Mercurys of that vintage were nice too. Perhaps I could find a convertible–fully restored. Not red though. Yellow. Yeah, yellow would be nice. With a black top . . .

It was barely light outside when Jeremy's call woke me.

"Jesus, Axel, I thought for certain you were dead."

"Nah, not this time."

"The Coast Guard is set to resume their search for you this morning."

"Well, if they find anyone it won't be me."

"Dozens of people saw you go over the cliff."

"Nope. That was Butch Cassidy and the Sundance Kid."

"You continue to amaze, Axel."

"All in a day's work, Jeremy."

"Your video is, of course, spectacular."

"Thanks."

"There's a bit of a problem though."

I could sense that. Exuberant Jeremy sounded uncharacteristically subdued. The guy was not tingling all over.

"Axel, you interrupted the wedding!"

"Yeah. That was, uh, not planned."

"Well, the word is that Richard doesn't mind. He had a good time anyway at the party and figures he dodged another marital bullet, as it were."

"Oh yeah?"

"But Tara's pissed, Axel. I mean really on the warpath. She's feeling deserted at the altar. The word is that Richard's publicist is going to announce this morning that the wedding is off."

"Uh-oh."

"It would have been better if you had waited until *after* the minister had done his thing."

"Sorry. So you can't get as much for the video?"

"It's not looking good, Axel. If your video gets out, Tara's lawyers will go after you and us."

"For what?"

"Well, at the very least, she'll sue to recover the costs of the wedding. And that was a very expensive affair. The florist bill alone came to six figures. Plus, damages of course. We're talking millions here, Axel."

"Damn."

"You don't want that video to get out, Axel. I've already destroyed what I downloaded here. I would advise you to take the file off your web location as soon as possible."

"OK," I sighed.

"We can't even sell the other photos now because Tara will assume they're the work of that mystery photographer."

"Other photos?"

"Yes, we smuggled in a tiny camera with one of the child tapdancers."

A gas jockey had been a spy!

"It was great work, Axel. You continue to amaze. How on earth did you get straight-on, close-up video of those people without their noticing? It was almost as if you were invisible."

"Uh, it's just a matter of the right disguise, Jeremy."

"Well, you're obviously a master at it. Keep up the good work, Axel. Just try to stay out of the action the next time."

"Yeah. Will do."

In my mind I saw a vintage yellow Ford convertible drive straight off a cliff. The despondent driver made no attempt to leap from the doomed vehicle.

Ten minutes after I hung up, Desma called.

"Axel! Are you dead?"

"Possibly. I feel dead. How do I sound?"

"Kind of depressed. The people on TV are saying you are definitely dead."

"Are they naming any names?"

"No, they're just calling you the unknown photographer. God, Axel, I thought for sure you were dead!"

"How did you feel about that?"

"Not at all good. Kind of awful in fact. Damn, Axel, I hope I'm not in love with you."

"It would make my day if you were."

"Yeah? That's sweet."

I told her about my near brush with visibility and the fortune that had just slipped through my fingers.

"Save that video," said Desma. "It could still be worth some money some day."

"How so?"

"Well, Tara wants to strangle you now with her bare hands. She's the laughing stock of the nation."

"I thought comedians liked to get laughs."

"Not that way. Not for losing her man in such an embarrassing way. Right now she'd cut off your balls and toss them to her snarling lawyers."

"That's a comforting thought."

"But let's face it. Richard's a fucking old man! Tara can be abrasive, but she's sort of attractive in an up-from-the-peasantry way. I hear she's half Bulgarian. Anyway, she's bound to meet someone better. Then she won't care and you can sell your video."

"But by then will anyone still be interested?"

"Just save it until Richard croaks. The guy's one cocktail and a cigar away from his next heart attack. It's always big news when a star like Richard dies. People will be clamoring to see your video."

The yellow Ford convertible swerved at the last second and veered away from the cliff.

"Thanks, Desma. You've cheered me up. Want to come over and spend the morning in bed?"

"I can't. I have to go do another fucking commercial."

"What's this one for?"

"Hair removal creme. I mean, do I look like a girl plagued with unsightly hair!"

The wedding disaster and my presumed drowning made a big splash in the *Los Angeles Times*. Eyewitnesses described the unknown photographer as a white male of average height with a pot belly and a camera strapped to his head. Rather distressing characterization. A paunch I could see, but "pot belly" struck me as needlessly cruel. Time to get serious about my diet. I had already sworn off beer. What was next–pizza? Donuts?

I was doing more fruitless web searches for "invisibility cures" when I heard someone lumbering down the corridor toward my door. Mr. Invisible leaped up from my desk just as Claudia entered with her passkey. Bruce bounded in behind her and circled joyfully around his long-lost master.

"I am speaking to you via that large rock, Claudia, from my office in Hollywood. Please remove that dog at once!"

"Yeah, I heard about your rock, Axel. And your shoe box. And I'm not buying any of it."

"There is no other possible explanation, Claudia. Please leave. You are not authorized to be here."

"I got an explanation, Axel. Try this on for size: you're invisible."

"Don't be absurd. And get that dog out of here!"

Claudia continued to ignore my orders.

"I read about it in *Reader's Digest*, Axel. You're one of those scientists at Cal Tech working on invisibility. Admit it! You're wearing an invisibility cloak."

"Wrong! I am speaking to you remotely via advanced micro technology."

"I want to borrow your cloak, Axel. Just for the day. Or I call a news conference and announce I've got an invisible man living in my building. A guy who everyone thinks drowned off Malibu."

"It's not a fucking cloak, Claudia. Here–feel for yourself."

I then permitted myself to be felt up by my landlady. No wonder chicks object to being groped. My actual explanation for my profound transparency did not diminish her enthusiasm for joining me in that state.

"You've got to make me invisible, Axel. I've wanted to be invisible for 30 years!"

I pointed out that invisibility was not to be trifled with.

Although it might prove a pleasant diversion for an afternoon, a lifetime of invisibility could be a severe challenge to anyone's lifestyle.

"I don't care, Axel. For me, it would be worth it. You've got to make me invisible or I'll blow the whistle on you. I'm not kidding. Let's get to it. What do I need to do?"

I spent a further five minutes trying to talk her out of it, but Claudia was obdurate. She wanted to be invisible and hang the consequences. So I wrote out the words and had her say them. Nothing happened.

"Well, there's another method," I admitted. "It requires close physical contact on the bed."

"How close?"

"Uhmm, hugging."

"Hugging, huh? I could do that."

We got on the bed (tremendous creaking and mattress sag), embraced each other (she was an armful), and said the words together. No change.

"Well, Claudia, this works better, uh, if the parties are, uh, undressed."

"Let me get this straight, Axel. You wish to see me naked?"

Actually I didn't, but I said I could see no other alternative.

"OK, Axel, but you're going to have to close your eyes."

I didn't tell her that I had already planned to do just that.

So we removed our clothes and embraced again on the bed. She felt even larger bare.

We said the words, magenta stars twinkled before my eyes, and I reappeared in all my stark nakedness as my landlady faded from view.

"Holy shit, Axel! It worked! Damn! I feel almost dainty. This is great!"

I grabbed for my pants.

"I hope you're keeping your eyes closed, Claudia."

"Not me, Axel. You're the first guy on my list to see naked."

I didn't dare ask who was second on her list.

While we dressed I explained how anything within about two inches of the body was rendered invisible.

"I get it, Axel. So a cell phone in a pocket is OK, but I better not carry my purse."

"Right. And people, of course, can hear you, so I make a point of treading softly."

"I can do that, Axel, but squeaky floors might be a problem."

I told her she had to watch out for carpet and grass as well.

After admiring her invisibility in the bathroom mirror, Claudia announced it was time to hit the road.

"Uh, are you going somewhere?" I asked.

"It's not far, Axel. You're driving me to an address in Encino."

"Uh, really, Claudia. Have you thought this out? This could be a major mistake."

"We're leaving right now, Axel. Get your car keys and let's blow this joint."

"Please, Claudia, let's stop and think about this for a few minutes."

"I've been thinking about it for 30 years! It's time to go!"


We left Bruce in Claudia's office. On the drive over the hill to Encino I pointed out that doing something this ill-advised might imperil Claudia's new relationship with Gus.

"Gus is a sweet guy, Axel, but NASA isn't going to be recruiting him any time soon. He must have got his smarts from his late father. His mother is fairly sharp, although hateful."

"Claudia, it's not good to be this impulsive."

"I'm the impulsive sort, Axel. Do you think I got this

large exercising firm control over my impulses? Shall I guess your birthday?"

"What?"

"That's one of my hobbies–guessing birthdays. Let's see, you look like an autumn sort of guy. I'm thinking October."

"Very good. I'm impressed. You know, there's still time to turn around."

"Forget about it, Axel. We're going to Encino. It is my destiny–and yours. Now, let's figure out the day. OK, I can see it's not a single digit."

"That's right."

"OK, I'm thinking 11, but I'm also seeing a two. Were you born on the 12th?"

"No, you were right the first time. It was the 11th. That's remarkable. How do you do it?"

"It's kind of a gift–like being tall. I'm pretty psychic."

I was beginning to feel uncomfortable.

"Claudia, are you staring at me?"

"I must confess I am, Axel. You're looking awfully tantalizing."

"That's another side effect I should have warned you about."

"A powerful urge to get laid?"

"I'm afraid so."

"Wow, this is *so* my lucky day! And to think I almost didn't rent you that apartment!"

Claudia guided me straight to the address. It was apparent she had been there before, although probably not past the high hedge that mostly obscured the modern stone and glass house.

"OK, Axel. Don't stray too far away. I'll phone you when I want you to pick me up."

"What should I do if you're arrested for trespassing or shot?"

"Relax, guy. This is not that big of a deal. When life opens a door for you, Axel, you got to be brave and go for it. Now open the goddam door."

I got out, opened the passenger door, and pretended to be checking the power window switch as Ms. Invisible Stalker climbed out, kissed me on the cheek, and strolled away.

I drove down the hill, parked, and–savoring my visibility–walked for miles along Ventura Boulevard through Studio City and Sherman Oaks. I browsed in bookstores, looked at $2,000 sinks in a fancy plumbing shop, ate lunch in a Japanese restaurant, bought a new shirt, had an ice cream cone, and relished the shadow I was casting on the sidewalk. I was back among the visible and I intended to stay that way. Call me a sociopath, but if I never heard from Claudia again that would be fine by me.

It was after 6:00 when she finally phoned. There were no police cars, fire engines, or news vans in front of the house when I pulled up and parked 10 minutes later. I opened the passenger door, saw my car sag on that side, closed the door, got in, and drove off. Silence from my passenger.

"Well?" I said at last.

"Well, what? I satisfied my curiosity."

"Any more details you'd care to relate?"

"Not really, Axel. It was very . . . illuminating and sort of touching."

"How so?"

"Uh, he kept something . . . that I mailed to him . . . when I was nine. All these years. I saw it in a closet upstairs."

"Jesus, Claudia, you were taking some chances."

"Yeah, it's kind of scary being out of control when your compulsions take over. But I didn't throw myself at him. You've got to give me credit for some restraint. And I left voluntarily. I didn't take up residence in his attic."

"So, are you over him now?"

"Get real, Axel. Is Santa Claus over Christmas?"

"So what's your plan for coping with being invisible?"

"You're right, Axel. Being invisible is a pleasant diversion for an afternoon, but not something you want to adopt as a lifestyle. We're going to your place and change me back."

"Uh, there's only one hitch in that plan, Claudia, I don't want to be invisible again."

"I appreciate your point of view, Axel, but you don't really have a choice here. I may be currently unseeable, but I still have my cell phone. A few calls from me and you're in a world of hurt for many years to come."

Damn!

"But all is not lost, Axel. I'm the smartest friend you have, although—considering your circle of acquaintances—that may not be saying much. But I do like you, I appreciate what you did for me today, and I'm prepared to help you any way I can. You're not alone any more, Axel dear. You now have a large and powerful ally."

I considered crashing her side of the car into a towering eucalyptus tree, but instead drove back to our building and awaited my doom.


After I fed and walked Bruce, we did the transference in the buff on my bed. The icy rod goosed my organs, and I gave an involuntary shudder as Mr. Invisible returned. Tall expanses of re-emerged pink flesh filled my vision. Claudia, however, did not release her clinch.

"Forgive me for pointing this out, Axel, but you appear to be in a state of arousal."

"Sorry. I hope you're not offended."

"Not at all. I am presently experiencing a parallel physiological response."

I considered the matter. I was again invisible—for how long I had no way of knowing. Darling Desma, I knew, had ruled Mr. Invisible off limits. Dearest Rachel hadn't even bothered to call and check if I was dead. The dating prospects for invisible persons were not encouraging. Many years of celibacy could be looming ahead.

"I know you keep a box of condoms under that pillow, Axel. Shall we employ one?"

"Sure, Claudia. Why not?"

And so we cemented our alliance, as it were. Propelled by unseen forces, we went at it with a fervor that few have experienced. I imagined that she was Desma multiplied by three; she perhaps pictured herself transported back to forbidden Encino bedrooms. It was all quite extraordinary, and left us panting and sweating.

"Wow," sighed Claudia. "That was better than sex."

Curiously, I had to agree with her.

"Was it that good with Diane when she was invisible?"

"How did you know she was invisible?"

"I got some scary vibes one day when I was going through her purse. That's why I said all those nice things later about her crummy movies. Is she still invisible?"

"No. She's back."

"Oh, I get it. And not having anything to do with you now. That's not very nice, Axel."

As usual, Claudia was remarkably well informed about my personal life.

"Well, she's afraid of becoming invisible again."

"I guess I can understand that. She's a girl with a lot to lose in the looks department. So how was she in bed?"

"My god, Claudia, don't you respect any boundaries at all?"

"I told you, Axel dear, I take a great interest in my tenants. Care for sloppy seconds?"

I had to admit I did. We slapped a fresh tire on my tube, and took the mattress for another spin around the track.

# Chapter 18

Some people never listen. In their narcissism they believe their specialness excuses them from following the rules. And because they don't listen they cause trouble. This morning I experienced an example of this when I opened my *Los Angeles Times*. On page one under the headline "Who is this man?" appeared a large, three-column, clearly focused, frontal view of me–camera strapped to my forehead, in the act of fleeing the wedding tent. The villain who defied the ban on cameras was the bride's Bulgarian-born father–may he yet live to be stomped under a thousand Russian jackboots.

I was still recovering from the shock when Claudia burst into my apartment with her copy of the paper.

"Did you read it?" she asked breathlessly.

"The story? Not yet."

"Tara is offering a $5,000 reward to the first person who comes up with your name."

"Damn! Well, that should take all of 12 seconds."

My cell phone rang. It was Desma with more bad news.

"Axel! The cops were just here!"

"What did they want?"

"Somebody ratted on me about the pin. I bet it was Steve's cow of a receptionist. That snotty bitch has *always* been jealous of me."

"What did you tell the cops, Desma?"

"I said my pin was a fake, but I was scared to tell them I lost it when my purse got stolen. I mean, would you believe that? That story sounds awfully fishy. So I told them we broke up and I gave it back to you."

"You didn't!"

"Well, you have nothing to worry about, Axel. I mean, you're invisible. But two Beverly Hills cops may be showing up there any minute now."

"Thanks for the warning, Desma! Gotta go! 'Bye!"

I cleared out just ahead of the cops. Claudia helped me carry my laptop, camera, financial records, cell phone, and other vital stuff (Desma's little gun) up to her apartment on the third floor. The cops went first to the apartment office. Claudia told them that she hadn't seen me since Saturday. She agreed to let them into my apartment with her passkey. They turned the place upside down, but didn't find the pin–or me. They said she should call them immediately if I returned.

After the cops left, Claudia joined me in her apartment for a powwow. Her place was an elaborate, multi-room, living shrine to a former TV star and the minutiae of his life.

"OK, Axel," said Claudia, buttering a bagel, "fill me in on this yellow diamonds caper."

I gave her the two-minute precis of my life in crime.

"So Diane, who you insist on calling Desma, flushed the fabulous earrings down the toilet?"

"Yes, it was a form of ritual sacrifice."

"I get it–in lieu of a virgin. But she still has the pin?"

"Yes, it's well hidden."

"Probably in her capacious vagina," commented the bagel chewer.

I could tell Claudia was having problems with my close and loving relationship with Desma.

"Clearly, Axel, you're better off dead. The world has to continue to believe that you drowned in Malibu."

"I don't have any problem with that. But we have to get

Gus and his mother on board."

"Leave that to me. The bigger problem is your damn cell phone that you've been chatting away on since your demise."

"Oh, right. The cops might check up on that."

"They will unless they're closely related to Gus."

"It may not be a problem, Claudia. My cell phone got cancelled a few months back for non-payment. I've been using a prepaid one I bought off a guy at the dog park."

"Where'd he get it?"

"I didn't inquire. But he was a big fellow with gang tattoos and a pit bull."

"Good, Axel. Well, that's a break. You must have been anticipating your future law-breaking. So, there's no connection of that phone to your name. Very good. Still, we better ditch it. So who knows you're alive?"

"Well, just you, Gus, his mom, Desma, and my photo agent Jeremy."

"Is Jeremy willing to lie to the cops?"

"I don't know. Probably. If he doesn't want to get sued by Tara, then he better hope the world believes I'm dead."

"OK, use my phone here to call Jeremy and Desma. We need them on board right away."

"Oh, wait a minute, Claudia. I just remembered: dozens of people saw me along Ventura Boulevard yesterday."

"Anyone who knew you?"

"No, just strangers."

"OK, let's look at this *Times* photo. Your face–what can be seen of it–is distorted by fear and panic. Frankly, you look like an escaped mental patient. I recognized you because you are a friend and we have balled several times."

I hoped she wasn't going to keep bringing that up.

"OK," I conceded.

"But I don't think the average person is going to connect this nut with the calm Axel Weston they encountered briefly in boring Sherman Oaks. You have a good face for crime; it's ordinary and unmemorable."

"Thanks. I guess."

My cell phone rang. I reached automatically to answer it, but Claudia grabbed it and stepped on it, crushing its tiny electrical parts.

"That might have been my wife," I pointed out.

"Ex-wife, you mean."

"Oh, damn. I just remembered. There's a Burbank police detective who can connect me with that number. Plus, Rachel of course."

I confessed to Claudia about Mr. Invisible's impulsive act with Rachel's bat.

"Entirely understandable, Axel. I would have done much worse under the circumstances."

I found that comment potentially worrisome.

We finally worked out a plan. If the cops inquired, she was to say she was passing my apartment early yesterday morning, heard my cell phone ring, used her passkey to enter, and answered the calls from Jeremy and Desma in hopes that they might know why I hadn't come home Sunday night. Then, later that day in Encino, she used her cell phone to leave an appointment message on my cell phone, which she had inadvertently left in her car. This morning–with my phone still in her purse–she answered the call from Desma.

"What a tissue of lies," I pointed out.

"Yeah. Let's pray the subject never comes up."

Claudia returned to her office while I made my calls. Jeremy was totally fine with playing along that I was dead. He said he imagined that a guy with a life as exciting as mine frequently had to discard former identities. I said yeah it was hard to believe I had started out three decades before as a Chinese schoolgirl. I'm not sure he got the joke.

Desma was watching a morning TV news show when I called.

"You know some old gal named Emma Smeesh?" she asked.

"Uh, yeah, Emma's a retired waitress in Glendale. She has a Pekinese named Fluffy."

"Well, she won $5,000 this morning for naming your name. Sorry I sicced the cops on you."

"They've come and gone from here. We may be in the clear, darling."

"Don't count on it, Axel. I have to go talk to some detective in Beverly Hills this afternoon. Myron's agreed to go with me. He's an entertainment attorney, but he's not going to let the cops walk all over me."

"Good. Don't worry, darling. I can take the rap for the robbery since I'm now officially dead. Remember, you haven't heard from me since before Sunday. All our phone calls since then were between you and Claudia."

I filled in Desma on my adventures with Claudia.

"That girl's trouble, Axel. You should get out of there."

"And go where, darling? Relocating to a safe place is hard when you're invisible."

"She's probably going to try to seduce you."

"Don't be ridiculous, Desma. She's, uh, very happy with Gus."

"I doubt that. Just remember, Axel: she's the spider and you're the fly."

Somewhere inside of me a journalist's heart was still beating feebly. To keep busy, I got out my camera and took several dozen shots of Claudia's amazing collection that covered every wall and overflowed every corner of her apartment. The gal was truly one of the great obsessives of our age.

Mr. Invisible was sharing a lunch-time take-out pizza with Claudia in her office when we spotted Rachel approaching. She looked quite satisfactorily distraught. I quickly returned my half-eaten slice to the pizza box and retreated to a corner as Rachel rushed in.

"Axel Weston! Have you seen him?" Rachel asked.

Claudia coolly chewed and swallowed. "And you are?"

"His wife! He's not answering his cell phone!"

"Nobody's seen Mr. Weston since Sunday. Have you seen today's paper?"

"Yes, of course! That's why I'm here. I had no idea he was missing. Why didn't somebody call me?"

"I can't really say, Mrs. Weston. Perhaps you should speak to the Coast Guard in Malibu. You might wish to begin making plans for a memorial service."

"Memorial service! But nobody's found a body!"

"They often don't, Mrs. Weston. Would you like to see Mr. Weston's apartment? Perhaps there's something in it you'd like to keep as a memento."

Rachel recoiled from my landlady. "Memento? What, what kind of a person are you?"

Claudia smiled her sweetest smile. "Just trying to do my job, Mrs. Weston. We all have to do our best to cope with unforeseen tragedies."

Rachel hurriedly wrote down her number on a pad on the counter.

"Please, just call me at this number if there's any news about my husband."

Claudia felt the need to correct her. "You mean your ex-husband?"

"Our divorce is not yet final–not that it's any of your business!"

Rachel slammed the door on her way out.

"She didn't have to get so huffy," Claudia remarked, sliding the pizza box toward me. "Do you like this pizza, Axel?"

"It's totally fabulous."

"Isn't it? I can't tell you how many places I tried before I found this one. And so close on Sepulveda. I must have driven by it a million times."

So far, we seem to be in the clear with the Baboos. Gus–like the rest of America–believes I went over that cliff and drowned. He's taken it so hard, he had to call in sick at the car wash–not that they had much need for him on a slow Tuesday. As far as his mother is concerned, she only dealt with some nitwit in a rock named Adolph, who Gus has decided must have been one of his late boss's office associates in Hollywood.

Claudia had individual pints of Ben & Jerry's ice cream in her office mini-fridge for dessert. Hanging out with her could be bad news for my gut.

"You need a new name, Axel. I can't keep calling you by a dead man's name. How about David?"

"No thanks. I need a short dynamic moniker that looks good on the big screen as the credits roll by. You know: screenplay by Jack . . ."

". . . Sprat," suggested Claudia.

"Come on. I'm not kidding. Screenplay by Jack . . . D. Ainger. Get it? D. Ainger?"

"I get it Jack. You're a dangerous guy. Care for another pint?"

"I can't, Claudia. I've got brain freeze as it is."

"Pussy," she said, reaching for another carton. "You should be glad I'm big."

"Why's that?"

"When your wife came in, she didn't question why there was an extra-large pizza, but only one person eating."

"You're right, Claudia. You saved my bacon again."

"That's right, Jack. And don't you forget it."

If there's one thing cops like to do, it's stand up in front of cameras and make portentous statements. The guys in blue really like to hog the limelight–almost as much as actors. First, some blow-dried Beverly Hills detective announced that possible drowning victim Axel Weston was a "person of interest" in the big Harry Weinstock diamond heist. Then, out in Burbank, Detective Myers piped up that the Malibu wedding crasher was also a "prime suspect" in a vicious assault upon a "male companion" of his "estranged wife." For a guy who committed all of his crimes while invisible, I didn't seem to be getting away with much.

With all the cops singing like canaries, my address became public. Soon our building looked like O.J. Simpson's house after they found the bloody glove. I retreated with Bruce to Claudia's apartment and watched gloomily out a window as my fellow journalists scrambled all over the premises for any scrap of information.

The L.A. cops came and put a big official crime-scene padlock on my apartment door. It's a good thing Claudia had gone back for more of my clothes. I don't think her underwear would fit me, although I suppose Mr. Invisible could just as well flounce around in the nude. The cops also towed away my car. I can imagine what it will look like after they finish searching for Desma's pin. All those months of hiding my car from the collection agency, and I lose it anyway after I pay it off in full. What a pain!

I checked in by phone with Desma while Claudia was making dinner. She seemed pretty upset.

"It's bad, Axel. They have surveillance tapes of me in the store right before and after the pin disappeared."

"OK, but they don't show you committing any crime."

"That's what Myron pointed out. I said I was just looking because you had promised to buy me something from the store."

"Good. That sounds plausible."

"And Myron stressed that I'm nowhere on the tapes the day the earrings disappeared."

"What did you say about the earrings?"

"Well, I never got a chance to wear them, so I said I didn't know anything about them. I said maybe you stole them to give to some other girlfriend and she flushed them down the toilet."

"What did the cops say to that?"

"Well, they're like totally stumped because you don't show up on any of the tapes. They don't have a clue how you did it, Axel."

"Good. That's a relief."

"I tried my best to get them to think you're dead. I wailed, I shrieked, I cried my eyes out."

"I'm touched, Desma."

"You should be glad I'm a highly trained actor."

"Oh, right."

"Where are you sleeping tonight, Axel?"

"The cops padlocked my apartment, darling. I guess I'm bunking here with Claudia."

"Barricade your door, Axel. It's your only hope!"

Claudia put her (size 16) foot down. No more calls to Desma's cell phone. She said the cops might be monitoring her calls. Good point, I suppose. Well, if they overheard that call, they should be breaking down Claudia's door any minute now.

# Chapter 19

OK, so sue me, I had sex again last night with Claudia. Under the circumstances, I saw no gracious way to decline. She had prepared a delicious dinner. She did the washing up. She provided for my every comfort (heated towels, choice of waxed or unwaxed floss, etc.). She even switched off all the lights so you-know-who wouldn't be watching us from every wall. There are times when a grateful guest is called upon to reciprocate for hospitality received. Besides, I soon could be facing long years of involuntary same-sex fumblings with a succession of thuggish cell mates. So why not get some of the real thing (in the large economy size) while I could? And, yes, it was just as spectacular as before. One nice thing about being invisible during sex is that no matter how absurd your position–and mating with Claudia posed some formidable logistic challenges–you can never appear ridiculous.

We both slept as if unseen anaesthesiologists were pumping ether into the room, woke up full of beans, and carved off another slice before breakfast. As the song says if you can't be with the one you love. . . Anyway, it made a welcome change of pace from worrying about the cops.

I checked out the paper while Claudia was frying my eggs and bacon to order. For some reason the *Times* was giving this dumb wedding-crasher story more ink than the kidnaping of the Lindbergh baby. And I used to think it was a decent rag. Manic reporters had exhaustively pursued every angle and turned over every rock. It was all there: alleged heists and assaults, months of drunken loitering at the dog park, my shocking credit history, the condo foreclosure with libelous allegations of slovenliness by the appalled new owner, photos of Rachel and her gimpy boyfriend, the brand of her baseball bat, my arrest two decades before for high-school high jinx (cherry bomb, toilet), and on and on. They had a quote from my former editor saying I'd been a promising reporter sabotaged by alcohol–that from a guy who routinely used to drink me under the table. There was an entire sidebar on lovely Diane Philips, her "spotty" acting career, her previous arrest for shoplifting a blender in Sears (news to me), and her connections to the sordid Axel Weston.

I tossed the paper aside.

"Claudia, you got anything to drink around this place?"

"Just coffee and orange juice, sweetie. Don't take it so hard. It will all blow over in a few days."

Right, assuming I don't blow my brains out in the meantime.

Unlike me, Claudia had the stomach to read every word.

"They're quoting the singer Grace Glover here, Jack. She was at the wedding. She said you materialized right in front of her out of thin air."

"Fucking eyewitnesses, that's all I need."

I'd been hoping that all eyes had been riveted on the Bulgarian throat singers when Mr. Invisible slipped up. Being an alleged singer herself, Grace may not have been so entranced.

"She's hardly credible, Jack. Everyone knows Grace has had drug problems for years."

After breakfast Claudia went down to her office to tackle the flood of applications from people suddenly clamoring to live in our building. I pegged them all as celebrity-obsessed morons.

I was toying with Desma's little gun when Claudia's

phone rang. I didn't answer it, of course, but listened as the caller left a message: "This is Jeremy. Get the hell out of there. Now!"

I erased the message, gathered up everything that I could hide on Mr. Invisible's person, borrowed a wad of bills from Claudia's P.F. cookie jar, and left. As I exited the back door into the parking lot, I heard the screech of braking tires in front of the building. I circled around and spotted several L.A. police cars and three of those unmarked but obvious government sedans used by the FBI. Their many occupants were hustling into Claudia's office and securing all exterior doors. As I hurried from the scene I could hear loud barking from my former dog, loyally defending my territory.

What is so rare these days as an intact and working pay phone? I finally found one at a gas station on Veteran. I removed the receiver from the hook, placed it against the side of the phone so it wouldn't appear to be floating in space, deposited my coins, and dialed Jeremy's number. He was happy to hear his message had been helpful.

"How did you know I was there?" I asked.

"Well, they towed your car. I figured you weren't too far away."

"So what's going down?"

"The word is they found some unusual surveillance video from a celebrity's house in Encino. The location was tied in to your cell-phone calls."

"How unusual?"

"I didn't get the details, but my source thinks they might be calling in the Feds."

"Yeah. They did."

"Can you tell me anything, Axel?"

"Partridge Family."

"Oh, yes. That's interesting."

"Check it out. Gotta go."

"Good luck to you. We're not saying anything here."

"Thanks. I appreciate that very much."

I clicked the hook, deposited more coins, and dialed Desma's number. She answered, sounding scared.

"Pack a bag, darling. And meet me in the tow-away zone in an hour."

"Oh, Axel! What's happening!?"

"In an hour. Be there. Don't let me down!"

I hung up and started hoofing it toward Beverly Hills. My laptop was fairly thin and light, but walking with it stuffed into my shirt was no picnic. I had no way of knowing if Desma would actually show. My backup plan was to call Rachel and throw myself on her mercy. I stuck to secondary streets that paralleled Veteran and then Olympic. Not much traffic or many pedestrians on those streets. A few loose dogs, one of whom–a nosy poodle mix–Mr. Invisible had to kick in the butt. He beat a hasty retreat.

It made sense. The more obsessive the fans, the better the security system. I wonder what Claudia looked like taped on the infra-red spectrum. Probably a real eye-opener to the security firm: this tall and bulky semi-transparent blob sneaking around on tiptoes. "Whoo-ee, Ed, too weird for us, let's pass this one off to the FBI."

Damn, there are a lot of red Miata convertibles in this town. The fifth one that came along mercifully pulled up to the curb. I flung open the door, hopped in, kissed the driver, and we were off.

"I missed you, Axel!"

A rare bit of good news. I said I missed her too.

"My name is Jack now, Desma."

"Jack. I like that. Your old name reminded me of tires and blowouts at high speed."

"Let's hope we don't have any of those. You got any gas in this thing?"

"Oh, yes. There's plenty."

I leaned over and checked her gauge. The needle was registering under a quarter tank. We filled up on Olympic and charged it to Desma's credit card. A purchase in the middle of L.A. wouldn't tell them anything, but we'd have to retire the card once we left the city.

"Where are we going, Jack?" asked my driver, cleaning the windshield. She looked slim and sensational in cerulean blue.

"Somewhere far from the madding crowd, Desma. Got any ideas?"

"Well, Myron has a weekend house in Carpinteria he hardly ever uses."

"Where the hell is that?"

"Up the coast past Ventura."

"Let's go. Did you bring your cell phone?"

"Of course."

"Turn that sucker off. It's like a giant neon sign advertising where you are."

I told Desma to stay under the speed limit, keep her eyes on the road, and drive defensively. What we didn't want was to attract the attention of those boys in blue. She agreed and said she'd had enough of cops to last a lifetime.

"Did you see that horrible story about me in the *Times*, Jack?"

"It wasn't that bad, Desma. Remember, there's no such thing as bad publicity. You looked great in the photo."

"Thanks. You think it might have made an impression on casting agents?"

"No way it couldn't have. You are definitely on their minds."

"Well, I was splashed right there on the front page. You don't get that kind of exposure being in a lousy stain-remover commercial."

"That's right. So what was your plan for sneaking out with a blender? That's a pretty bulky item."

"It was all my boyfriend's fault. God, what a cad! He said I was looking fat. So I was reading in *Vogue* about the smoothie diet. I was buying the jerk a cordless drill for his birthday when this impulse came over me. You think it will wreck my career?"

"Nah. It was years ago. People don't care. Almost everyone has shoplifted at one time or another. It's the national pastime."

"Thanks, Axel, I mean, Jack. You're making me feel much better. God, I missed you."

We could have gone up 101, but I had a morbid desire to revisit the Pacific Coast Highway. We made good time getting to Malibu.

"Oh, look, Desma. There's where I drowned."

Traffic slowed from rubbernecking tourists as we drove past the scene of Tara's disastrous wedding.

"You know who used to own that house, Jack?"

"Who?"

"Tommy."

"Tommy, your billionaire hedge-fund manager?"

"Yeah. He had to unload it when he lost his pile."

"So you've been in it, huh?"

"Once or twice."

"Did you do it with Tommy in that big bedroom upstairs with the incredible view?"

"That's for me to know, Jack honey, and you to worry about."

I looked over at her and smiled. That was the first term of endearment I had ever heard from those beautiful lips.

Desma bought a sack of mini-burgers in Oxnard and found a private spot by the ocean to park for lunch. We dined in the car with the top up, but with the windows rolled down to catch the cooling breezes. It was a nice change from solitary confinement in Claudia's apartment.

"Where did you sleep last night?" asked Desma, sucking on her straw. She was washing down her burger with a tall strawberry sun tea.

As a journalist I had witnessed innumerable people destroy their lives through inappropriate and excessive candor. Telling the truth probably makes sense in some contexts, but not in this one.

"On Claudia's couch, darling. It was about a half-foot too short for real comfort, but I managed OK."

Little details like that help to add to your credibility.

"She didn't try to throw herself at you?"

"I don't know. She may have been dropping some hints, but I ignored them. I just steered the conversation back to Gus, her boyfriend."

"Chicks hate to be reminded of them when they're trying to be seduced."

"I figured as much, Desma. Yeah, that was my strategy."

"So you never slept with her at all?"

Now was not the time to falter when the interrogation became so direct.

"Nope. Never had the pleasure."

"She didn't get horny when she was invisible?"

"Well, if she did, she didn't mention it," I lied.

"I hope you're not lying to me, Jack."

"I have nothing to hide, Desma. If I'd slept with Claudia, I'd tell you all about it. Sleeping with that giant would probably be an experience one would want to get off their conscience."

A chuckle from my interrogator.

"She's not that unattractive, Jack. Tall girls can be really striking. She could be cute if she trimmed down."

An obvious snare. I dodged around it.

"Well, darling, you have a better imagination than I have. Do you want this last burger?"

"No. You can have it. Did Claudia cook dinner for you last night?"

"No, she nuked some leftovers. She's not much of a cook."

"I've dated so many lying weasels, Jack. I sometimes have trouble trusting people."

"I know how that is, Desma. Trust is something you have to build brick by brick."

"It's harder to trust someone when they're just a voice

beside you–when you can't look into their eyes."

I didn't mention that even if I had been visible beside her, I'd have made sure I was wearing dark sunglasses while denying my torrid sex history with Claudia.


Carpinteria was a sleepy little beach town about a dozen miles south of Santa Barbara. It had a modest business district a few blocks long up from a stretch of sand that a large sign advertised as "the world's safest beach." The houses I passed were just as modest. Probably 50 years ago they were affordable to an average family. According to Desma, now even the two-bedroom cottages near the beach were going for a million plus. But the neighborhoods still looked cozy and unostentatious. All the folks seriously putting on the dog were up the coast in fancy Montecito and Santa Barbara.

Myron's weekend house was painted a bilious pink (to discourage break-ins, said Desma) and set back from the street behind an overgrown garden. We parked the Miata out of sight in the ramshackle two-car garage. Desma retrieved the key from under a bird feeder, and we went in through the back door. It was about a thousand square feet, circa 1940s, furnished like a lot of weekend houses with castoffs that could acquire cigarette burns or get stolen and nobody would care. It smelled just musty enough to remind you that the ocean was only two blocks away.

"What do you think?" asked Desma, putting down her bag.

"Very nice. Let's check out the bedroom."

That room looked like it had been decorated by someone's Aunt Minnie, except for two walls displaying dozens of framed photographs of rockets. There were U.S. rockets and Russian rockets. English and French rockets. Plus rockets from China, Brazil, North Korea, Japan, Israel, etc. There was even a photo of the late Saddam Hussein smirking beside his own impressive Iraqi rocket.

"Myron's into rockets, huh?" I asked.

"That would be his elder son Jeff."

"These are all rather phallic, you know," I pointed out.

"Remind me what that word refers to," Desma leered.

We pulled down the pink chenille bedspread and undertook a leisurely refresher course in that subject. Among the essentials I had rescued from Claudia's place was a stash of Desma's rubber reliables. One was pressed into duty to withstand the many G-forces of my own personal rocket blast. It was the first time I had ever made love to two women in the same day–and neither of them my wife. Quite a stretch for a guy cursed with the monogamy gene.

"I wish I could see you, Jack," said Desma, snuggling against me. It was women like her who made applied nudity such a compelling sport.

"This way has some advantages, darling. You can imagine you're lying here with George Clooney. Or Elvis. Or Genghis Khan, the scourge of Asia. Or, of course, Myron."

"Please, honey, I'd rather not. Myron said the D.A. would probably offer me a plea deal to testify against you. I might get off with probation."

"Well, your testimony would be the only real evidence they would have against me. But I don't see them hauling an invisible defendant into court."

"Hey, that's right! How could they prosecute you?"

"Prosecution is the least of our worries, darling. The government doesn't like the idea of invisible people running around free. We could start giving seminars on how to be invisible. No jewelry store in the land would be safe."

"Oh, right. I suppose so. Damn, what'll we do?"

"What we do is we lie low. We hunker down. We blend in. We disappear off the radar screen."

"Me too?"

"You know the magic words, darling. You've been there and done that. You're a target now too."

"Damn! What'll I tell my agent!?"

"Not a word, darling. Sorry, not one word."

While Desma wrote out her grocery list, I counted up our cash: $1817 from me and $38.53 from Desma. Good thing she had made a stop at the ATM yesterday for the impressive sum of $20. I'd been too anxious to get out of town. We both should have stopped at ATMs in L.A. and sucked out the maximum bucks permitted. We couldn't last long on the road with less than two grand.

I kissed Desma, suggested she limit her purchases to budget items, and she left for Vons nearby on the main drag. While she was gone, I searched the house. A desk drawer in the other bedroom proved to have a false bottom. I pried up the panel and discovered Myron's .45. Next to the gun was an envelope containing 36 $100 bills. These I added to my stash; the gun I left where it was. Myron might want to shoot himself with it when he discovered the theft. I found another $3 in change and a dried-out joint under the couch cushions. There was an aging $50 bill taped to the back of the walnut headboard in the main bedroom. From the condition of the yellowed cello tape it could have been there for decades. Probably someone's rainy day fund. Well, it was raining on my parade, so I took it.

Vons had cornish game hens on sale; Desma roasted a pair for dinner. No beer for me, but she bought a pint of off-brand bourbon for her own emergency use. We toasted to "happy days" with tap water and enjoyed an excellent dinner. Afterwards we walked over to the beach in the dark. The western horizon still glowed faintly pink. A string of oil platforms along the Santa Barbara Channel sparkled with a lacy light. Too many houses overlooked the beach for strolling in the sand. Instead, we walked along the street that paralleled the beach, then took a risk and continued on up past the stores and restaurants on Linden Street. Quite a few tourists and locals out and about on this warm night, but we steered our way around them.

When we returned, we were both ready for bed. Desma

had some bad news. She would sleep with me, but she wouldn't sleep with me. I was banished to the lonely single bed in the other bedroom. I complained, I whined, I puled, but she was unyielding. We lay there apart in the dark listening to dim ocean rhythms and chatting desultorily through the wall until we both fell silent.

Desma bought me a *Los Angeles Times* from a coin-op rack down the block. It's always unsettling when the boys in blue stop talking. You could sense the reporters' frustrations as their sources clammed up. The front-page story reported that Axel Weston's building had been sealed off and all the tenants relocated temporarily to hotels. The building manager, Claudia Stasse, had been detained for questioning. Also taken into custody was Jeremy Hollis, a partner in the Z77 photo agency. A police spokesperson declined to say why Mr. Hollis, a British national, was being held. Nor would she say why the building had been sealed, although she did state that the missing pin and earring had not been found, and the building was not closed off because it was contaminated in any way. Good. At least the world knows that dastardly Axel Weston hadn't been cooking up methamphetamine in his bathroom.

I must admit that the arrest of Jeremy came as a surprise. It appears that calling my cell phone was the kiss of death. I hope his bladder is standing up to the pressure. The *Times* article carried this quote from Tara: "If Axel Weston destroyed my wedding at the behest of the vile predators at Z77, they can expect no mercy from my lawyers." It also reported that the police were searching for Weston's companion, actress Diane Philips, who allegedly had disappeared.

"Is it bad, honey?" asked Desma, nibbling on a piece of toast.

"Oh, nothing we can't handle, darling. Any more coffee in that pot?"

"Sure."

She refilled my cup. The gal was a gem in the kitchen and the bedroom. What a combination.

"Desma, do you think you could change your appearance?"

"Why?" she asked, alarmed. "What's wrong with it? Do I have stains? Unsightly hair?"

"You're perfect, darling. As usual. A little too perfect. You look like a movie star."

"Thanks, honey. I try my best."

"I know you do. But you kind of stand out in a crowd."

"Oh. You want me tone down the effect? I could do a mousey look and walk with a limp like Talia Shire in 'Rocky'."

"The mousey sounds good, but I think we could dispense with the limp for now."

Thankfully, Myron's wife had wretched taste. Desma pawed listlessly through a selection of ghastly weekend clothes hanging in the closet.

"I don't know, Jack. This isn't mousey. This is Alzheimer's victim on acid."

"No, Desma, I think we can work with this. Here, try on this wig."

Desma recoiled from the wig as if it were last month's road kill.

"You picked that thing off the closet floor, Jack. I am *not* putting it on my head."

After I shampooed the ratty brown wig in the sink, wrung it out in a towel, and blew it dry, Desma reluctantly consented to place it on her head. She studied her reflection in the bathroom mirror.

"God, Jack! I look like Susan Tyrrell in 'Fat City'."

"That was an excellent film, Desma, one of John Huston's best. Who was the actor who played the broken-down boxer?"

"Stacy Keach. Didn't you love the scene where he poured the peas straight from the can onto her plate? God, that was low-life living at its most authentic. Is that the look you're going for here, Jack?"

"Sure. About as far from Hollywood glamor as you can get."

"OK, Jack. Whatever you say. You're directing this epic."

I surmised that Myron's wife was around Desma's height, but considerably bulkier. Not in Claudia's weight class, but certainly matronly. Her dispirited prints and toxic knits draped loosely on Desma, nicely obscuring her exquisite form.

Desma coordinated a nightmarish orange blouse with a greenish skirt from hell.

"The secret to this look, Jack," she said, selecting a severely contrasting sparkly belt, "is to dress like you're blind."

Next, Desma redid her make up, going heavy on the green eyeshadow and smearing on flame red lipstick with an unsteady hand. She stepped back from the mirror so I could take it all in. She shifted her hip into a slouch and chewed imaginary gum.

"Here it is, Jack baby. The full Bakersfield. Want to mosey on down to the pool hall and buy me a cream sherry?"

"Damn, Desma, you're perfect!"

Desma fluffed up her wig.

"Yeah. I am kinda at that."

"We need a name for this creature. How about Tammy?"

"Tammy it is, Jack. Come gimme a kiss."

I kissed her somewhere wide of the lipstick smear, and Tammy gave me a friendly grope to the balls.

After lunch Tammy dived into the garage and pulled out an old tandem bike. I inflated the tires with a rusty hand pump, and determined they were holding air. We packed a blanket and some snacks into the rusty basket and were off. Tammy piloted from the front seat. She steered us on a long meandering course along the beachfront, and up and down the quiet residential streets. It was an ideal way for an invisible person with a paunch to get some exercise on a sunny summer day in a scenic beach town.

We wound up at the state beach park a few blocks from downtown. The grass–threadbare from budget cutbacks–was too sparse to give away Mr. Invisible's presence. Tammy spread out the blanket and we lay down to enjoy the sun. A couple dozen beach-goers were lounging along the sand, but we had the grass to ourselves. Every so often Tammy would sneak me a corn chip or a piece of cheese. Several single guys, undeterred by Tammy's appearance, paused by our blanket to chat her up. She told them she was waiting for her biker boyfriend, recently released from Soledad state prison, to return from his beer run. That sent the lonely fellows on their way.

I stroked her warm thigh and thought about our situation. The problem was I was floundering in the dark. I didn't know what exactly that tape of Claudia showed. It must have piqued their interest in a big enough way to call in the FBI and seal off the building. I also didn't know if Claudia and Jeremy were sticking to the "tissue of lies" story or if the truth had been water-boarded out of them. Claudia, I figured, could be pretty stubborn, and Jeremy didn't actually know I was invisible, although he might have suspected as much. I had to assume that the cops knew I was alive, and were hunting for me and Desma. Beyond that, I was just speculating. I also felt bad for my dog. I hoped he'd been rescued by Gus, and wasn't wandering lost or impounded in some cage.

"Whatcha thinkin' about, baby doll?" asked Tammy.

"Your sweet ass."

"Wanta go back to my place and get sweaty?"

"Can I do it Bakersfield style?"

"How's that work, Lyle?"

"Spread-eagled and naked acrost the hood of my pick-up."

"Dream on, ya big lug."

Afterwards, we lay entwined on the bed and I contemplated the rocket photos.

"So what's with this Jeff guy and his rockets?" I asked.

"I don't know much about him. Myron doesn't like to talk about him. They're estranged."

"How can people be estranged from their own children?"

"It happens, Jack. Some people aren't destined to get along. Being married is a very close connection, but you're estranged from your wife."

True enough. She was once the most important person on the planet for me and now we were severed–apparently forever. In fact, at the moment she thought I was dead.

"So did you sleep with Claudia, Jack?"

"Yeah. Fuck it. I did."

"I thought so."

"Are you pissed?"

"I don't know. I figured you were lying to spare my feelings."

"Yeah. You'd cut out on me and I was fucking invisible. I mean, guys have to get it where they can get it."

"I don't really understand that."

"Male sexuality is simple, darling. We're programmed to: 1. Locate target. 2. Stick it in. 3. Drive it in as deep as possible. 4. Deliver the load. It's a lot more complicated for you chicks."

"That's your theory, huh?"

"Yep. Chicks are multi-core work stations, guys are Commodore 64s."

"So what is female sexuality all about, Jack? In your expert opinion."

"You really want to know? It's simple: observe lesbians."

"Observe lesbians?"

"Yeah. There on display is essential female programming unobscured by all the male/female bullshit. What's the first thing that happens when two lesbians meet?"

"Uh, you tell me."

"They move in together and start elaborate nest building."

"You think so, huh?"

"It's a well-known fact. 'Build Nest' is not a command that appears anywhere in a guy's coding."

"So that's your rationale for screwing Claudia?"

"Well, that's the best I can come up with and I'm sticking to it."

She snuggled closer and kissed me.

"Well, Jack, I have to give you points for originality."

"It's all true, Desma. I'll never lie to you again."

"Uh-huh. What a comforting thought. All my troubles with men are over."

"Stick with me, baby. It's strictly the sunny side of the street from now on."

# Chapter 20

More unsettling news in the *Los Angeles Times*. I may have to switch to another paper. Perhaps I'll give the little Carpinteria weekly a try.

"Hey, Tammy. It says here Claudia Stasse escaped yesterday evening from a secure federal lockup facility."

Tammy–modeling violently clashing plaids–paused with a pancake in mid-flip. "How on earth did she do that?"

"My guess is she acquired better command of the words. She became invisible and slipped out in the confusion as they were looking for her."

"That must be embarrassing for the FBI guys."

"Yeah, they're probably as annoyed as hell. They're not accustomed to losing track of prisoners her size."

Tammy put three more blueberry pancakes on my plate. It's a good thing my gut was presently invisible.

"But why would she try to escape, Jack?"

"Search me. Maybe she didn't like the cuisine."

The article also reported that Jeremy had posted bond and been released on bail. He was quoted as having "no comment" on reports that his firm had wired substantial sums to Axel Weston's bank account shortly after the Briny X and Teresany photos had appeared.

A conversation with that Brit might prove enlightening, but I could think of no safe way to accomplish it.

After breakfast, I got out my laptop and transferred into

it all the photos I snapped in Claudia's apartment. I was surprised to see my computer was detecting an unsecured WiFi signal from somewhere in the neighborhood; I used it to get on-line. I didn't dare check my e-mail, but I went through an anonymizing website to obscure my tracks as I cruised to the Z77 photo agency site. It offered a function for the public to upload potentially marketable photos. I sent the whole batch to Jeremy. I figured he needed a boost after all the trouble I put him through. Claudia was certainly newsworthy now, and the world might pay to get a peek at her obsessions.

I also logged onto my offshore account and instructed my bank to send $5,000 in travelers checks via overseas express mail to D.M. Philips, care of General Delivery, Main Post Office, Fresno, California. I had no idea if they would do such a thing, but I thought it was worth a shot.

"Hey, Tammy," I said. "You ever want to go to Fresno?"

Tammy scratched her wig and cracked her gum.

"Damn, Jack. Going to Fresno has always been one of my dearest dreams."


In the garage was a rusty old Japanese pick-up with a fiberglass shell over the bed. Tammy said Myron used it for hauling garden supplies, although the garden gave little evidence of having been tended in the current century. The keys were in the ignition and the battery was dead. I found a tin box of rusty tools and managed to swap in the fairly new battery from the Miata. The little truck started on the first try. Chalk up another triumph for Japanese industry.

"Are we stealing Myron's truck?" Tammy asked.

"We have to, darling. Driving your car is way too risky."

The gods had somehow permitted Myron to have sex with Desma. For this glimpse of paradise, no recompense could be too great. I figured the sacrifice of this truck (and the wad of $100s) was entirely inconsequential.

"It's pretty skanky, Jack. Can I wash it first?"

"Sure. But don't spray too hard with the hose. You might blow holes in the sheet metal."

While Tammy sudsed up the truck, I contemplated its expired registration sticker on the license plate. Nowhere in my search of the house had I come across a letter from the DMV with the new sticker. The absence of one could get us stopped by the highway patrol. The Miata, however, did have an up-to-date sticker–adhered to a thick wad from previous years. I sent Tammy to Vons for a package of straight-edge razor blades and some epoxy glue.

Working the razor blade carefully all around the edges, I managed to pry off the stack of stickers in one piece. I stirred together two little squiggles of glue, smeared the gob on the back of the stickers, and applied them to the truck's plate. Road legality had been achieved. I also checked to make sure the taillights and turn signals were working. Cops were always looking for excuses to pull vehicles over. Thankfully, Tammy avoided another common provocation–driving while black.

It took us about a half hour to pack up our stuff. I couldn't squeeze into any of Myron's boy-sized clothes, so I'd been borrowing from his sons' wardrobe in the other bedroom. I tossed a selection of their socks, underwear, sport shirts, etc. into an old suitcase I found in the closet. The master-bedroom closet yielded a matched set of molded American Tourister luggage, circa 1962, into which Tammy packed her many eye-bruising ensembles. Food from the refrigerator we packed into a styrofoam cooler we dredged up from the pantry. Canned goods and cooking stuff went into a cardboard box. At Tammy's suggestion, we hauled out the single mattress from my bed–which just fit into the back of the truck. Using sheets and blankets from the house, we made up an inviting mobile bed. You never know when you might have to pull over to the side of the road for an emergency ball.

Tammy left her car keys and this note on the kitchen table: "Hi Myron. We borrowed a few things and your old truck. Please be understanding and don't tell anyone. Love ya, D."

On the way out of town we stopped for gas, and Tammy inflated all the tires to the correct pressure. She checked the oil and added some coolant to the radiator overflow tank. The little truck seemed to be running fine. It was very basic inside: AM radio (working), heater controls, but no air conditioning.

We headed north on highway 101; Tammy poked along in the slow lane with the big semis. Carpinteria had been a pleasant refuge, but I figured it was risky to stay in one place for very long. Plus, there was always the possibility that Myron or one of his family might barge in on our party. Still, we would miss that blue ocean and its temperate breezes. I could see why the wealthy were always elbowing their way up to the edge of the surf to build their McMansions.

As all routes to Fresno from the coast were circuitous, we had about 300 miles to drive. We took 101 to Santa Maria (famous for acquitting Michael Jackson), then headed east. Every mile in that direction brought the temperature up a degree or so. Hot dry air blasted through the open windows. Traffic, though, was light and the brown hills reminded me of the parched landscape in old western movies. I was finally seeing a bit of my adopted state. Every few minutes I daubed the driver with a wet hand towel swiped from Myron's bathroom.

"It's like an oven in here, Jack," complained Tammy. "You know my car was comfortable and had air conditioning."

I pointed out that people had been driving cars for over a half-century before A/C became common. They even drove through sweltering places like Arizona and Nevada in August. Movie stars routinely drove Cadillacs without A/C to Palm Springs as late as the 1950s.

"Sure, Jack, but I doubt Kim Novak ever made the trip wearing a hot old wig and polyester knits."

On highway 33 near Taft (a town formerly named Moron) a patrol car pulled us over. It was a local sheriff, not the highway patrol.

Tammy decided to start the conversation with some sarcasm.

"Howdy, officer. Was I speeding?"

The deputy was all business.

"Can I see your driver's license?"

Tammy rooted around in her purse and produced her I.D. The deputy studied the photo and looked over at Tammy several times.

"I got a makeover at K-Mart the day I got my picher taken. Pretty nice, huh?"

He handed back her license.

"Can I see your registration?"

More rooting in the glove box produced a wadded up registration. The deputy unfolded it and checked it over.

"Ma'am, who is Myron T. Landers?"

"My asshole of a husband."

"This registration is from two years ago."

"Really? Well, I got current tags, but I guess Myron forgot to put the paper in the cab."

"Ma'am, do I have your permission to look in the back of your truck?"

"Sure thing, officer. Be my guest."

"Could you step out of the vehicle and open up the back?"

Tammy complied and watched calmly as the deputy searched through our bags and boxes. He was hoping to score a drug arrest, but was coming up empty. I knew he wouldn't find Desma's little gun because it was in my pocket. The situation was tense, but I couldn't imagine a circumstance in which I could shoot anyone–except possibly myself. There was always the possibility he might find Desma's diamond pin, if indeed she had brought it along with her. Its present whereabouts were unknown to me. Eventually, everything was packed away again, and Tammy returned to the cab.

The deputy took out his ticket book.

"Ma'am, I'm going to have to give you a citation for not carrying your current registration."

"Officer, you ever have a bladder infection?"

"Beg your pardon?"

"I got a bad one now. If I don't get to a toilet in the next three minutes, I'm going to wet my pants."

"I can't help that, ma'am."

"I got a serious mucous discharge that's about to trickle down my leg. I can show you if you want."

That did it. The deputy folded up his book, advised her to carry her current registration at all times, and beat a hasty retreat. Tammy waved as he pulled out and sped off down the highway.

"You were great, darling," I said. "You don't really have a bladder infection again do you?"

"No, crackerjack, but we better give it a rest for a while. We don't want to pester your poor little wife for any more pills."

I was relieved that the deputy hadn't recognized the name on Desma's license or entered any of our data into his computer. We had passed the first test. Tammy did not look like a missing movie star.

We nearly made it to Fresno, but Tammy began to flag. We pulled off the road in Lemoore, a sun-baked town in the flats of the San Joaquin Valley about 30 miles south of our destination. It was the sort of wind-swept town you expected Clint Eastwood to ride into on a horse with murder on his mind. We stopped at an old motel called the Hrazdan Inn. The clerk, who looked like someone's Armenian grandmother, asked Tammy why she wanted a room with two beds if she were traveling alone. Tammy said she had multiple personality disorder and needed to keep everyone segregated by sex at bedtime. She got a double room across the courtyard from the office and some curious looks from the clerk. After driving all day, Tammy had to haul in the bags and go for our take-out order from the local Chinese restaurant. I hated that she had to do all the work, but what could I do? At least she got an invisible sex slave out of the deal.

Tammy was spooning the cashew prawns onto our borrowed Myron plates when we heard a knock on the door.

Immediate adrenalin rush of fear and panic. My hand went automatically to the gun in my pocket.

"Who is it?" called Tammy.

No reply.

She looked over in my direction, shrugged like the jig was up, and opened the door.

There was no one there.

"Hi, guys," said Claudia. "Damn, that smells good. Aren't you going to invite me in?"

Tammy stepped back as an unseen person swept in, making large foot-shaped impressions in the thin motel carpet.

"God, I'd kill for a glass of water," said Claudia. "Riding on the back of those flatbed trucks in this heat really dries a body out. I felt like a grape being turned into a raisin."

Claudia downed her eight daily glasses of water all in one go, then turned her attention to dinner. I got one prawn and a little bit of the mixed vegetables with tofu. (Claudia doesn't care that much for tofu.)

Of course, the first thing we asked was how she found us.

"Well, I'd always been a little psychic. I usually know ahead of time when the phone is going to ring, that sort of thing. Anybody mind if I finish the pork?"

Tammy told her to go ahead.

Claudia continued between bites. "I think being invisible gave my whole clairvoyance thing a boost. There I am, fleeing federal custody when I spot this truck loaded with concrete pipes stopped at a light. So I wedge myself into one of the sections and hang on like I'm inside a blasting wind tunnel all the way to Las Vegas. But I've never had much luck in Nevada, so I hop another truck carrying giant spools of cable. This one hauls me to a trucking terminal in Lemoore. Now I'm getting somewhere, I think, because my worst enemy in junior high was a girl named Lee Moore. So there I am sweating my ass off in beautiful downtown Lemoore–wondering what the hell I should do next–when who should drive by but Diane Philips wearing a dead possum on her head."

"It's a disguise," I pointed out. "She's impersonating a redneck from Bakersfield named Tammy."

"Oh, yeah?" said Claudia. "I was born in Bakersfield. And guess what my mother's name is?"

It was all too weird and creepy to deal with on a practically empty stomach. I asked Claudia what happened with her and the cops.

"OK, there I am warming up a danish in the office microwave, and the next thing I know I'm face-down on the carpet and some cute cop is slapping on handcuffs and reading me my rights. I'm hauled downtown and all these guys in bad suits and government haircuts start grilling me like I'm Mrs. Osama bin Laden."

"What did they want to know?" I asked.

"What do you think? Your name came up prominently. So I stuck to the program and said I hadn't seen you since Saturday, etc. Then they play this tape of my invisible self exploring a certain house in Encino. Fuck that shit, I'm thinking. What's the point of being invisible if you show up on a tape looking like something from a Ghostbusters movie? But I stay cool and tell them the tape is an obvious fake. I say it's some amateur CGI put out by someone trying to cash in on the Tara-Richard wedding publicity."

"And they bought that?" I asked.

"Hey, these guys have very rational minds. They're desperate for some logical explanation for all this wacky L.A. stuff that has hit their fan. They don't want to think that people are walking around invisible. So they let it slip that the original of the tape is on its way to Washington for analysis. I figure that gives me a little time. But I know when the report comes back, I'm going to be in deep doo-doo. They're going to transfer me to some maximum security dungeon to be poked and prodded by guys with clipboards and large I.Q.s. So I ask to go to the ladies' room and start saying the words like my life depends on it. Anyway, it works and I make a break for it. God, it was hot. I must have sweated off 25 pounds. Hey, Tammy, you feel like making a run for ice cream?"

Tammy and I walked across the highway to a convenience store while Claudia took a shower.

"What are we going to do, Jack?"

"Well, we're going to have to start ordering more food."

"Are we going to take her with us?"

"Something tells me she'd be a tough person to ditch."

"Damn. Why did you involve her in this?"

"I didn't, darling. Claudia involved herself. She's like a runaway freight train coming right at you. And you can't jump off the tracks."

Tammy bought their largest carton of double dutch chocolate and two hotdogs. We ducked behind the store, gobbled down the dogs in the fading light, then returned to the motel. Claudia had washed out her clothes and hung them up to dry on the shower rod. We surmised that our unexpected guest was lounging on one of the beds in the nude.

Tammy was smart this time. She dished up servings for us before she turned the carton over to Claudia. I figured I'd at least broach the subject.

"And what are your plans, Claudia?" I asked.

"I thought I'd go on being a fugitive from the FBI, Jack. What are your plans?"

"Uh, similar."

"Good," said Claudia. "That's settled. Tammy, do you have anything that would fit me? I'm traveling sort of light."

"You're welcome to look in my bags, Claudia."

"I already did. I was hoping you had something more in the truck."

"No, sorry," replied Tammy coldly.

"We'll have to stop at the mall tomorrow," said Claudia, scraping the bottom of the carton with her plastic spoon. "How you fixed for cash, Jack?"

"Not well. We'll have to look for a Wal-Mart. Or, better yet, a thrift store."

"OK, but if I'm dressed like Tammy, I'm not going to be putting my heart into becoming visible again."

"Have you said the words?"

"Up, down, and sideways. Your invisibility genie really likes to tease."

"What do you suppose we're doing wrong?" I asked.

"I wish I knew. You must have tapped into some vestige of black magic, Jack. The words sound just enough like some ancient spell to work occasionally. But we've just blindly grabbed onto a little corner of the power. The rest of it we don't comprehend and can't access. We just know enough to get ourselves into deep doo-doo. Still, you got to love the side effects."

"Side effects?" said Tammy.

"You know, all the manic energy, the mental lift like you're mainlining some new form of heroin–not to mention the aphrodisiac aspects. I suppose you guys are balling constantly."

"Uh, no comment," I said.

"Don't be shy, dudes," said Claudia. "I spotted some pills in Tammy's purse that speak louder than words."

"I wish you'd keep out of my stuff," said Tammy.

"What are you going to do, Tammy dear," she chuckled. "Call a cop?"

Bedtime posed another dilemma. There were three people and two beds. Claudia wanted to sleep with me. I certainly didn't wish to sleep with her. I wanted to sleep with Tammy. And she didn't want to sleep with either of us. I suggested to Claudia that she consider bunking down in the back of the truck.

"Not on your life, Jack. It's still about 95 degrees out there. That wheezing motel air conditioner is the only thing between us and death from heat prostration."

There was only one thing to do. The man would have to be a gentleman and sleep on the floor. As Tammy was dragging in the mattress from the back of the truck, the clerk ran over from the office and demanded to inspect the room. Claudia and I ducked into the bathroom, where its vinyl floor wouldn't give us away.

"You only paid for one person," insisted the clerk.

"Lady, you see anybody here besides me?" asked Tammy.

"Who ate all that ice cream and Chinese food?" she demanded, pointing at the empty cartons.

"I told you. I got multiple personalities. I got one girl who's a really big eater."

"Whose brassiere is that?" demanded the clerk, pointing to the shower rod from which depended the world's largest bra.

"It's mine," admitted Tammy. "I used to have a weight problem. I hang it up to remind me not to eat so much."

"I get it," replied the nosy granny. "So now you only eat one gallon of ice cream. Well, you can't bring that mattress in here. It might have bugs."

"You mean it might pick up some bugs."

"You get that mattress outta here or I'm callin' a cop."

The mattress went back out to the truck, the clerk left muttering to herself, Tammy claimed one bed, I bedded down with a large naked person in the other bed. I laid down the rules before I switched out the light.

"OK, Claudia. No hanky panky. You stay on your side at all times."

"Jesus, Jack, it's not like we haven't done it a million times before."

"That is a gross exaggeration, Claudia. And you know it. You're just trying to drive a wedge between me and Tammy."

"Will you both shut up!" exclaimed Tammy. "Some of us here are tired and disgusted."

"Relax, Tammy," said Claudia. "We'll work something out. How about we each get Jack every other night?"

"I hardly think so," said Tammy. "Jack and I are engaged to be married."

That was the best news I'd heard all week.

Claudia was skeptical.

"You're engaged to an invisible fugitive who happens to be married already?"

"I'm in the process of getting a divorce, Claudia. You know that. Now go to sleep and don't touch me!"

"OK, Jack. But just remember: It works for the Mormons."

Did you ever have an erection that was so granite-like in its stiffness that it woke you from a dead sleep? So I pop awake and try to get my bearings in the dark. I have sagged into some kind of sinkhole in the mattress. I am lying against a massive warm thing, perhaps someone's back. My tool is pleasantly enclosed in a vibrating warmth. The vibrations seem to coincide with the sounds of snoring. Yep, every throaty exhalation produces a corresponding tingle in my rod. The sensation is pleasant in the extreme. Uh-oh. A realization begins to dawn. I fear an untoward trespass has occurred. Can I extract myself without arousing my host or other sleepers? Inch by inch I undertake a stealthy withdrawal, timing the measured retreat to the body rhythms of my victim. Eventually, I undock from the mother ship and retreat to the far edge of the mattress. So what the fuck happened to rocket-man Jeff's pajamas? I feel around. Yes, I'm still wearing them. My busy tool had slipped between two buttons and gone adventuring on its own. Damn. Why couldn't pajama makers take precautions and equip these things with stout zippers or industrial-strength Velcro?

# Chapter 21

When we reached Fresno, a bank sign was flashing the time: 11:23 a.m. and the temperature: 104 degrees. Heat lay upon the stunned and supine city like a giant, bloated beast. Actually, the Fresnoians we observed seemed undisturbed by their customary summer weather, but the three visitors in the roasting little truck were certainly stunned and nearly supine. Nevertheless, we dragged ourselves from thrift shop to thrift shop, acquiring a meager collection of unfashionable garments in size Gargantuan. Petulant Claudia insisted on sneaking in with Tammy to oversee her purchases, while Mr. Invisible sat outside in any shade I could muster and read the *Fresno Bee*.

Splashed across the front page was a full-color photograph of Claudia's living room–credited in the slug line to Z77 Agency. That should help Jeremy pay for his lawyers. The article discussed in length Claudia's fascination with you-know-who, and quoted the actor as saying he appreciated the interest of his fans but hoped they'd keep in mind that it was just a TV show. That will teach the guy to be so magnetic on the screen. The story noted that Ms. Stasse was still at large and quoted "male companion" Gus Baboo as urging her "to return to the folks who love you." There was no mention of my former pup and his fate.

Fresno seemed like a mid-sized city that had grown into a large city solely through the accretion of housing tracts, strip malls, and shopping centers. We drove along endless commercial avenues and eventually checked into a budget motel just off the freeway on West Shaw. There we partook of a large Mexican lunch purchased from a nearby taco truck. Since Claudia and I dare not eat in restaurants, all of our meals–even breakfast–were of the take-out variety. I tried to think of it as being on a perpetual picnic.

After lunch I asked Claudia if she would excuse herself so as to afford my fiancee and me an hour of privacy. Frankly, my libido was still a bit overwrought from the previous night's stimulations.

"And where would you have me go?" asked Claudia, re-reading the *Fresno Bee* article for the fifth time. She loved that her collection was getting the media attention it deserved, but worried that it was not being adequately guarded by the police from raids by other P.F. fanatics.

"You could take a walk," suggested Tammy.

"Yes," I agreed. "You could explore greater Fresno."

"It's 110 degrees in the shade out there," replied Claudia. "And there ain't no shade."

"We all have to make sacrifices," said Tammy. "This trip is supposed to be a like a honeymoon for Jack and me."

"Get real," said Claudia. "You two are on the lam from the law. Desperate fugitives should be concerned with survival not screwing."

In the end, we agreed on a compromise. Claudia hauled the TV into the bathroom and agreed to lock herself in for the full duration of Oprah's program. She did so while Tammy and I enjoyed a blissful interval of intimacy. On the second go-around I felt my monogamy gene clamp down tight on Diane, Desma, Tammy Philips. She was the woman for me; I was officially and genetically over Rachel Burke, which is just as well since the latter believed herself to be my widow. My complicated love life finally had sorted itself out.

Later that afternoon Tammy drove slowly past the downtown Fresno post office while Claudia did a psychic reading on the situation. Claudia was riding shotgun, I was observing her astral cogitations from the bed in the back through the cab's sliding rear window. We were all sweating like Nazi slave laborers.

"What do you think, Claudia?" I asked.

"I'm not picking up any danger signals. But you and I should probably case the joint before Tammy goes in. Even if we get caught, at least it will be air-conditioned."

Claudia and I walked all around the block and then through the lobby of the post office. We saw no one who looked like a plainclothes detective, spotted no sharpshooters on nearby rooftops, saw no government cars or command post vans, and detected no psychic disturbances beyond the usual ones emitted by bored postal employees. We went back to the truck and sent Tammy in for the mail.

No letter or package.

Damn. We would have to hang around Fresno and try again tomorrow.

We went back to the motel and turned the A/C on full blast. The motel didn't offer WiFi, but it did have a cable movie channel. So we watched TV, and Claudia and I competed to see who could make the most bitingly sarcastic comments. The victor by a mile was the tall bulky girl, no doubt the butt of a lifetime of other people's offensive comments. If they ever turned my script into a movie, I wouldn't want to watch it sitting next to Claudia.

I can see now why Bonnie and Clyde robbed banks while on the lam. You needed to find something to do to relieve the tedium.

"Why didn't you have the checks sent to someplace nice like San Francisco?" asked Tammy, as we chowed down later on take-out Armenian food.

"You think we can find a motel room in that town for 28 bucks a night?" I asked. "Besides, every FBI agent in the country would love to go to San Francisco on their government expense accounts and hang around waiting for us to show up. How many of those guys do you think are begging to go to Fresno in July?"

"I know why Jack chose Fresno," said Claudia, slurping down another exotic chee kufta.

"Why's that?" I asked.

"Because Tara is appearing here tomorrow night at Fresno State," she replied.

"Well, that's the first I've heard of it," I said.

"That's funny," said Claudia, "because you chose a motel that's right across the freeway from campus. It's so close, we could walk there."

"Why would I want to go see Tara?" I demanded.

"That's obvious," replied Claudia. "You broke up her marriage. Now you want to go throw yourself at her. Face it, Jack. You and Tara have some unfinished business."

Time slows down in Fresno. Giant braking mechanisms on the outskirts of the city apply tremendous pressure to the earth, slowing its rotation. The hands of my watch barely crawled. Fantastic yawns bubbled up lugubriously from one's toes and stretched open the mouth to unbelievable size. After the passage of several eons, it was time again for bed. The sleeping arrangements were the same as last night. I borrowed some safety pins from Tammy and surreptitiously reinforced my pajama closure.

We turned out the lights, and Claudia threw down the gauntlet.

"I need it bad," she announced. "I intend to get some and I do not intend to beg. Tammy, you were invisible. You know what it's like."

Tammy alarmed me by conceding Claudia's point. Immediate confusion in my monogamy center.

"But, Claudia," I pointed out. "I love Tammy."

"That is beside the point," said my bedmate. "Tammy, would you mind going into the bathroom?"

"Oh, hell," she replied. "I'll just stuff cotton in my ears."

"Tammy," I said, stricken. "Don't you love me?"

"I do, Jack. As long as you assure me that you're not doing it for your own pleasure, I guess I won't mind. You'll recall a lot of my previous boyfriends were married. I'm used to sharing."

Damn, this was all very unexpected. Before my mind could fully contemplate the consequences I was clamped in a powerful nude embrace. My pinned-up pajama bottoms were being forcefully yanked from my person. The rest was standard applied biology, stimulated by the invisibility genie. Two more condoms were applied strenuously from our diminishing stash. For Tammy's sake I tried desperately not to have too good of a time. I'm not quite sure I succeeded.

While sharing a shower with Tammy the next morning I asked why she hadn't objected more forcefully to last night's boyfriend swapping.

"It's pointless to resist, Jack," she whispered. "Not when Claudia gets like that. She's bigger and stronger than both of us put together."

"What should I do, darling?" I asked, helping her wash her chest.

"Get rid of her, Jack. She's spoiling everything."

I recognized that tone of voice. It was the same one Desma employed when she told me to abandon my dog.

I thought of Desma's little gun. Homicide was never something I'd perceived as being within my purview. How far into this criminality business was I prepared to go? The whole idea seemed preposterous. Claudia, I knew, was someone who would die about as promptly and meekly as Rasputin. I could empty the entire gun into her gut and only have time for a sincere apology before she twisted off my head.

No mention of us on the front page of today's *Fresno Bee*. But I read with interest a brief article on an inside page about a memorial service held in the chapel of a Burbank hospital for notorious wedding crasher and drowning victim Axel Weston. Rachel looked genuinely bereaved in the photo surrounded by sympathetic dog-park pals. Hovering in the background was Detective Myers, who may have been hoping that I'd show up for the eulogy so he could arrest my ass. Sorry to disappoint him. The story noted that a video of the service was made available almost instantly on Youtube. I look forward to checking it out. Not many folks have the opportunity to watch their own funeral service.

After another month-long Fresno morning (next time I go on the lam I'm bringing along some books), we downed a take-out lunch from the taco truck, then headed back downtown. Again, we psychically and physically cased the post office, then sent in Tammy. An ominously long wait in the heat beside our little truck. Finally, Tammy reappeared and gave us the story.

"They had me talk to a supervisor. God, I was getting nervous. An overseas envelope came in for me, but she said Fresno doesn't have a main post office any more. So she interpreted 'main' to mean 'big' and sent it over to their larger facility on East Olive. She said it's in transit and we can pick it up tomorrow."

Another day in sun-fried Fresno!

Not as bad as death by firing squad, but close.

We drove to East Olive Avenue, located the post office there, then at Claudia's insistence hustled over to Fresno State and bought an over-priced ticket for tonight's show. Only a few were left in the very last row; the ticket seller advised Tammy to bring her binoculars. Claudia and I, of course, will be sneaking in–assuming I don't work up the nerve to shoot our pushy pal before then.

> "This beast is fierce and that's no lie,
> He's our mascot and for him we'll die,
> He's a bull of a dog with teeth so sharp,
> Get in his way, and you'll be playing a harp!!!"

That poem appeared on a plaque under a massive bull-dog sculpture in the lobby of the performance hall, a building sized to accommodate Genghis Khan and his entire horde.

"Oh look, Claudia," I whispered as we passed the bronze canine, frozen in mid-snarl, "does that remind you of anyone?"

"You better be referring to Bruce and not me," she whispered back. My invisible hand was clamped firmly in her vise-like grip.

We had said good-bye to Tammy outside and waited until the great throngs of Tara fans had entered and been seated before we sneaked in. The show was just starting when we slipped into the main auditorium and headed toward the stage. Somewhere in that vast sea of faces was Tammy–probably wondering like me what she was doing there.

"Hello, frenzied state!" called Tara, a tiny figure at the center of a dozen spotlights on the enormous stage.

Big roar from the crowd.

"Oh, wait, I'm in a frenzied state, you're Fresno State!"

Another roar. Tara strolled back and forth with her corded microphone like a caged lioness of comedy.

"Hey, anybody here getting married?" she asked.

Laughter and applause.

"Want to rent a wedding gown cheap? Only slightly used! I'm offering a discount for virgins!"

Another big laugh.

"OK! All the virgins in the crowd please stand up!"

A few fraternity types stood up and waved.

"Liars!" bellowed Tara, laughing along with her audience.

Claudia tugged me up the stairs leading to the stage. Tara was dressed all in black and beginning to sweat a bit. The adrenalin had to be flowing in buckets to face a crowd that huge.

"Did you hear a guy died at my wedding?" she asked.

"Of course, I suppose a lot of you think a guy dies at every wedding."

Big applause and cheers. Relentless Claudia dragged me over until we were standing right behind Tara, then released my hand.

"Actually," Tara continued. "There would have been two guys dying at my wedding, but my gun misfired."

Tara tugged on her microphone cord while waiting out the laugh.

"My dad offered to settle matters the way they do in Bulgaria. But what would I do with some old guy's dick? I mean it wasn't doing me that much good when it was attached to his body!"

Tara was having more trouble with her cord.

"Yeah, in Bulgaria it's a tradition. They got whole cabinets full of them. Old dried up wrinkly things. Over there that's what they call marriage counseling. Hey, what's with this damn cord?"

Tara shaded her eyes with her hand and peered out into the darkness.

"Hey, Richard, if you're out there, stop yanking on my cord!"

Tara planted her feet and gave a fierce tug on the cord. Someone let go and Tara nearly went flying over the edge of the stage. She recovered and staggered back to her stool.

"Damn! Where was I? Oh yeah, Bulgarian wedding traditions. Virginity is a big deal there. It's a big deal here too, but only if you're 12. No, wait–I'm in conservative Fresno–make that 13!"

Tara brushed something away from her ear. I knew I should leave, but I felt rooted to the spot. I felt pinned to the stage by the enormous energy of the crowd.

"Actually, I was pretty heartbroken on my wedding night." Tara flinched and gasped. Something was tugging on her dangling gold loop earring. The gal was a trouper; she lurched on to the next joke. "I was so looking forward to being wife number five! I mean, think of all the practice that guy'd had!"

Tara danced backwards and looked all around her as the audience laughed.

"OK, Fresno, I'm getting a little weirded out. Let's stop playing games up here!"

Applause from the audience; they assumed it was part of the act.

"Say something, Axel," I heard Claudia say. Tara heard it too.

"What was that!" exclaimed Tara, looking all around her. "Who the fuck is here?"

Tara's microphone tilted sideways in her hand, and Claudia's deep voice boomed out over the sound system. "We interrupt this boring monologue to bring you a message from the late great Axel Weston. Axel, take it away!"

Instant silence in the vast hall. Something willed me to walk over and grasp the microphone, still gripped by the stunned comedian. My cool hand touched her warm one.

"Hi, Tara," I said. "This is Axel Weston. You're a lovely person and a funny gal. I'm sorry I broke up your wedding. I can assure you it wasn't intentional. I hope you'll forgive me and I wish you all the best."

As far as I was concerned, that was a sincere apology from the heart. Then Claudia spoiled everything by rudely depantsing the comedian in front of 18,000 flabbergasted fans. All layers went down, displaying the full montyette. Not that I looked, but one couldn't help but notice that she was fully shaved.

Somehow we made it past all the rampaging security guards and got out of the building. We rendezvoused at the motel, Tammy tossed all our stuff in the truck, and we escaped up route 99 in the hot darkness.

Girlish laughter from the bed in back. I slung open the sliding window.

"Damn, Claudia, that was incredibly stupid!" I hissed.

"Hey, don't complain, Jack. I got us out of Fresno, didn't I?"

"Yeah, sure you did. And now every cop in the world knows where we are. And now we can't pick up those checks. What are we supposed to do when the money runs out?"

"Lighten up, Jack," Claudia replied. "We're fucking invisible. We're not supposed to lead boring lives. Don't worry, I'm not going to let you starve. I need meat on your bones. Want to join me back here while Tammy drives?"

I slammed closed the window and didn't reply. I fingered the gun in my pocket. One shot to the back of the head. That might do it. And since the victim was invisible, we wouldn't have to worry about disposing of the body.

Not a bad plan except for one thing. How do you aim your gun at the back of someone's head if you can't see them?

Fortunately, even invisible people have to pause to answer the call of nature. While Claudia was taking a tinkle in a truck stop just beyond Lodi, I told Tammy to floor it. We zipped out of the lot and headed south on 99 back the way we'd come—not north toward Oregon as we had discussed with Claudia. I was hoping that deception might confuse her psychic detection powers. We got off the freeway a few miles later in Lodi and headed west on highway 12. We crossed the Sacramento River at Rio Vista as the pink dawn illuminated the vapors rising off the water. We gassed up in Napa and drove on until Tammy could barely keep her eyes open, finally checking into a budget motel by the 101 freeway in south Santa Rosa. We didn't have to turn on the A/C as we collapsed on the bed. We were out of the heat at last.

As I drifted off to sleep an old song played in my head: "Oh! Lord I'm stuck in Lodi again." Perhaps I had psychically tuned into a song Claudia herself was humming. She, I sensed, was not having a boring day.

# Chapter 22

We slept until late afternoon and both woke up ravenous. I grabbed a quick shower while Tammy headed across the street for take-out burritos from another of California's ubiquitous taco trucks. Or perhaps it was the same truck that just followed us around because we were such good customers. Tammy also brought back a copy of the *Santa Rosa Press-Democrat*. To my surprise, the Fresno high jinx didn't make the front page. There was just a brief mention in the Page 2 gossip and entertainment column. The snarky report suggested that the interruption in Tara's performance was merely a "tasteless stunt," staged by a comedian "desperate to prolong the publicity from her aborted wedding." The media may believe poor Tara depantsed herself, but would the FBI?

Since the motel offered free WiFi, I fired up my laptop and checked Youtube. There were a half-dozen murky cellphone videos of the Fresno incident, but all were taken from too great a distance to show much useful detail. I downloaded the best one and also copied the Axel Weston memorial video for viewing at my leisure.

Our immediate problem was still Claudia. I figured if she got caught, she might be so annoyed with us as to give a description to the cops of our poky little truck. We needed a new vehicle. I was highly untrained for car thievery. I couldn't jimmy a door or deftly disable the steering wheel lock with a screwdriver. Hot-wiring ignitions was a skill unlearned by me. But I had read in the paper that the county fair was underway in Santa Rosa. A Google search revealed that the fairgrounds was just a few miles away.

Tammy paid eight bucks for a space in the huge lot, parked nearly full with hundreds of vehicles–their owners far away at the tops of Ferris wheels or admiring displays of amateur handicrafts. She waited in the truck while Mr. Invisible strolled up and down the aisles. The laws of probability held true. Eventually, I came to a car with the keys forgotten in the ignition. It was a green Volvo station wagon–not new, but not ancient either. The tires appeared to be good. I inspected the underside. No vital fluids were dripping on the asphalt. It had been waxed recently and the interior was not torn up. The license plate tag was up-to-date. It bore all the signs of conscientious Yuppie ownership. Some telltale stickers on the bumper, MEAN PEOPLE SUCK and EVOLUTION IS A FACT–GOD IS A THEORY, would have to go soon. I checked that no one was in the vicinity, cracked open the door, and grabbed the keys.

Tammy drove the Volvo to an industrial street a few blocks away, then we hoofed it back for the little pickup. We returned and she quickly transferred our stuff. We had hit the jackpot. Under a tarp in the back of the Volvo was a complete kit for camping: tent, sleeping bags, air mattresses, cookstove, cooler, gas lantern–the works. Also two backpacks full of personal items.

"I think we may be spoiling someone's vacation," Tammy pointed out.

"Well, I suppose we're confirming for them that mean people do indeed suck."

We left Myron's mattress in his truck, but brought along the bag with Claudia's thrift-shop clothes. If she showed up, we planned to claim that we thought she was aboard when we breezed out of that Lodi truck stop. Retaining her stuff might lend credibility to our story.

We bid a fond farewell to Myron's truck. It was slow, it was decrepit, it was uncomfortable, but it had always started right up and got us where we were going. I told Tammy to leave the keys on the seat.

"But, Jack, what if someone steals it?"

"So much the better, darling. They can take the rap for vehicle theft instead of us."

Wallowing in rich but sensible Swedish luxury, we sailed north on the 101 freeway through the wine country of Sonoma County. The engine purred, no warning lights flashed on the dash, and the gas gauge revealed that the tank was over three-quarters full. The seats cradled our every bulge and curve with Scandinavian efficiency. We were on the lam in style.

In Cloverdale we stopped for take-out Chinese food. We ate in the deepening twilight behind an abandoned car dealership, then I got out my razor blade and scraped off the bumper stickers. We didn't want any born-again cops stopping us because they objected to our religious views.

Tammy said she wasn't feeling tired, so we continued on. North of town we headed west on Highway 128 toward the coast. This two-lane road wended over forested hills and through serene valleys turning deep purple as the sky faded to black. The peaceful beauty was a welcome change from the bleak flatness and unremitting heat of the Central Valley.

"Why do you suppose people live in Fresno, when they could live here?" I asked.

"That's life, Jack. Someone has to package all those raisins."

"I suppose, Tammy. But does it take a half million of them?"

We spent the night in a rundown but pricey motel in a little town called Boonville. Any wide spot in the road in California that attracted tourists felt free to gouge the traveler. We parked the Volvo where it couldn't been seen from the highway. Only single-bed rooms were available, so Mr. Invisible camped on the floor on one of our new air mattresses. Not super comfortable, but restful sleep was an established perk of invisibility.

In the morning I moved up to the bed and got reacquainted with my fiancee. Afterwards, Tammy hauled in our new backpacks and we checked out what the Crime Santa had provided. I got some nifty binoculars, a guidebook to the birds of the West, some thick socks, several Stanford polo shirts, hiking shorts, underwear, toiletries, Ipod with earbuds, and over $800 in cash. From the gal's pack, Tammy extracted a jogging bra (not her size), panties, shorts, t-shirts, sandals (all her size), toiletry kit, a trashy novel, condoms (not our brand, but welcome), miniature digital camera, and $26 in cash.

"Why do you chicks never carry any cash?" I demanded.

"Guys have to pay, Jack. Get used to it."

"But why do we have to pay?"

"Because we've got what you want."

"Oh, right. I forgot."

Tammy switched on the camera and we reviewed the photos. Our benefactors had been to San Francisco and gone wine-tasting along Napa's Silverado Trail. They appeared to be in their early thirties. An earnest couple who were taking a well-deserved vacation. Putting faces to our victims was a mistake; Tammy switched off the camera with a sigh.

"We should make it up to them, Jack."

"I know. We'll try if we can. I'm sure the car is insured and probably the contents for theft. Life is tough, Tammy. We're having a hard time too."

Another hour's drive brought us to the spectacular Mendocino coast. I assumed it was spectacular; thick fog obscured any views of the ocean. It lifted as we approached the picturesque village of Mendocino, where we had a gourmet take-out lunch and then strolled along its quaint streets with the other tourists. I resisted the urge to blow our bundle on an engagement ring for Tammy or heist one from the many posh shops. Tammy bought some groceries in the village market and picked up a *San Francisco Chronicle*.

We headed back down Route 1 and scored a nicely private camping spot in Van Damme State Park. While Tammy put up the tent (the directions falsely claimed it was "self-erecting"), I sat on a folding stool and read the paper. A front-page story reported on a car that had mysteriously rolled free at a truck stop near Lodi and somehow traveled–apparently driver-less–for many miles. It was finally halted when the highway patrol raised the drawbridge at Rio Vista. When officers approached the car, they found no sign of any driver. Authorities in Sacramento were investigating the strange occurrence, but had no further comment.

Damn, Claudia hadn't been fooled by our Oregon dodge. What was that woman–part bloodhound?

Tammy made a fine dinner of campfire chili and salad. A beer would have gone nicely with that, but I contented myself with admiring the scenery. The fog returned and wicked away any residual Fresno heat. Summer on the Northern California coast is not unlike winter in Fresno. We bundled up and huddled around the fire. Later, while searching the car for a flashlight, I found a loaded and very lethal-looking Walther P99 pistol under the driver's seat. I showed my find to Tammy.

"Why would folks with a loaded .45 hidden in their car not remember to take their keys?" I asked.

"The gun was his, Jack. He's kind of a security freak. She was probably driving. As I recall I didn't have to adjust the seat when I got in. She was so concerned about bringing the sunscreen lotion for him, she forgot her keys. Now he's giving her endless grief. That's married life for you."

"Yeah, tell me about it."

All those moments accumulate until divorce sounds like a promising solution. I hoped it would be different this time.

"You want the tent or the car?" asked Tammy, sounding chilled and dispirited.

Oh right, cuddling in the cozy tent was not on the menu. I told Tammy the choice was hers; she chose the car. We folded down the rear seat and laid out her air mattress and sleeping bag. I kissed her goodnight and gave her the little gun.

"If Claudia shows up and wants to cause trouble, don't be afraid to use this," I advised. "I'll take the .45 with me into the tent."

"OK, Jack. I hope I don't plug you by mistake."

"Yeah, try not to."

I turned out the lantern and we retired for the night–both fully armed in the spirit of the American West.

I hadn't slept in a tent in decades. Even locked and loaded I felt a bit vulnerable. Bugs were (mostly) excluded, but anyone could come along and step on your face. The moisture in your breath condensed on the chilly nylon and made everything damp. Irregularities in the ground tele-scoped up through the air mattress. Your position was not entirely level, so muscles had to remain tensed to prevent rolling. Still, you were out there in nature where the air was fresh except for the fumes from the generator droning away in the next campsite. I switched on my new Ipod and lis-tened with the earbuds to Mr. Volvo Gun Nut's music. He was into old rockers: Santana, Neil Young, and Creedence Clearwater Revival. Unlike some people I knew, Mr. Fogarty was still stuck in ol' Lodi again.

More chilly fog the next morning, making it difficult for campers to rise and face the day. The spartan campground provided toilets but no hot showers. Damp, cold, and stinky was the theme as Tammy fired up the portable stove and set to work on our eggs. No newspaper rack for miles. I sat at the dripping picnic table and stared off into space until a mug of coffee was set in front of me. It was one leg of the holy trinity: coffee, newspaper, cigarette. I'd given up ciga-rettes long ago and newspapers had been shrinking for years. Probably someday they'll wither to the size of postage stamps and then disappear entirely–like Mr. Invisible.

The fog lingered until 10:30, then was gone in 30 seconds. It was God's morning magic act. I felt revived by the sun and asked Tammy if she wanted to take a walk. But she was absorbed in Ms. Volvo's trashy novel and declined.

"You need anything from town?" I asked.

"You're invisible, Jack. What can you bring back?"

"Well, I'm fully capable of heisting small items. How about another diamond pin?"

"No thanks. I'm fine."

She returned to her book; I didn't kiss her good-bye.

I trooped down to the highway, then hiked the three miles north to Mendocino. Cars whizzed by, but there weren't any pedestrians about, so I didn't make an effort to walk quietly. I got hot after a while, but when you're invisible you can't just take off your jacket and sling it over your arm. At one point I stopped to relieve myself against a redwood tree. The stream became visible about two inches from its source– a startling optical illusion had anyone in the passing cars been paying attention.

A young couple on the patio of the Mendocino Bakery were staring into each other's eyes instead of minding her brioche, which went quickly into my pocket as I walked by. I was leaning against a building on Albion Street and sneaking torn bits of pastry into my mouth when I saw a familiar figure approaching. She was wearing dark glasses and a head scarf, but I recognized her immediately. She continued on down Albion; I followed about 10 paces behind. She turned down Kasten, continued on to Main, crossed the street, and headed down one of the many paths that crisscrossed the grassy headlands overlooking the ocean. She walked out to one of the farthest points on the bluff, paused a moment, then strode resolutely toward the precipice. I grabbed her from behind as she was one step from the edge, and pulled her back. She turned and faced me.

"I didn't know if you intended to shove me or save me," gasped Tara.

"Jesus, you gave me a fright. Don't do that again."

"I should let you know: all evidence to the contrary, I don't believe in ghosts."

"That makes two of us. Want to go sit on that bench?"

"OK."

We sat on a metal bench that was safely back from the cliff's edge. She took off her sunglasses and peered in my direction. She had one of those in-between showbiz faces: not beautiful enough for leading lady roles, but rather too pretty for comedy. I liked her dark, semi-Bulgarian eyes.

"I'm sorry for what Claudia did at your performance," I said.

Tara gazed about in alarm.

"Is she here too?"

"No, we ditched her a few days ago in Lodi. She stole that driver-less car you may have heard about."

"So are there hundreds of you running around or what?"

I gave her the condensed story of Axel Weston and his adventures with invisibility.

"OK, Axel, I guess I have to accept that you're invisible since you're sitting right next to me and I can't see you. But why are you following me?"

"I don't know, Tara. It's not a conscious act on my part. I think whatever is making me invisible wants me to go where you go. Why I don't know. Have you ever had anything to do with invisibility?"

"Only in the early years of my career. I couldn't get a break anywhere. I was as invisible on the comedy scene as you could get."

"You weren't consulting any . . . uh, palm readers, mystical oracles, voodoo priests–that sort of thing?"

"None, Axel. I'm not superstitious in that way at all."

"So what was the cliff dive about?" I asked.

"Oh that. God, my life is a mess. It could solve a lot of my problems."

"I feel terrible about this, Tara. If it weren't for me, you could be on your honeymoon now."

"Actually, Richard was one of my larger problems. You kind of cleared that one up for me."

"So what else is wrong?"

"What isn't is a better question. Please, let's not dwell on my insecurities."

"So what are you doing in Mendocino?" I asked.

"Oh, I often come here. It's my place of refuge. I tell my manager I need to disappear for a while, I switch off my cell phone, and drive up here. It's too unstimulating for Richard, so I hadn't been here for over a year."

I noticed the time on her wristwatch.

"Uh, Tara, I need to get back. Will you be OK?"

"Sure, Axel. I'm fine. The impulse has passed. I was hoping fate would intervene and it did. Anyway, it was nice meeting you at last. I'm glad you're not dead."

"Yeah, I feel the same way about you."

She laughed.

"Hey, why don't you come to lunch? Diane's a great cook and she'd love to meet you."

"Remind me, is she invisible too?"

"No. She was, but she's back to normal now. How about it?"

Tara was resistant, but I finally talked her into it. We drove back to the campground in her Mercedes Slk 350. We pulled in next to the Volvo and I found this note under a rock on the picnic table:

Dear Jack,

Some people from down the row are giving me a ride to Ukiah. I can catch the bus to L.A. there. Please don't try and come after me. I've concluded that life on the road is not for me. I'm going to turn myself in and face the consequences. I won't tell them about you or give them any information. I borrowed

some $$$ for the trip. Forgive me for leaving
you like this. I do care for you and hope to
see you again someday when all this is over.
Love and best wishes,
D.

"Bad news, Axel?" asked Tara.

I handed her the note and collapsed on the picnic bench.
It was a blow to the gut I hadn't been expecting.

"Oh, I'm sorry, Axel."

I was too distraught to reply.

"Axel, are you still there?"

"I'm here. Sorry, I'm, uh, trying to deal with this. I'll be
OK in a minute."

Tara sat down beside me and took my hand. We watched
a pair of blue jays swoop down and steal tidbits from around
the dead campfire.

"Damn, Axel, you're kind of stuck here. I mean, you
can't really drive that car."

"I could, but it would probably spook my fellow driv-
ers."

"What are you going to do?"

"Uh, well, gee, I'll figure something out."

"I don't see any solution, Axel. You'll have to come with
me."

"That's OK, Tara, I'm not your problem. I'll get by."

"Hey, I've got a huge suite. There's plenty of room. I
mean you'd probably be following me around anyway."

Tara was persistent. Eventually, I got to the point of in-
quiring about the floors in her hotel.

"Uh, let's see. They're wide planks. The inn pretends to
be an oversized horse barn, but they charge you like it's the
Ritz."

"Any carpets?"

"Just a few oriental rugs, but we could avoid those."

Tara snooped around the campsite while I packed a bag.

I took Mr. Volvo's gun (Tammy must have taken hers), binoculars, Ipod, and some of his clothes. Also my laptop and camera. The rest I left where it was. That's the good thing about being an invisible guy on the lam: you can walk away from your messes.

"There's a dead animal behind this bush," called Tara. "No wait, it's somebody's wig."

The final resting spot of Tammy of Bakersfield. I would miss that colorful gal.

Tara offered to buy me lunch, but I explained how restaurants didn't work for Mr. Invisible.

"Pish posh, Axel, we'll go to Café Blunderbuss. They have these little private rooms upstairs. Normally, they only open them for dinner, but they stretch the rules for us famous types."

"Is there really such a place–Café Blunderbuss?"

"Oh, that's just my pet name for it. I'm big on pet names."

After much obsequious fawning by the owner and staff, Tara was seated in a pleasant little room under the eaves of an old house that had been converted into an upscale café. I sneaked up the rickety stairs behind her and the waiter–the squeaks of my footfalls blending with theirs. Tara told the waiter that the salmon special sounded so yummy she wanted two servings of it, plus two bowls of the cream of carrot soup. She also ordered a bottle of German reisling. When everything was delivered, she told the waiter that she didn't wish to be disturbed and that she would ring the little buzzer if she needed anything.

"How's this, Axel? What you need is some wine to wash away love's disappointments."

I explained how I was enduring my second month of sobriety and had to stick reluctantly to water.

"God, Axel, I admire your forbearance. I'd be getting totally wasted now if I were you. Do you mind if I have a little glass to recover from my near brush with the briny deep?"

"Go ahead, Tara. I don't mind."

The grub was many powers of ten finer than a take-out burrito. The nice thing about dining with Tara was you could ask her a question and then rest your vocal cords indefinitely.

"I figured out what's happening with you," she said at one point.

"What's that?"

"You're being controlled by time travelers from the future. They want us to meet so that I can have your baby and she can grow up to save the world."

"You think?"

"There's only one problem. You might mention to your handlers that I'm on the pill. Oh wait! It could be that I'm following you! My manager arranged that Fresno gig at the last minute. And my decision to come up here was totally spur of the moment. God, isn't destiny strange? And right when we met, Diane splits out on you."

"Yeah, she did."

"Oh, I'm sorry. I didn't mean to rub it in. Being dumped is the worse thing in the world. I mean, let's face it, we're both a couple of dumpees."

I told her that I had also recently been dumped by my wife.

"Ooh, doubled dumped! Axel, that's bad. I would be a total mess! How do you function?"

"Believe it or not, being invisible helps. It comes with this natural mood elevator."

"Man, I've got to try it!"

"Sorry. No more free lessons. I've had too many disasters from this whole business. So how did you become a comedian?"

"You really want to know? OK, growing up I had no interest in comedy. Woody Allen? Bill Cosby? Jerry Seinfeld? Sorry, wrong number. From age one I want to be a dancer. I do the ballet lessons, the recitals, I'm the second coming of Margo fucking Fonteyn. Then at age 12, I start getting breasts.

I'm happy. Sure, breasts are nice, most girls have them, boys seem to like them. Great! Breasts it is. Only my breasts don't stop growing. I'm not getting your petite ballerina tits here. I'm going for the full Jayne Mansfields. It's like I'm in a horror movie: "Breasts from the Planet Gigantica."

"You look pretty normal to me," I pointed out.

"Oh, checking me out, huh? No wonder you're invisible. You're one of those perverts who likes to stare."

"No, I'm . . ."

"Don't interrupt. I have three words for you and I don't want any wisecracks: breast reduction surgery."

"Oh. OK."

"Not only are my tits massive, they start about one inch under my chin. So no matter what kind of little modest blouse I wear I'm always flashing this Liz Taylor meets Sophia Loren decolletage. You can imagine the reaction of the boys in my junior high. That I lived through the humiliation is truly a miracle. So while my breasts are spreading over the continent like a new ice age, I'm also changing down below. Mother nature is equipping me to have 12 children. Only with this pelvis I can have all 12 at once–sideways! There goes my ballerina body. If Tchaikovsky wrote a ballet about enormously breasted lady wrestlers, I'd be a cinch for the lead. So dance is out. I can't sing, I can't act, but after all those recitals I'm addicted to performing. What's left? Naked pole dancing or comedy."

"And you chose. . ."

"Naked pole dancing, of course. I only do comedy as a sideline."

Tara paid for lunch with her platinum credit card and added a tip that was double the bill.

"I've worked as a waiter," she remarked. "It's a thankless job and these people deserve way more than they get."

She took me back to her inn for an emergency shower. On the drive there she said she couldn't believe the campground didn't offer bathing facilities.

"That was your mistake with Diane, Axel. Roughing it in the woods is fine as long as you have a nice, comfortable house to come back to. But you guys were on the road. You don't deprive a lady who has no home of her daily hot shower. That's asking too much."

"Yeah. You're probably right."

"I know I'm right. I'm speaking to you as a fellow homeless person."

"What?"

"That's right. I have no home. One of the things I have to do when I go back to L.A. is haul my stuff out of Richard's place and find an apartment. I'm just like you, Axel. I'm living out of my car!"

I didn't point out that she was also living in a sumptuous suite in a grand rustic inn with ocean views through every window and wood-burning fireplaces in both the sitting room and bedroom. The luxurious marble shower shot temperature-controlled water at you from head to foot and offered a choice of cleansers, lotions, and shampoos at the press of a button. After that decadent bathing experience, I wrapped myself in one of the inn's absurdly thick terrycloth robes and enjoyed a cappuccino (ordered from room service) with Tara in her pine-paneled sitting room.

"Don't you hate these awkward B.O.L. moments?" she asked.

"B.O.L.?"

"Buddies or lovers. This is the moment when the die is cast. Are these two people, thrown together by fate, to be pals or spit-swappers? He's a recent double-dumpee, she's a complete mess. He's invisible and wanted by the F.B.I. She'd been getting it on with a guy who was older than her father. She can't make a move because she has deep veins of insecurities that years of therapy have not yet begun to uncover. Plus, to make matters worse, his previous girlfriend was a total knockout."

"You're kind of irresistible, Tara, in a talkative sort of way."

"Yeah? I'm available for groping, should you get the urge."

I took her hand and led her into the pine-paneled bedroom. I don't know why she was so insecure. She had a deliciously voluptuous body and knew precisely what to do with it. She declined my offer to don a condom. We merged in a marvelous way that went on and on. Very unusual, I thought, for a first time around.

"What's with the bare look?" I finally got around to asking her, as we lay together on the king-size bed.

"That's the style these days, Axel. Shag carpeting is no longer in. Actually, I had a bush that could only be penetrated after extensive foreplay involving a machete. Do you mind the pre-pubescent look?"

"No, it's fine. You were great. So how did it feel to be depantsed in front of 18,000 people?"

"Oh, it was just another day at the office."

"Really?"

"You can't imagine what it was like in my junior high, Axel. Daily non-stop torture. I'm like an Iraqi prison survivor. Stuff like that doesn't phase me now."

"Then why the walk off the cliff?"

"I'm a moody bitch, Axel. It's only fair to warn you. The shit builds up and I get in holes so deep I can't see any way out. I woke up this morning and really thought it was my last day on earth. Now I'm all toasty and warm in bed after just having great sex with an invisible man. Kind of a different scenario than planned."

She expounded on that theme for about ten minutes, then paused. I shot out another question.

"Tara, I've got to know. Why 'Rose Marie'?"

"'Rose Marie,' right. OK, so Richard is planning this fabulous wedding. I go along because I'm hypnotized by his magnetic blue eyes and Jupiter-sized charisma. I have to pinch myself hourly. Tara the toad is actually marrying this famous star."

"You're not a toad!"

"Please, tell me that frequently. So, finally I begin to wonder—why such a grand wedding? Then it occurs to me. Richard isn't getting any parts. Producers aren't sending him scripts because he's such a pill to work with. There's not a sound stage on earth big enough to contain his ego. Our wedding is his ticket back to the center of the stage. He's constantly stewing over what to wear. As a joke—and I mean as a deeply sarcastic suggestion—I mention 'Rose Marie.' Well Richard loves it! He loves the uniform of the Canadian Mounted Police. He doesn't care that his bride looks about as much like Jeanette MacDonald as Nelson Eddy did. So he gets to parade around in snappy scarlet, I get the frumpy frills."

"But you wanted the wedding to go on, Tara. You didn't care that I'd just plunged to my death in the Pacific ocean."

"Sorry, Axel. You're right. Very ungracious of me. But by then I was in total bride mode. No person with a cock and two balls has any concept of what that is like. It's like your mind is taken over by some alien force. Suddenly the color of your bridesmaids' shoes is the most important issue in the world."

"Why no photographs if Richard was doing it for the publicity?"

"Just to kick the hysteria up a notch. Richard's a master at that. He knew cameras would be sneaked in. He was tickled pink when you ran off that cliff. An actual death in the middle of his wedding. Talk about publicity! The hoopla was so great, he didn't have to go through with our marriage. The bride was expendable."

"Yeah. Tough on you."

"And remember I was still in total bride mode. It takes a while to snap out of that state. What a debacle! And to think I owe it all to you, dear Axel."

I kissed her; her warm fingers curled around my invisible member.

"Would it amuse you greatly, Axel, to probe my ample pelvis again?"

"I can't think of anything I'd rather do."

The inn prided itself on its vegetarian cuisine. As Tara and I picked over the remains of a lavish room-service supper in her sitting room, someone knocked on the door. It was a deputy sheriff. I froze in my chair as Tara welcomed him into the room.

"Good evening, officer," she said. "What can I do for you?"

"A stolen vehicle was located in the state park. A ranger reported seeing your car parked today at that same campsite."

"Oh dear. Am I in serious trouble?"

"Well, ma'am. We'd like to know what you were doing there."

"Some friends of mine are coming up to visit. They asked me to check out that park as a possible camping spot. I told them it was totally unacceptable. There are no bathing facilities!"

"Were you visiting the woman with the green Volvo?"

"No, I only parked in that location because there didn't seem to be anyone around. Are you going to arrest me?"

"No, ma'am, but I would like your autograph."

Tara produced a photograph from her bag and signed it for the cop. He shook her hand in gratitude and left.

"You saved my ass," I said, kissing her.

"Well, it's a nice ass."

"I'm impressed by your quick thinking, Tara."

"It's from years of being heckled by drunks in obscure comedy clubs. The mental processes become honed to a sharp edge. You're pretty much ready for anything."

"I don't want to get you in trouble, Tara. I should go."

"You may already have gotten me in trouble, Axel. I lied."

"About what?"

"Being on the pill."

"Then having unprotected sex with me was not very wise."

"Just doing my bit for your handlers, Axel. I want to have a baby. Are you shocked?"

"Kind of surprised."

"That's one of my obsessions. I'm not getting any younger. Don't worry, you don't have to have anything to do with it if you don't want to."

"You're serious about this then?"

"Terribly serious, Axel. Please don't tell me you've done anything criminal like gotten a vasectomy."

"No. I'm just as God made me."

"And he made you very fine, if I'm any judge. And I believe I am. So please don't go. I don't mind the danger."

"What if you have a baby that's invisible?"

"Then I'll be very, very seriously annoyed with you."

# Chapter 23

Although Tara objected, I figured I should take a lesson from Desma's experience and sleep separately on the fold-out bed in the sitting room. Tara said she felt so relaxed she was going to skip her sedative. She led a tension-filled celebrity's life and always carried a bottle of prescription sedatives in her purse. She must not have been that relaxed because she shook me awake in the middle of the night.

"Tara, what's wrong?" I asked, rising with a start.

"Axel, I need to see you."

"About what?"

"I mean, I need to see you. Put on your robe and let's go."

I looked at the digital clock on the mini bar. It was 3:47 a.m.

I followed her out the door and down the stairs. I hoped she wasn't going to be one of those restless chicks who liked to schedule activities in the wee hours. She led the way to a large indoor swimming pool, which–not surprisingly–was deserted. She flipped a switch. Blinding overhead lights. She turned those off and tried another switch. Underwater beams illuminated the pool with a soft light.

"Much nicer."

Tara dropped her robe. She went into the water wearing only swim goggles. I checked the place for security cameras, didn't see any, and jumped in after her. The water was pleasantly warm. Tara swam over and pushed me under water. I swallowed a mouthful of brackish chlorine and flailed my way back to the surface.

"I saw you, Axel! I saw you!"

"Yeah, you almost saw me drown. Damn, give me a warning before you do that the next time."

"Oh, sorry, darling. I can see your outline underwater!"

"Oh. That must be a rare thrill."

"You actually exist, Axel. I haven't been imagining all this!"

"I'm glad to hear it."

She yanked on my dong and I chased her across the pool. After a half hour of water play, she climbed out and sat on the edge of the pool. I swam between her legs and did her with my tongue. I showed no mercy and didn't stop until she unwound the full explosion. Then she dragged me out of the water, stretched me out flat on a towel, and started in with her tongue and mouth to return the favor. I was about to give her a sticky mouthful, when an early-rising elderly couple walked in. They stopped and stared in wonder.

Tara calmly rose, slipped on her robe, and casually grabbed mine as well. Mr. Invisible rolled off the towel and rose as silently as I could.

"Sorry, folks," said Tara. "I like to do my yoga in the nude."

I slipped out the door with her and we ran back to her room. We collapsed laughing on my fold-out bed.

"I'll bet they never saw that yoga position before," said Tara.

"Shall we finish what you started?" I asked.

"Sure. But let's not waste it, Alex. Come inside me."

I complied, but warned her that my sperm count was probably down to single digits.

"That's OK, big guy. It only takes one."

We slept together on my bed until after 10:00 with no invisibility mishaps. We took our time getting up. I followed her into the bathroom and watched her shave her stubble with a man's electric razor.

"Axel, what's the biological function of pubic hair?"

"I have no idea, but you could definitely charge admission for this show."

"I know. I have no modesty at all. But take a look at this pelvis. Is that a baby-making machine or what?"

"I'm no expert, but I'd say you've got everything it takes."

We had to interrupt her program to return to the bedroom for another run around the track. I knew invisibility made me horny, but I wondered what was lighting her fire. Eventually, I rolled off and lay there gasping.

"Well, that was the last one, Tara."

"Last what, sweetie?"

"Sperm. You've got the whole batch now. The tank is empty. The sperm have left the building."

Tara found my invisible balls and gave them a squeeze.

"Come on, guys. Don't let the team down! Get up and fight for motherhood and the flag!"

Some wedding questions still gnawed at my soul.

"So the little gas-station attendants–what was that all about?" I asked.

"Another inspiration of Richard's. He has this 60-foot bell tower on his property in Bel-Air with a meditation room at the top. The neighbors screamed when it went up, but he had quietly gotten a zoning variance. So he goes up there and rings his bells like Quasimodo and gets inspired. It all came to him in a vision. Their dance was to be like a Busby Berkeley extravaganza with coordinated spritzing of the little spray bottles and waving of the yellow silk bandanas. As a finale, flames would shoot up and the ministers were going to rise up through a trapdoor in the platform."

"You had multiple ministers?"

"Only two: Bette Midler and Whoopi Goldberg in long silver robes and matching blond wigs. Richard had them ordained by mail just for the occasion."

"Yeah, I saw them walking around later. I wondered why they were dressed like angels."

"It's probably just as well you showed up. I was worried sick about those shooting flames. One of the stand-ins had been seriously injured the day before while testing the effect."

"Yet Richard still intended to go through with it?"

"Yeah, that's what worried me. He had the technicians move the explosive charges over to the side."

"Which side?"

"You have to ask? It was the side I was sitting on."

We decided there was no point to getting dressed. Tara phoned room service and ordered their deluxe breakfast for four. While we waited, she told me about her first marriage.

"Henry was very sweet. He was Chinese, you know."

"No. I didn't know that."

"It was right after I got out of UCLA. I had lots of computer problems. My computer would crash, so I would call Henry. He was a grad student at Cal Tech and mucho smart. He would come over and fix my computer in about two minutes. Well, I've always found competence in men to be a turn-on. So after a while I started sticking a hairpin in the back of my machine just to see Henry. Now Henry was very single-minded and rather endearingly obtuse. I mean, I'm throwing myself at him. This is before I had my tits reduced and I'm about as subtle as a speeding Humvee."

"Henry wasn't interested?"

"Well, eventually I resigned myself to the situation and just ripped his clothes off. He got the picture then. So we got married about six months later. Now I may not be the first Bulgarian in the history of the world to marry a Chinese person, but my parents reacted like I was."

"They weren't thrilled?"

"What's a word for opposite of thrilled?"

"Hmm, appalled?"

"Yeah, they were appalled. Henry's family was even more appalled. They pretty much ran screaming whenever they saw me and my tits approaching."

"It didn't work out, huh?"

"Nah, I got busy trying to break into comedy. I never saw the poor guy. And I wasn't making it as a proper Chinese wife."

"Where's Henry now?"

"He's very high up at Apple. When Steve Jobs gets an idea, Henry is one of the first guys he consults. Very rich too, as I'm sure his second wife and their numerous 100 percent Chinese children appreciate. So tell me about the ditzy dame who dumped you."

Over breakfast I told her about Rachel and my days as a reporter in the midwest.

"A nurse, huh? That means you need lots of mothering. Were you breast fed, Axel?"

"Yeah, but Mom cut me off without a drop at age eight. I never got over the trauma."

It was a very lazy day. All our energy was siphoned off into human reproduction. My monogamy gene was in a state of total confusion. I had one of those four-hour erections like they warn you about on TV, although I hadn't taken any pills. Several more miracle ejaculations went into Tara's baby-making machinery. We just couldn't keep our hands off each other.

We did throw on some clothes long enough to return to the Café Blunderbuss for dinner. There was a party of five in the other upstairs room, so we had to restrict our conversation to whispers. For the "baby's sake" Tara ordered organic apple juice instead of wine. I pointed out that many couples our age required years of effort to get pregnant.

"I know, Axel darling, but they don't have time travelers from the future watching over them."

"Right. Well, if they're watching, they're getting quite a show. Are you, uh, sore?"

"Not at all. Are you?"

"No. Just a dull ache in the balls. They're kind of stunned down there."

"It's good for them, Axel. They need to feel the sting of the lash every once in a while. So, did you ever get anyone pregnant?"

"Not that I know of. How about you?"

"No. I've always been careful–until I met you."

"Richard didn't want kids?"

"He's got five adult children–all world-class brats. Not one of his spoiled hoodlums would deign come to our wedding. He did the world a favor and got a vasectomy after wife number three."

"Not a good husband choice for someone who wanted a baby."

"Tell me about it. God, I don't know what I was thinking. Have I thanked you for breaking up my wedding?"

"Not lately."

She gave me a long kiss. I felt my monogamy gene stir and unclamp from absent Desma.

We were finishing breakfast the next morning in Tara's suite when two FBI agents dropped in. One of them did most of the talking. I listened from the bathroom, where I darted at the sound of their knock.

"Did you know we wished to speak with you, Ms. Yordanyotov?"

"Call me Tara. No, I had no idea. What's this about?"

"You have not been in contact with your manager, a Mr. Matthew Debome."

"No, I'm taking a bit of a break. I guess Matt doesn't know where I am."

"And your cell phone is turned off. Why is that?"

"Uh, so people don't annoy me with calls. I am taking what is termed a vacation."

"I see. We've been trying to get in touch with you to inquire about the incident in Fresno."

"Right, yes. That was kind of dumb."

"Were you contacted at that time by Axel Weston?"

"Of course not. He's dead."

"We have reason to believe he is alive, Ms. Yordanyotov. The person who interrupted your performance was not Axel Weston?"

"No, it was sort of a dumb gag that got out of hand."

"So whose voice was that? You were interrupted by a male and a female on the stage."

"Oh, I did those voices. It was all part of my act. It was supposed to be something of a parody."

"You can do Axel Weston's voice?"

"I can do a man's voice. I've never actually heard Axel Weston speak."

"Would you mind doing his voice for us now?"

"Hello, gentlemen," said Tara in a credible imitation of me. "Would you like me to disrupt your wedding?"

"Very good. And the disrobing that took place on the stage?"

"Oh, that was a bit of a wardrobe malfunction. The panties were supposed to stay up. I'll use double-sided tape the next time."

"So you have no knowledge of the current whereabouts of Axel Weston?"

"I didn't even know the creep was alive. I need his address for my lawyers."

"We have reason to believe he may be in the vicinity. His fingerprints were found on a stolen car just a few miles from this location."

"Oh dear. Well, I imagine that he'll be easy for you to find."

"Not that easy, Ms. Yordanyotov. We have reason to believe that he's invisible."

"You're joking!"

"We're very serious."

"But how is that possible?"

"That's what the Bureau wishes to find out. If Mr. Weston contacts you, please call us immediately at this number. And don't mention the invisibility aspect to anyone. It's confidential."

"Right. I understand. Well, I hope you catch the bastard."

The other agent spoke for the first time.

"Are you sharing a breakfast with someone?"

"No. Just me. I'm ashamed to say I ate it all. I'm kind of depressed from the failure of my marriage."

"We understand," said the first agent. "Call us if you hear from Mr. Weston or his associate, a possibly invisible female named Claudia Stasse."

"Oh, yes, I've read about her. I certainly will. And thank you so much."

Tara found me in the bathroom and gave me a torrid kiss.

"How did I do?"

"Excellent, Tara. But we better get out of here."

"We'll go back to L.A., honey. You can help me find a nice private house for us."

"You sure you want me along?"

"I'm positive. So don't ask me again. I'm supposed to be the one with the insecurities, not you."

"OK. But before we go, we've got to wipe down every surface I might have touched."

"Including my delightful breasts?"

"I'm serious, babe. Let's get to work."

Tara sneaked my bag and stuff down to her car, then returned to the inn, called for a bellhop to carry down her bags, and checked out. She kept the top up on her car to make room for the bags. Her Mercedes (which she named "Steffi" because it was sporty and German) featured an elaborate mechanism that folded the hard top down into the trunk like a convertible. There was no Swedish reserve in the luxurious fittings of her car. We would be traveling in grand Teutonic style and comfort.

I suggested that we take twisty Highway 20 east to connect to 101 in Willits. This road was much less traveled than the route Tammy and I came in on. About 40 minutes into the drive I had Tara pull over into a turnout for an old logging road. We waited there 10 minutes. Only six vehicles passed us coming from the coast; none of them looked like a government car. I concluded that Tara wasn't being followed.

"It's pretty private here, honey," she said with a leer. "Have you ever done it in a Mercedes?"

"We just did it two hours ago."

"Oh. Can't get it up again, huh?"

I could. And did.

The sun was blazing in Willits, where we turned south on 101. Stretches of the road were still the old undivided highway. I dialed the temperature down to 68 and plugged Mr. Volvo's Ipod into Tara's bone-shaking sound system. She drove like a careful mom (for the baby's sake) while all three of us were serenaded by the rock stars of two generations ago. Tara usually listened to recorded books on long trips, but she said she would spare me the "chick lit" CDs that filled her center console.

It was good to be on the move again. Every day spent in one place made me more wary that Claudia might be bursting in on us. She'd found me the first time in less than a day. I worried that her arrival was imminent, way overdue, and wouldn't be welcome.

Traffic got heavy in Santa Rosa and slowed to a crawl through Marin County. We crossed the Golden Gate Bridge (my first time), and Tara bought take-out Vietnamese food in San Francisco. We parked in a semi-deserted section of Golden Gate Park and ate our lunch crouching low in the seat. Then Tara's GPS directed us to I-280 south and we made good time heading down the peninsula to San Jose and beyond. We stayed on 101, which was slower but more scenic and perhaps less patrolled than the I-5 alternative. No budget motels for Tara; we spent the night in an oceanfront hotel in Pismo Beach. Being famous, she got the best room on the top floor. Being glamorous, she drew the attention of all eyes as we crossed the carpeted lobby. Nobody noticed her invisible companion.

The room-service dinner was not in the class of the Mendocino cuisine, but my pricey steak was cooked just the way I requested it. The waiter was Latin and liked to flirt with pretty guests.

"Did you order the second dinner for me, Miss Tara? he asked. "I could take my break now."

"Sorry, it's for me. I need to gain 20 pounds fast for a movie role."

She softened the rejection with a $50 tip. The guy was lucky I didn't trip him on his way out.

Tara was so bushed from all that driving she fell asleep right after dinner–no sedative required. I'd been hoping to persuade her to go down to the lobby to get me a *Los Angeles Times*. I thought of sneaking down myself, but two minutes later I was asleep on the other bed.

We made up for the celibate night the next morning in her bed. Somehow we always seemed to be perfectly in tune with every caress and stroke. As we lay spent in each other's arms I brought up the issue of my name. I suggested that she remember to address me as Jack instead of Axel.

"Jack, huh? That's pretty dull."

"I suppose you gave special pet names to all your old boyfriends."

"Only to their weiners. Is that terribly immature?"

"Probably. Give me an example."

"Well, one fellow could wink with his dick so I named it Lucille."

"Could you elaborate on that?"

"OK, so you know how dicks have this opening at the tip?"

"Right, I've noticed."

"Well, he could wink at you with his opening. It was the *cutest* thing."

"OK, if you say so."

"Flaccid or erect, he could do it both ways."

"That's more than I need to know. And the leap to Lucille?"

"You know, Lucille Bluth on 'Arrested Development.' She would drive her son nuts by winking at him."

"Right. So, have you come up with a name for mine?"

"I don't know, Jack. I might not do one for you."

"Why not? Don't I rate?"

"You rate too much, darling. Your equipment is way too important to give it a silly name."

I was touched. That was one of the nicest things anyone had ever said to me.

A fresh *Los Angeles Times* rolled in on the room-service breakfast cart. Only one small box on an inside page was of interest: the second earring had been found at the sewage treatment plant. No mention anywhere in the paper of Diane, Claudia, or me. Perhaps the whole thing was beginning to blow over.

In the parking lot of the hotel it occurred to me to inspect the underside of Tara's car. I pointed out to her the small black box adhering to the sheet metal of the chassis.

"What's that, Jack?"

"If I had to guess, I would say it's a tracking device."

"Damn! FBI?"

"Or some other government entity."

"Well, let's get rid of it!"

"We can't, Tara. If I took it off, they'd figure you had something to hide."

"What should we do?"

"When we get to L.A., we'll park this car and rent another one. Or perhaps you can borrow one."

"My dad will lend me one of his clunkers."

"Good. We like clunkers."

Two hours later we were rolling past the freeway exits

for Carpinteria. I thought about my time in that pleasant little town with Desma. I had fled north from L.A. with one woman and was returning with another. Both had put themselves greatly at risk to help me out. Mr. Invisible was a lucky guy.

We checked into a hotel in Beverly Hills that was set up for extended stays. The suite Tara booked had a full kitchen, so we wouldn't be dependent on room service. Ordering all those double meals might start to seem suspicious. And there was an exit directly from our floor to the parking garage–bypassing the carpeted lobby. The corridors were carpeted, but the busy pattern in the low pile helped disguise footfalls. I offered to chip in some for the rent, but Tara said I could pay her back with future midnight diaper changes.

As the bellhop left with his generous tip, Tara took a deep breath, switched on her cell phone, and discovered she had 83 messages. She switched it off.

"God, I hate my life, Jack. Let's go catch a plane to Bali."

"I might have some trouble going through airport security."

"Fuck, let's go back to Mendocino."

"It'll be OK, darling. How come you don't have a personal assistant to do your grunt-work?"

"Oh, I've had them in the past. It's just too weird. They know all the intimate details of your personal life, but every Friday you have to hand them a paycheck. It's a totally alien form of human connection."

"What about all those other stars who have them?"

"They have them, Jack, because they have monstrous egos, are completely self-centered, and are very likely sociopaths. I, on the other hand, am a fairly normal person. You could help me now by saying something sweet."

"Corn syrup."

She swung her handbag at me. I ducked, took her in my arms, and kissed her.

Tara decided to deal with her messages by ignoring them. She did spend five minutes checking in with Matt, her manager. To give her some privacy, I went into the bathroom and said the words. The many mirrored surfaces confirmed that I was still invisible.

Tara came in looking for me.

"Matt knows a good real estate agent who can find us a place to rent. Where would you like to live? I'm always hot so we can't go too far inland. And anywhere within 20 miles of Costa Mesa is out because that's where my parents live. Do you hate the idea of Venice?"

"It's pretty densely populated, Tara. We need a place that's private and the neighbors aren't nosy."

"You're thinking of what–a 400-acre horse ranch in Oxnard?"

"That might work."

"We'll compromise on Santa Monica north of Montana or Pacific Palisades. How does that sound?"

"I could do that."

"Good. I'll tell the agent we need minimum four bedrooms with pool and maid's quarters–emphasis on the privacy. Tennis court?"

"I could probably scrape by without one."

"OK," smiled Tara. "That's one chore down. Let's go try out our new bed."

We had to make it a quickie because Tara needed to get on the freeway to Costa Mesa before rush hour. Trying to get anywhere in car-clogged L.A. between the hours of 4:00 and 7:00 p.m. is an exercise in masochism. I told her if it got too late, she should spend the night at her parents' house.

"Oh, are you planning to phone an escort service? Call up Diane? Have a reunion with your wife?"

"None of the above and you know it."

"Did I mention I have insecurities, Jack? For example, I'm presently dating a guy who's invisible."

"What can I do to help?"

"Three little words. That's all it takes."

As Rachel could attest, I had a long history of trouble

with brief, declarative sentences from the heart. I swallowed and said the words. Why was it always such a struggle and sounded so phony coming from my lips?

"I love you too, darling," said Tara. "Next time don't make me hold a gun to your head."

"I'll try. It's nearly four."

"What do you want for dinner? I'll phone room service now and have them deliver it later. I'll tell them to knock on the door and leave the cart in the hall."

I chose from the menu, she phoned, I kissed her.

"What was that for, Jack?"

"For being so thoughtful and generally great."

"Thanks. Repeat that hourly and we'll do fine."

After Tara left I scouted out the hotel. I checked the various exits and scoped out possible escape routes. Being back in L.A. had elevated my paranoia level. Hundreds of cops and agents could be marshaled in minutes to surround any building. Tara's responses during the FBI visit had been perfect, but I had made a major mistake letting her car be seen at the campsite where the stolen car was found. And how did the cops connect the stolen Volvo to me so quickly? Thousands of cars go missing every day in California. The police couldn't have the investigative manpower to run fingerprint tests on all of them. Had I left some identifying item at the campsite? I had assumed Desma had taken her little gun, but perhaps she had stashed it where I didn't see it. The deputies might have found it and traced it to Myron. Or had Desma done the unthinkable and dimed me to the cops? Or had Claudia tracked me to Mendocino and made the call herself? Why hadn't I heard from that woman? For all I knew, she could have jumped off that bridge in Rio Vista and drowned in the Sacramento River.

Every question raised new issues. I had too few facts; I was still floundering in the dark. I was getting more paranoid by the minute.

# Chapter 24

Tara's loaner car from her dad was no clunker. It was one of the last of the big Buick Roadmaster station wagons and in primo condition. Conveniently, it had a front bench seat so invisible passengers could enter and exit from the driver's side–avoiding suspicious door openings. Tara had told her parents she needed to borrow the wagon to shlep her stuff from Richard's place. No, they didn't question why a person in her income bracket would be hauling her own household goods. They just assumed they raised her right.

Tara's real estate agent was hot to take a meeting, but Tara requested she fax a list of potential rental houses to her hotel. She would drive by them first to see if any of them were "at all suitable."

The fax was delivered by a tip-happy bellhop (word had gotten around), who went away smiling. We finished our cereal and coffee (donated by Tara's mom) and were soon cruising around some of the west side's swankiest neighborhoods in the cavernous Buick. We stopped in front of an expansive faux chateau on Corona del Mar. I liked the palm trees, the manicured grounds, and the sweeping views of Santa Monica Bay. The rent, though, seemed a bit steep: $18,500 a month.

"Guy put a star by this one," commented Tara.

"Your real estate agent is a chick named Guy?"

"Why not, Jack? There are guys named Chick."

"Is Guy her first name?"

"It's Guy Biffle, Jack. We're lucky to get her. She's famous."

We were living in a place that fostered such a culture of celebrity that even real estate agents could achieve fame.

"If we rented this place, Tara, every morning we'd have to get up and stuff over $600 in the rent kitty."

"Yeah, it does seem a pit pricey. And it's rather exposed to the street. It has six bedrooms, a wine cellar, and an underground garage for your classic car collection."

"I don't have any classic cars, although someday I wouldn't mind owning a yellow 1949 Ford convertible."

"Not a snazzy Cord or an Auburn?"

"Nope, just vintage basic transportation. Let's drive on before somebody calls a cop."

A house on Amalfi Drive seemed the most promising–assuming one could get over the pretentiousness of the street name. It was well-hidden behind an ivy-covered fence, offered a "filtered" water view, had four bedrooms, "decorator" kitchen, and the pool house could double as maid's quarters. The rent, with a one-year's lease–was a mere $6,300 a month.

"This place looks like a bargain, Jack. We should jump on it."

"You can afford that sort of tariff, darling?"

"I'm doing pretty well, honey. I just signed for three more specials on Comedy Central. Matt's booking me all over the fucking globe. And my prenup with Richard specified a heavy penalty for unilateral cancellations. His own attorneys stuck in that clause. The bastard was afraid I was going to back out!"

I was appeased. I could live in the lap of luxury knowing Richard was picking up the tab.

By 8:00 that night the deal was done. Tara had toured the place with Guy (I declined to come along), and found it acceptable–although needing some interior TLC. The pool was fairly small, but it was solar-heated and had a spa. The security system was basic and did not monitor the infra-red spectrum. Being half-Bulgarian and no spendthrift, Tara negotiated the rent down to an even $6,000. Guy said she would get the keys as soon as the paperwork went through–in two days, but possibly sooner.

We celebrated by having a four-course banquet delivered to our hotel room from Chez Rodeo. They don't normally do deliveries, but all things are possible when you're famous and charming. While we dined on linguini with lobster tomato mint pesto sauce and tempura prawns, Tara commented that it was a shame that Axel Weston couldn't take advantage of his own fame as a notorious drowning victim.

"You're right," I agreed. "I'm nearly as famous as you are, Tara, yet I have to hide out like some criminal."

"Well, you are a bit of a criminal, darling."

"I'm an oppressed minority, darling. We invisible folks are constantly being harassed by the police."

"That's right, Jack. You're a pioneer in the struggle for invisible rights."

"I'm as visible a spokesman as they've got."

"Which is, alas, not that visible. But I know Axel Weston will leave his imprint on history. Invisible statues will be erected to your memory."

"And will there be invisible pigeons to mess on them?"

"I'm sure there will be, darling. If there's any justice in this world."

The two FBI agents returned early the next morning. This time they brought along a buddy. Tara was not as friendly as before. She let them in, but suggested in the future they do the polite thing and call her for an appointment.

"You still have your cell phone switched off," said the more talkative agent.

"You could have called the hotel phone," Tara pointed out. "How did you know where I was?"

"We're just interested in your own safety, Ms. Yordanyotov," he replied, not answering her question. "Mind if Agent Buorman looks around?"

"What's that thing on his head?" Tara asked.

"It's an enhanced vision device, Ms. Yordanyotov. This will only take a minute or two. It's just routine."

"Did you catch that bastard Weston yet?" Tara asked, sounding nervous.

"Not yet. But we have his girlfriend. We're hoping she divulges his location."

"You arrested Claudia Stasse?" asked Tara, trying to sound misinformed.

"No. A young lady named Diane Philips. We caught her yesterday mailing a package to the Harry Weinstock store in Beverly Hills. It contained a missing diamond pin."

"How do you know she's connected to Axel Weston?"

"We know, Ms. Yordanyotov. We're putting all of the pieces of the puzzle together. It's a most unusual case."

"Looks like somebody had a party here last night," commented the second agent. He must be their Special Agent in charge of noting food consumption.

"I just found out that I'm pregnant," said Tara. "I've been eating like a horse."

"And who's the lucky father?" asked the first agent.

"That is none of your business, I'm sure," Tara replied coldly.

"Here's the receipt," noted his partner. "You ate $287 worth of food."

"So call me a glutton," said Tara. "Are you people through here? I need to take a shower."

"Picking up anything?" asked the first agent.

A third male voice replied, "No. The place is clean."

"Sorry to disturb you, Ms. Yordanyotov," said the first agent. "Have a nice day."

I counted to 100 slowly, then pushed open the refrigerator door and gulped in some air. It had been getting very stuffy in there. Not to mention chilly. And crowded with my bag and laptop. Previously, I had had the foresight to remove several refrigerator shelves and hide them in the oven.

I embraced Tara and placed my hand over her mouth while shaking my head.

I whispered in her ear, "Don't say anything, darling. They may have left behind a bug."

She whispered in my ear, "God! I was terrified they were going to open that door."

I whispered back, "Are you really pregnant?"

Her whispered reply, "I hope so. I'm now officially 24 hours late."

Without speaking, we wiped down the suite, then bailed. Tara didn't phone down for a bellhop. We went out through the parking deck; she loaded our bags into the Buick, and we headed up North Canon Drive toward the hills. She stopped and bought a *Times* from a rack. She continued on up Coldwater Canyon Drive and pulled off at a vista spot where the view was expansive and conversations could be private. We both searched the car for bugging or tracking devices and came up empty. We scanned the newspaper and found no mention of Diane's arrest. I took that as a bad sign.

"That was privileged information, Tara. They told you so you would pass it along to me. They must be pretty confident that we're in contact."

"Possibly. I suppose."

"They've got me, darling. It's my fault Diane is in this mess. I can't let all this ruin her life. If I turn myself in, they'll go easier on her. It's me they want."

"That's not going to happen, darling. If you do that, I'll drive back to Mendocino and walk off that cliff."

"Don't talk like that, Tara. I need you to be strong here for me."

"We're going to Plan B, Axel. You can forget Plan A. We'll get Diane a lawyer. Richard has a very good one–he's always getting Richard's kids out of jams."

"How much good can a lawyer do her?"

"Let me finish. Didn't you say if you could find a volunteer to be switched, you might be able to become visible again?"

"That's right. It worked several times with Claudia."

"OK. So we find someone and do the switch. Our lawyer works out a deal: Diane will talk if all charges against her are dropped. The Feds agree, we divulge the location, and they grab an invisible guy."

"Only he wouldn't be me, Tara, because the fingerprints wouldn't match."

"So big deal, it's not you. I doubt the Feds are going to mind. They'll get their invisible person to play with. That's all they care about."

"And you really think we can find a volunteer for such a mission?"

"I've got one, Axel. Only it's more like I'm volunteering him than he's volunteering himself."

"You're really that pissed at Richard?"

"Forget Richard! I'm talking about a guy who deserves much worse treatment than this. I'm talking about a guy who is as low as a human being can get."

"OK, so who is this villain?"

"Kenny Tinker."

"And Mr. Tinker is?"

"The fiend who instigated and directed the systematic and daily torture of the woman who is expecting your child from grades five through eleven."

"Why did he stop at grade eleven?"

"That's when he finally flunked out."

"He was just a kid, Tara. OK, so he was a nasty kid. We couldn't do something this cruel to him for acts he committed as a juvenile. People grow up. They change."

"Not Kenny. He's only gotten worse. I still have friends from high school. They keep me informed. He had two brief marriages that blew up because of domestic abuse. Several girlfriends since then have had to get restraining orders against him. Last year he broke his mother's arm."

"Why isn't the creep in jail?"

"His mother refused to prosecute. She claimed it was an accident. The guy is a total lowlife, Axel. He's got 'white power' tattoos and swastikas."

"He has a swastika tattoo?"

"Yeah. At least one big one on his shoulder."

Kenny was losing his advocate here. I have trouble with guys who adorn themselves with the insignia of a regime responsible for the deaths of nearly twice as many people as currently reside in California.

Tara continued her case for the prosecution. "There have been many unexplained killings of pets in Kenny's neighborhood. And last year Halloween candy from his mother's home was found to have been tampered with."

"Kenny tried to poison trick-or-treaters?" I asked, aghast.

"I kid you not. He only got away with that because his mother blew three grand on a lawyer."

"Perhaps we should get Kenny's lawyer for Diane."

"OK, Axel. Are you agreed? We snatch Kenny and do the switch?"

"Forget snatching anyone, Tara. Do I look like a Mafia enforcer? Do I work for Murder Incorporated?"

"Well, Axel darling, I know you've got a gun in your coat pocket."

"That's just for show, darling. We'll do this like civilized people. We'll look up Kenny. And we'll make him a deal."

Since their clients were mostly criminal types, Steiner & Guerra, Attorneys at Law, did not feel the need to put on the dog like many other L.A. law firms. They occupied a modest suite of offices over a drugstore on an unglamorized block of Wilshire. Tara parked in the drugstore lot and headed upstairs. Mr. Invisible sneaked into the store behind an old lady pushing one of those wheeled walkers. I found the correct aisle, checked that the coast was clear, and pilfered a pregnancy test kit. Never had I imagined that I would some day be shoplifting such an item. I exited behind the same old lady and waited beside the passenger door of the Buick. Tara came down about 20 minutes later. She let me in the car and we drove off down Wilshire.

"It's all set, Jack. Ted Steiner was in court, but his partner said they would take the case. He agreed that they would keep my involvement in retaining them strictly confidential. Nobody's going to know–not even Diane.

"You told him the whole story?"

"As much as he needs to know, darling. I told him he should try to make a full-immunity deal for Diane based on her disclosing the location of Axel Weston. He should tell Diane that Axel's on board with the plan and that she shouldn't be concerned that she's betraying him."

"Good, Tara. Diane has to agree to cooperate with us on this or she's screwed. Did you give him a way to get in touch with you?"

"I told him to leave a message with my parents and I'll call him back."

"Good, darling. We can't use your cell phone because it will give away our location."

"God, I love having a reason to turn off my phone. We should get in trouble more often."

"You know, Tara, this scheme might get the Feds off my back, but I'll still be on the hook for the diamond heist and stealing that car."

"Don't worry, Axel. Ted's a very good lawyer."

"Well, he may be able to finesse the Weinstock robbery, but the cops got my fingerprints off that Volvo. I may still have to go away for a few years."

"Don't even think that, darling."

"Believe me I don't want to, but the facts are against me. Could you stick by a jailbird?"

"You're not going to prison, darling. I won't let them take you."

"Tara, even the boyfriends of celebrities sometimes go to jail."

"Not happening, Jack. Let's change the subject."

Tara turned on the I-110 freeway heading south. The big Buick floated along like the boat it was.

"Did he request a retainer?" I asked.

"Of course. But they're giving me a deal because Richard's such a good customer."

"Was it more than $10,000?"

"It was, but don't worry about it, darling."

I was on the hook for a lifetime of diaper changes. I'd cleaned up a lot after Bob, but I suspected that diapers could be considerably more repellent. I took out my drugstore bounty and showed it to Tara. She took it entirely the wrong way.

"What the hell is that for?" she demanded.

"Uh, it's a pregnancy tester."

"Oh, you don't trust me, huh? You think I'm lying! You think I'm trying to entrap you!"

"Not at all, darling. I just thought you might want to know for sure."

"Here's something you need to know about me, Jack. I prefer to operate in life from a position of hope. Not despair!"

"Uh, OK. Shall I pee on it instead?"

Tara grabbed the kit from my hand, rolled down her window, and tossed it out on the freeway. It seemed like the act of a woman whose hormones were in an uproar. I concluded, therefore, that she probably was pregnant.

We rode on in silence. Tara took I-110 to I-405 south past endless L.A. sprawl. Eventually we crossed the border into Orange County. In all my months in California I had never ventured this far south. Rachel and I had talked of going to Disneyland, but we never quite got it together to make the trip. We bought that ugly condo and got mired in Glendale goo.

"Are you hungry, darling?" asked Tara, breaking the ice.

"I could go for something big and bleeding."

Being a native, Tara knew all the best eateries in Costa Mesa. She got two large take-out orders of ribs from a place on Harbor Boulevard, then drove to a nearby park. On the way she went past her old high school, scene of all that youthful trauma.

"That's Estancia High. Go Cardinals!"

"How come they don't have a picture of you out front?" I asked.

"Too many teachers still hate me. They had a problem with my sarcasm."

"Which is now earning you the big bucks."

"Yeah. Ain't revenge sweet?"

Throwing caution to the wind, we found a private spot in the shade of some trees and had a picnic on the grass.

"How come this park is so deserted?" I asked.

"This is Costa Mesa, Jack. Everyone's at the mall."

The spicy ribs were delicious. After our messy lunch we cleaned up with the lemon-scented wipes so thoughtfully provided, then leaned back against a tree and necked. In between kisses Tara apologized for yelling at me in the car.

"Not a problem," I assured her.

"God, I'd kill for a piece of floss," she said, picking her teeth with a fingernail. "Did you know I lost my virginity in this park?"

"Then this is hallowed ground!"

"Not really. It was your usual disaster. His name was Mitchell. A classy name for a very unclassy guy. I was in love with him for about ten minutes. Which was about as long as it took him to tell everyone in school that he had nailed me. Ah, Mitch, may flesh-eating bacteria attack your puny dick."

"We could do Mitch instead of Kenny," I suggested.

"No way. Mitch was a fleabite, Kenny was six long years of torture."

Kenny's mother lived in a 1950s tract home on a bleak street bordering the industrial section of Costa Mesa. Tara parked across the street and pondered the weathered and neglected little ranch.

"God, I can't believe I'm about to talk to Kenny Stinker. Jack, if you ever doubt that I love you, please recall what I did for you on this day."

"I appreciate your sacrifice, darling. Shall I cover you with my gun?"

"No. That won't be necessary. Well, here goes nothing."

Tara slipped on her sunglasses, exited the car, walked to the front door of the house, and rang the doorbell. She rang the doorbell again. As she was peering in through the dirty front window, the door opened, and an emaciated-looking woman greeted her. They spoke for a few minutes, then Tara returned to the car.

"She kicked Kenny out. She didn't want to give me his address, but I managed to convince her I wasn't a bill collector or a knocked-up girlfriend. He's living in a trailer park a few blocks away."

The trailer park was a one-lane affair between two warehouses. All the trailers were small single-wides from some distant era. This time I insisted on following behind Tara as she walked up the row from the street. Space #18 was occupied by a once-flamboyant, now derelict trailer that sported actual 1950s tail fins. Tara picked her way across the cluttered patio and knocked on the battered aluminum door.

"Who is it?" demanded a male voice from within.

"Hi, Kenny," called Tara. "It's a friend from high school."

Mr. Tinker himself opened the door. He was a tall sunburned guy with a greasy mullet haircut and one diamond (probably fake) earring. His casual trailer-lounging attire consisted of a soiled wife-beater T-shirt, cut off to expose his muscular torso, and heavily stained sweat pants. Part of a swastika was exposed on his pimply shoulder. Other offensive tattoos were also in evidence. The oaf was clearly surprised by his visitor.

"Holy Shit! It's Tara Lordytov! What happened to your fucking tits, girl?"

The die was cast. Kenny had sealed his doom.

"Uh, I had some surgery to reduce them. How ya' doin', Ken?"

"Great. Come on in."

Even ten paces away I could detect Tara's shudder. She didn't budge.

"Uh, I can't stay, Ken. I just came by to see if you might be interested in some work."

"You want me break the knees of that old actor dude? What's his name?"

"Uh, no. I'm working with a film company. They're testing some new 3-D technology. We're looking for some participants. It only takes a few hours. We're offering a thousand dollars."

Kenny was intrigued but suspicious.

"So why do you want me?"

"Uh, we need guys around your height and muscular. I remembered that you used to work out."

"I still do. Can't you tell?"

"Yeah, you look like you're in great shape."

"So, Tara, is this a real deal or did you just come by lookin' for a fast fuck?"

More nails in Kenny's coffin.

Tara opened her purse and took out an envelope.

"Here's $500 in cash, Ken. You get the rest of the money afterwards."

"Also in cash?"

"That's right. There might be a bonus for you too."

Kenny stepped down from the doorway and took the envelope. He peered into it and smiled.

"So what's this test? Is it gonna hurt?"

"No, it's easy. It's just testing some 3-D effects. There's no pain involved."

"So when do you want me?"

"I'll pick you up tomorrow night. Say 7:00?"

"You got it."

"And, Ken, we need you here on time and sober."

"Not a problem, Tara. I don't drink."

When we returned to the car, I told Tara I had seen her pal Kenny before.

"You're kidding, Axel."

"Nope. Remember I told you somebody bashed me in the leg in Santa Monica?"

"It was Kenny?"

"I only got a one-second glimpse, but I'm about 99 percent sure that your Mr. Tinker was the dude swinging the pipe."

We checked into a budget chain motel a few miles away. Tara stripped off her clothes and went immediately into the shower. After a while I began to fear she was going to drain all of the hot water out of the building. Eventually she emerged, warm and steamy, and we made love on the budget bed.

"God, what a day," she sighed, when we had finished. "Remind me why we chose this dump instead of someplace nice."

"If we went to someplace fancy, darling, you'd be recognized. Here people just assume you're someone who resembles that famous person."

"Or else they assume it is that famous person–only now her life is on the skids."

"Do you feel that way?"

"No, darling. I've just got Kenny Stinker poisoning. I'll be all right when this is over."

"He's amazingly repulsive. I'd hate him even if he hadn't broken my leg."

"He's lower than a Dachshund's crotch. I got a million Kenny stories. Want a few more?"

"Sure."

"OK, in the second grade I brought my hamster to school. It must have been for show and tell or something. So when school is over, my beloved pet is missing. The cage is there, but my buddy Baxter is gone. Big trauma for Tara. So over the next few days I hear these rumors. Kenny was too big and scary even then to take on, so I beat up this kid named Bryan to get the facts. Kenny ran my hamster through his mother's meat grinder."

"He didn't really."

"He did. Bryan turned the handle while Kenny stuffed the little guy–alive mind you–down the opening."

"That's horrible."

"Yeah. I should have strangled him then."

"I thought you said Kenny started torturing you in the 5th grade."

"Well, he was nasty to everyone before then. The 5th grade is when he started to zero in on me. Want to hear some more?"

"I can take it if you can."

"OK, fast forward to my sophomore year in high school. I'm in the drama club production of 'Bye Bye Birdie'."

"Did you have the Ann-Margret part?"

"Get real. Remember, I couldn't act. I could sing if you overlooked the flat notes. Dancing I could do, but any movement of my tits was deemed too provocative for a high-school production. I played Doris McAfee, the mother. With my build I always got the mother or grandmother parts. Anyway, it's opening night and the curtain is about to go up. Suzy Eimann brings me a Coke to help me relax. I have the usual jitters, but even then I considered myself a pro. But I take a few swigs. So about midway through the first act I start to feel a little nauseous. But I'm a trouper, the show must gone on. There I am belting my way through 'Hymn for a Sunday Evening' when I suddenly throw up."

"You didn't."

"I did. We're talking extreme projectile vomiting all over myself and fellow cast members in front of an audience of 900. I mean I heaved it all out. I scraped the bottom of the barrel. I barfed up cake from my previous year's birthday."

"Wow, what a nightmare."

"The kindest thing would have been just to shoot me right there. You know, put me out of my misery."

"I detect the dastardly hand of Kenny."

"Yeah. Turns out he had doctored that Coke. Suzy was in on it too, the little bitch. Her father owned a drugstore. They both got suspended. I got another lesson in Humiliation 101."

"That's awful, darling."

"Yeah. Scarred for life. Bruised as deep as you can go. That's why I went into comedy. I found my tribe at last. Speaking of all things neurotic, I need to call my mother."

Using the motel phone, Tara called her mother, who reported that a man named Ted Steiner wanted her to phone him. Tara dialed the number and got an update from Ted. He had seen Diane, but she needed a confirming sign that he was there at the behest of Axel.

"Tell him to say Grata dressing room and Carpinteria," I said.

Tara relayed the instructions and told him he could call her anytime day or night at the motel phone number. She thanked him and rang off.

"So what happened in the Grata dressing room and Carpinteria?" Tara asked.

"Oh, nothing that would be of interest to you. Say, what does it take for a guy to get some dinner around here?"

Since we needed to stick by the phone, Tara called out and had Costa Mesa's best thin-crust pizza delivered. The delivery boy inquired if she was Tara, the comedian.

"Nah, I'm better looking than that bitch," replied Tara, handing him a chintzy non-celebrity's two-dollar tip.

"That will teach the jerk to recognize people," said Tara, passing me a napkin and a slice. The pizza was excellent. We sat on the bed and stuffed ourselves.

"Damn, Axel, why did you let me toss that pregnancy tester?"

"You need to call me Jack, darling."

"Oh, right. Sorry."

"We could go to a drugstore and get you another one."

"We'll do it after the business with Kenny is over. There's no sign of my period. And I'm usually quite regular. I'm feeling optimistic here, Jack."

"My handlers will be pleased."

"And how about you?"

The signs were pretty clear. My monogamy gene was rooting for Tara.

"I also will be pleased."

After dinner, I fired up my laptop and we watched the video of my memorial service. Gus Baboo gave the halting eulogy. He said that I had been a good person, a loyal friend, and a generous employer. He pointed out that I always cleaned up after my pet at the dog park. And I even went the extra distance and cleaned up after other people's dogs. Several other dog-park pals stood up and added their praise. Emma Smeesh said I'd always had a smile for Fluffy, and she was praying that I would lay off the beer in my next life. I was a bit disappointed that Rachel didn't get up to speak. I did see her shed a tear or two. And she hadn't brought a date–I could take comfort in that.

"Your wife is very beautiful, Jack," observed Tara.

"You think so?"

"And, of course, Diane Philips is gorgeous."

I didn't like the drift of this conversation.

"You outshine them all, darling. By far! I am totally and completely stuck on you."

It wasn't three little words, but it was as near as I could come.

# Chapter 25

The next day was spent getting ready for that evening's performance. We decided it would have to take place elsewhere. After doing some research on Yelp.com, Tara rented a room in Costa Mesa's worst-rated motel–which turned out to be just down the block from our own. We got a moldering ground-floor room at the far end of the building. With any luck, we wouldn't have any immediate neighbors.

Next, we bought some supplies at a local hardware store. Tara wore her head scarf and dark glasses so she wouldn't be recognized. Our final stop, after a quick lunch, was a medical supply store. I sneaked in along with Tara to help her pick out a machine. The choice was an easy one. We went for the multi-parameter health monitor that featured a dizzying array of digital readouts, flashing LEDs, buttons, and switches. The salesman told Tara she couldn't go wrong with that machine.

"How much to rent it for a day?" inquired Tara.

The salesman looked startled. "Uh, we usually rent these by the month."

"The prognosis for Aunt Marge is not good," she replied. "We only need it for a day."

The salesman was willing to compromise on a one-week rental. Tara plopped down the $500 deposit in cash (courtesy of me and my pal Myron), signed the contract, and the salesman loaded the bulky machine into her Buick.

"I hope your aunt recovers," he said.

"Yeah," replied Tara, "we're all praying for a miracle."

We unloaded the machine at the funky motel and plugged it into an outlet next to the double bed.

"If we were at all curious, Tara, we would attach ourselves to this machine and monitor our bodily functions while having furious sex."

"Sorry, Jack. I wouldn't get in that bed if George Clooney was begging me for a lay."

"Hey, I have to take off my clothes tonight and get in that bed with Kenny Stinker."

"Shut up, Jack. You are totally grossing me out."

We went back to our budget motel, and Tara checked in with Ted Steiner. The deal was on. He said "way more people" were interested in Diane than would be expected on a grand-theft/burglary rap. But emergency meetings had been held. Diane would walk free; all he needed was an address. Tara told him to expect the call later that night.

We were much too wound up to worry about dinner. We rehearsed our lines until it was time for Tara to go pick up our victim.

"You sure you don't want me to come along?"

"I'll be OK, Jack. I can handle Kenny."

"OK. One final thing. Just remember, whatever happens tonight, we have to stay calm. We don't want your big friend getting alarmed and running amok."

"Right. Stay calm. Are you calm, Jack?"

"I'm attempting to stay calm. Here's my gun. Only use it if you have to."

"I'd have no problem shooting Kenny."

"Well, try to restrain yourself. We need him alive."

Tara dropped me off at the funky motel, then drove on to the trailer park. I switched on the machine and got everything ready. I shed my clothes and hid them in the closet. Less than 20 minutes later, I heard the Buick pull to a stop outside the door. Operation Invisible Tinkering had commenced.

Kenny had spruced up for the occasion. He had shaved, his mullet appeared somewhat less greasy, and he was dressed in a flashy shirt, black pants, and leather jacket. I may be prejudiced, but he looked to me like a low-rent pimp. "Stinker" was an appropriate nickname; his sickly sour body odor soon pervaded the motel room. Kenny nervously eyed the health monitor.

"What the hell is that?" he asked.

I decided for maximum credibility I would speak with an upper-crust English accent.

"Good evening, Kenneth," I boomed, startling him. "My name is Jack Armstrong. This machine is our new R12-10-17 model that we will be testing with your assistance. I am speaking to you from our laboratory in Hollywood, California. Can you hear me clearly?"

"Yeah, it sounds like you're standing right next to me."

"Excellent. And how are you this evening?"

"Not bad. Is this gonna hurt?"

"Not at all, Kenneth. Are you comfortable? Can we get you anything?"

"Can I smoke?" he asked.

"Certainly, whatever you like."

Kenny's hands were shaking as he lit a cigarette and sucked in deeply.

"Kenneth, what we will be experimenting with tonight is the projection of 3-D spatial illusions. Do you know what an illusion is?"

"Yeah. Of course."

"Good. I think you'll make an excellent subject, Kenneth. What I want you to remember, Kenneth, is that nothing that you will be perceiving is actually real. It is all an illusion projected into your mind by our machine. Do you understand what I am saying?"

"Yeah, it ain't real."

"Correct. Even if what you are experiencing seems unsettling, you must think of it as a new sort of movie or video game. Except that now *you* are the star. That is what makes our new technology so exciting. That is why Tara has invested in our venture."

"That's right, Kenny," she added. "I've tried it. It's fabulous."

I went on with my soothing spiel. "Many companies around the world are interested in our technology. We have demonstrations scheduled in New York, London, and Tokyo. If you prove to be a good subject, Kenneth, would you be willing to travel with us to these destinations and others?"

"I don't know," said Kenny, cagily. "It'll cost you."

"We are prepared to pay you a generous salary. And all of your expenses will be paid. I am certain we could come to terms. Now, Kenneth, are you ready to begin?"

Kenny stubbed out his cigarette on the motel carpet and grunted his assent.

"For maximum effect, Kenneth, we must ask you to remove all of your clothing. If you prefer, I can request that Tara leave the room."

"Let her stay," said Kenny, winking at Tara and stripping off his clothes. "Chicks like to see me naked."

He may have thought so, but Tara turned to face the wall. The body odor was even more oppressive with Kenny modeling all of his tattoos and pimples in the buff. As I directed, he slipped into the bed and got comfortable under the covers.

"Now, Tara, will you please connect the spatial projector to Kenneth's temple."

Tara wiped Kenny's temple with an alcohol swab and taped down one of the machine's monitoring electrodes.

"Now, Kenneth, I want you to do exactly as I say. You must keep your eyes closed at all times. Only open them when you are directed to by me. Your ability to follow my instructions to the letter will determine whether you will be invited to join our team. Do you understand?"

"Yeah, I'm keeping my eyes closed up tight."

"Excellent. Now, we are going to begin with a mirror projection of your own body. Tara, please turn on switch 17C."

Tara reached over and flipped a switch on the machine.

"Now, Kenneth, you should feel another body enter the bed and embrace you."

I swallowed hard and climbed into the bed. I couldn't imagine that women sometimes did that willingly with this guy.

"Jesus," exclaimed my repulsive bed-mate, "I feel it!"

I turned my head away and lowered my voice. "Don't pull away, Kenneth, you must grasp the projected body image firmly. It is only a mirrored reflection of your own body."

"It doesn't smell like me," noted Kenny. "And it has cold feet."

"Good. Our altered effects are working perfectly. Now, Kenneth, you may open your eyes."

Kenny popped open his peepers and looked at the void beside him in amazement.

"As you can see, Kenneth, it is all a projected illusion."

"That is fucking incredible!"

The guy had toxic cigarette breath too. And I could see that flossing was not part of his daily health regimen.

"Now, Kenneth, are you prepared to go on to the next stage?"

"Bring it on!"

"Excellent. You and I, Kenneth, are going to read some words that Tara has written on a card. We are going to say them slowly and in unison. You must take care to pronounce each word exactly as written. Do you understand?"

"Yeah, Jack, I understand."

"Good. After we read them, you must shut your eyes and keep them closed until I tell you to open them. You must not open them under any circumstances. Do you understand?"

Kenny shut his eyes. "I understand."

"Right. Only you have to keep them open until after we read the words."

Kenny opened his eyes. "Oh, right."

"Tara," I said. "Please flip switch 9X and hold out the card."

She did so, and our victim and I read the words together. I felt the rod goose my organs and vivid orange stars twinkled and flashed throughout my field of vision. I could sense that I had made a transition, but something was clearly awry. My entire body felt suddenly alien and strange. I looked over. The person I was grasping had disappeared. That was the good news.

"Damn," sighed Tara. "It didn't work."

"Kenneth," I said, "are you keeping your eyes closed?"

"Yeah, Jack. They're closed."

At that point Tara started shrieking. I felt the body beside me go tense; I grasped it firmly.

"What's happening, Jack?" Kenny asked with my voice.

"Stay relaxed, Kenneth," I said as soothingly as possible in his voice. "Keep your eyes closed. Tara is merely excited because things are working so well. Tara, please step outside and wait for me there."

Tara stared at the bed with an expression of pure horror. I repeated the command. She clutched her head and stumbled out the door. I struggled to stay calm and go on.

"My voice sounds different, Jack," said Kenny. "How come you sound like me?"

"It is all a projected illusion, Kenneth. We can alter voices at will. We developed that technique especially for use in video games. Now, Kenneth, I am going to remove your projected double from the bed so that he can assist me. Please remember to keep your eyes closed."

I got up from the bed and dressed hurriedly in Kenny's clothes.

"How are you feeling, Kenneth?" I asked. "Are you in any pain?"

"No, I'm fine. I feel a little weird. I had kind of a cold feeling inside, but it went away."

"Good. Our temperature alteration effect is working splendidly. You're doing very well, Kenneth. You're the best and most cooperative subject so far. I'm very pleased. Now, Kenneth, I'm going to ask you to put your arms behind your back. Can you do that?"

I saw the bed covers move.

"Good. Now, I'm going to put another projection device around your wrists. This will help amplify the spatial effects."

I located Kenny's arms by feel and slipped a stout nylon tie around his wrists, binding them together.

"How is that, Kenny. Is it uncomfortable?"

"No, Jack. It's fine."

"Excellent. Now keep those eyes closed tight. I'm going to put a similar device around your ankles."

I quickly bound Kenny's legs with another nylon tie.

"Now, Kenneth, I'm going to ask you to swallow six little tablets–keeping your eyes closed all the while. These contain a harmless marker that will help us trace the projection effects in your body. Do I have your permission to do this?"

"Sure, Jack."

I located his mouth and gave him six of Tara's sedatives. I heard him swallow the mouthful.

"Good, Kenneth. Now I'm going to switch on one of our best effects. We call this the relaxation effect. You will feel your body begin to relax. The sensations will be pleasant and you may possibly go into a relaxing sleep. At all times remember to keep your eyes closed. When you awaken you must remember what I'm going to tell you. Can you do that for me?"

"Sure, Jack."

"If anyone asks you your name, you must say it is Axel."

"Axle like the car part?"

"Correct. If you tell anyone that your name is Kenneth

Tinker, our entire experiment will be a failure. We won't be able to invite you to join our team. We won't be able to pay you the large salary. And we'll have to get someone else to go on our demonstration trips. Do you understand?"

"Sure," he said sleepily. "My name is Axel."

"Correct. And remember, any change that you perceive in your body is only a projected illusion. It is not real."

"Right, Jack. It ain't real."

"Good. Now, you just rest here. I'm going to take a brief break and talk to Tara. I'm going to tell her what a wonderful job you're doing. Are you keeping those eyes closed?"

His reply came from the far edge of consciousness. "They're closed."

I backed away from the bed and went out through the door. Tara was leaning against her father's Buick and pointing Mr. Volvo's gun at me.

"Stop right there!" she commanded.

"It's me, darling."

"Please! Don't say that!"

"I'm afraid it's true."

"Then get inside and say the words again!"

"I can't. It's too late. I already gave him the sedatives."

"But why! Why!"

"I don't know, darling. Something screwed up. It's not something I wanted, believe me. But I sensed right away it was final. Those words aren't going to work again. I'm stuck."

"Tell me why I shouldn't kill you right now."

"Because I love you. Because there's some kind of weird destiny at work here."

"I could never be with you. You realize that."

"I hope that's not the case, darling. We have to think this out. We're giving them Axel Weston. The fingerprints are going to match. I'm free."

"Free? Free to live as Kenny Tinker!"

"I may have his body, darling. But it's still me. The old Kenny Tinker is no more. He's invisible. He's out of your life."

"My life? My life is fucked!"

"Come on, darling. Put down the gun. We've got things to do."

Tara lowered the gun.

"Just don't come near me! And don't touch me!"

Kenny was sound asleep when we went back into the room. The health monitor went out much easier than it had come in. I simply hoisted it up with my powerful new muscles and carried it out to the Buick. I closed up the tailgate, and Tara drove off to stash the machine at her parents' house. I didn't know if she'd be back.

I went in and sat in a chair beside the bed. The invisible figure on the bed was snoring away as Rachel used to complain that I did. My hand reached automatically into Kenny's jacket and pulled out the pack of smokes. I was familiar with those pangs. I lit one and took a deep drag. Damn, I would have to quit smoking all over again.

I retrieved a glass from the bathroom, pressed it against the other sleeping Kenny's hand to leave some fingerprints, poured an inch of cola into it, and dissolved the contents of another sedative tablet into it. This I left with the cola can on the bureau for the evidence guys to find. I also transferred the cash from my old wallet into Kenny's, leaving behind one $10 bill.

I'd finished the cigarette by the time Tara returned, but the smell still lingered.

"Did you smoke a cigarette?" she demanded coldly.

"Uh, yeah."

"My Axel did not smoke!" she exclaimed, as if one cigarette proved my falseness and treachery.

"Well, I smoked at one time, darling. This has been a stressful evening. You could cut me some slack here."

"You're getting no slack from me, buster!"

She sat as far away from me as she could in the cramped motel room, and we went over what we would say to the cops. I asked her what she'd done with the card.

"What card?"

"The cards with the words, Tara."

"Oh, I tore that up in the car. I tossed the pieces out the window."

"Is that the truth?"

"Of course it's the truth! Get off my back!"

"You can't say those words, Tara. It's too dangerous."

"I have no desire to become invisible. OK, satisfied? Are you ready?"

I nodded and she dialed the number. The Costa Mesa police showed up in less than three minutes. They did as they had been directed: they secured the premises and stood by until the Feds arrived. The helicopters swooped down in less than 20 minutes. The street in front of the motel was closed off and they landed there. It was the same agents as before and a big posse of their associates. Kenny's sleeping form was secured with government-issue shackles and he was whisked away by helicopter to parts unknown. Tara and I were separated and interrogated in different rooms in the motel.

I got the second agent, the food-consumption expert. I told him the story: Axel Weston was a nut who was obsessed with Tara. He broke up her wedding and followed her to Fresno, where he disrupted her performance. He befriended Diane Philips knowing she was a pal of Tara. He even stole jewelry to give to Diane, thinking it would help him get closer to his target. Tara couldn't tell any of this to the cops because Axel threatened to kill her family. Finally, in desperation, she hired me–an old high school friend–and I helped her lure Axel to the motel room, where we gave him a drugged drink. When he fell asleep, we bound him with the nylon ties and called the cops.

After I finished answering the agent's questions, he left and I smoked another cigarette as two other agents watched over me in silence. Then his partner came in and I told him the same story all over again. I hoped my story was matching

Tara's. The agent kept coming back to the same questions: Why hadn't we brought them in? Why had Tara been so evasive with them?

"I told you, man," I said, adopting Kenny's vernacular. "Tara was scared shitless. I mean that dude was fucking invisible. He could have killed anybody he felt like. We found that loaded .45 in his coat pocket. That guy was armed and dangerous."

"You are not to mention his invisibility to anyone," said the agent. "Do you understand? You are not to speak to the press or the media. You are not to tell your friends or anyone."

"My lips are sealed, dude. I hear you! I don't need no trouble with you guys!"

I didn't see Tara again that night. After midnight I was driven by a Costa Mesa cop to Kenny's trailer. The cop seemed to know who I was and where I lived. He appeared to regard Kenny as an odious person unworthy of acknowledgment. Perhaps the cop had a few trick-or-treaters of his own at home.

The third key on Kenny's set unlocked the trailer door. I turned on a lamp and looked around. It was even worse than I–an expert on slovenly living–had been dreading.

# Chapter 26

The trailer was about 35 feet long and had the stan-dard layout: living room in front, bedroom in back, kitchen and bath in the middle. Every visible surface was cluttered, filthy, and/or repellent. It smelled like sweat, smoke, old carpet, mildew, and piss–all overlaid with a concentrated Kenny sourness. Most of the living room was taken up by a large weight bench and an elaborate set of weights. Kenny liked to keep his muscles in tone, if not his house in order.

I didn't know if I'd be able to get any sleep; I was still operating on FBI-interrogation adrenalin. I sat on the weight bench and had another smoke. The pack was about half full. When I smoked the last one, that would be it. I wasn't going to buy any more. That's how I'd quit in my other body. I just stopped.

I went in the grungy bathroom and drained Kenny's lizard, which was large and circumcised. Too bad. Axel had also been circumcised. Had one of us been uncut, I might have been able to settle that argument over whether it made a difference in bedroom pleasures–assuming I would ever get another woman to sleep with me. The prospects seemed dim.

I stripped off Kenny's pimp clothes and checked myself out. I was about six-two and weighed around 180. Big feet with ugly yellow toenails. They went with the back pimples. No needle marks on the arms, I was relieved to see. I wasn't jonesing for a fix or booze. It appeared my only addiction was to cigarettes. I should probably be tested, though, for VD and HIV.

The good news was my paunch was gone. My brown hair was thick and did not appear to be thinning. I had no disfiguring scars or healed up bullet holes. My ass was neither white nor lumpy. I could see without glasses and I didn't appear to be color blind. I had zero fillings in my teeth. Was it possible that Kenny had never been to a dentist?

I had WHITE POWER tattooed on my left arm and a big black swastika on my right shoulder. There was a heart enclosing the words "FUCK YOU" under my left armpit. I had a small silver ring through my right nipple. Two letters had been tattooed in bright red on the end of my dick. That must have hurt like hell. Assuming the urethra opening stood for "O," the letters spelled WOW in one direction and MOM in the other. Perhaps it was intended to distract the viewer from the show immediately below. Kenny had a severe problem with scrotal sag. It was as if the two fat testicles were trying to get as far away from him as possible. I bounced and swayed with every step. Hell, I needed a bra for my balls.

I was operating with Kenny's brain, but I did not appear to be stupid. I spelled "ratiocinate" in my mind and then "paroxysm." I knew what the words meant. I was still a college graduate.

I looked in Kenny's wallet. According to my driver's license I was 32–the same age as Tara. I was five years younger than before. A free gift of five years. Those last two dissipated years had been cancelled out–erased from my time span. I was getting a fresh start to undo my messes. Only with one slight hitch: I was now Kenny Tinker.

The unmade bed in the back was too disgusting to lay even Kenny's body on. I stretched out on the weight bench and got a few hours of fitful sleep. I got up and took a shower in the scummy tin box provided for bathing. No shampoo in evidence. I washed my mullet with the bar soap. I suppressed a gag and cleaned my teeth with Kenny's ratty brush, then dressed in the cleanest clothes I could find. Even though it promised to be a warm day, I put on Kenny's only long-sleeve shirt, which was thick flannel. I would be covering up fully until I could afford to get his offensive tattoos removed.

I walked four blocks to a Mexican diner that was open for breakfast. I read the *Los Angeles Times* over my huevos rancheros. There was no mention in it anywhere of the events of last night. I doubted that the FBI would be calling a news conference today to announce that they had captured an invisible man. The local *Daily Pilot* carried one paragraph noting a brief street closure caused by a drug arrest at a local motel. No names were mentioned. It was a story that was going down a deep, dark hole.

Back at the trailer park, I nodded at neighbors who were about, but got only sullen stares in return. Kenny was not a popular tenant. There were two car keys on Kenny's ring, but they were plain hardware-store copies without the car brand logo. I didn't know if any of cars parked in the littered rear lot was mine. I offered a bored-looking kid five bucks to wash my car. He filled a dirty bucket with water and splashed it over an old Pontiac Grand Prix painted in flat-black primer. Too bad. I'd been hoping for the orange Mustang with the flashy mag wheels.

In the trunk of my Grand Prix was a three-foot length of heavy steel pipe such as a thug might employ to bash someone in the leg. I hefted it by its duct-taped handle and swung away, putting another dent in Kenny's fender. No doubt he'd been paid in cash for the job, by whom I will probably never know. The deed had been avenged in the curious way this was all working out. It was as if my discovering those words had activated the "Start" cam on an intricate clockwork of intertwining destinies. And how many gears, I wondered, were yet to unwind?

The engine started right up and the gas gauge was indicating nearly full. The ashtray was full to overflowing and the car reeked of smoke. The rock CD blasting out of the stereo was so offensive, I tossed it–Tara style–out the window. Having been born into my new body only a few hours before, I had no place in particular to go. I drove west through Costa Mesa and turned north on the Pacific Coast Highway. It ran along the ocean in Huntington Beach, then turned inland to slog through Long Beach and industrial Wilmington. We picked up the ocean again in Redondo Beach. A traffic light nearly every block, but I didn't mind. I cruised through Hermosa Beach and Manhattan Beach–all those beach towns I had heard about all my life but had never been to. I drove through El Segundo and passed the airport. In Venice I found myself on Lincoln Boulevard. I turned at the corner and parked across the street from Desma's building.

I smoked a cigarette, then got out of the car, and crossed the street. I went up the fire escape, stopped at the top, and looked across the roof. Her sliding door was open and she was giving a bowl of food to a scruffy gray cat. She was dressed casually, but everything was in perfect order. She looked up at me and scowled.

"Hey, you! Get out of here!" she exclaimed. "This is private property!"

"Sorry. I was looking for a friend."

I turned to descend, but she spoke again.

"Hey! Who are you?"

"Nobody."

She shaded her eyes with her hand and peered intently at me."

"Do I know you? Have we met?"

"Not in this lifetime. I'm glad they released you."

"How did you know about that? Who are you?"

"I'm nobody. I gotta go. Do me a favor and find somebody decent to love. You deserve it."

"Axel?"

"Sorry, I don't know anybody by that name. I gotta go. 'Bye."

I went back down the fire escape. She watched me from the roof as I got into my car. She waved, but I didn't wave back.

Kenny's cell phone rang as I was shopping for used clothes and underwear in a Venice thrift store. It was an older woman.

"Kenny, where the hell are you?"

"Uh, who is this?"

"Don't get smart with me, dipshit. It's your mother."

"Oh. Hi, Mom."

"Where are you? You promised to take me to my hair appointment!"

"Uh, sorry. I had to go to Venice on business. You'll have to reschedule."

"Then you'll just have to forget about this month's check!"

"Sorry, mom. It won't happen again."

Kenny's mother hung up on me. Another in a lifetime of disappointments from her flaky son.

I took the freeway back to Costa Mesa. After exiting, I stopped at a drugstore and bought unwaxed floss, toothbrush and paste, shampoo, deodorant, vitamins, athletic supporter, garbage bags, and a bottle of Pin-X. The druggist said this would take care of Kenny's pinworm problem. The asshole had a bad case of rectal itch.

I filled four garbage bags with detritus from Kenny's trailer. These I tossed into the park's overflowing dumpster. The bedding, other linens, and useable clothes I took to a coin-op laundry and processed at the hottest setting. I washed the dirty dishes piled in the sink, emptied the many ashtrays, and cleaned the bathroom as best I could. I swept the floors and ratty carpet with a broom. I considered an experimental peek inside the grungy refrigerator, but decided to leave that horror for another day.

I had dinner in a Chinese restaurant. I decided Kenny needed more vegetables in his diet. I hoped that this in combination with vitamins and improved hygiene might clear up the back pimples. I felt they clashed excessively with my swastika. As an experiment I also ordered a beer. It looked great in that tall chilled glass, but it tasted like dirty socks. I couldn't gag the stuff down.

Kenny's cell phone rang as I was finishing my meal. This time it was a guy calling.

"Is this Ken?"

"Speaking."

"Are you booked for Saturday night?"

"I don't know. What's cooking?"

"I'm having a party with about 60 guests. How much would it cost?"

If Kenny was a pimp, that sounded like a big order.

"Uh, how much do you want to pay?"

"I can't pay more than two bills, man. And I'm not expecting any trouble."

"Uh, which ad is this in regards to?" I asked.

"The one in the *Recycler* for party security. Aren't you Ken, the bouncer?"

"Yeah, but I'm booked up solid. Sorry."

I wasn't just a semi-employed thug after all. I had a profession. I was a free-lance party bouncer.

My fortune cookie read: "You are ever the center of attention because of your admirable character." I hoped it was a message from my unseen handlers.

I went back to the trailer, pumped some iron, then crashed on my freshened and sanitized bed. I went to sleep thinking of Rachel. I wondered what she was doing and if I had seen the last of Axel's wife. I also wondered if my monogamy gene had transferred with me, or if I was destined to resume Kenny's program of promiscuous couplings with inappropriate partners.

The FBI looked me up the next day; I was not surprised by their visit. Two agents I hadn't seen before invited me out for a drive in their government sedan. We went to a federal office building in Santa Ana, where the original two agents were waiting for me. They looked like they hadn't been getting much sleep lately.

"Hello, Ken," said the lead agent. "How have you been?"

"No complaints."

"Have you discussed this matter with anyone?"

"No, sir. You said not to."

"Good. Have you been in contact with Ms. Yordanyotov?"

"Nope."

"Why's that?"

"Well, she hired me for a job and the job's over. That chick hangs with movie stars, not guys like me."

"Ken, we've been talking to Axel Weston. His story is rather startling. He says he's actually you. He says you and Ms. Yordanyotov used a machine to make him invisible and take over his body."

"I'd like to have some of what that guy's been smokin'."

"So you don't know anything about such a machine?"

"Not me, sorry. It sounds like something out of a movie. It don't sound real."

"You haven't invented or employed such a machine, Ken?"

"Shit, man, I flunked out of high school. You can look it up. I can barely get my cell phone to work. I don't know about Tara, but I can tell you she wasn't much of a science brain back in high school."

"Why do you suppose he would make up such a story?"

"The guy's probably embarrassed. He thought he was going to score a piece off Tara, and he got snookered instead. We nailed his ass, so now he's out to make trouble for us."

"Axel told us about some words that were employed in connection with the machine."

"Words, sir?"

"Yes. A short sentence of nonsense words. Do you know anything about such words?"

"Nope. What were they?"

"He doesn't remember. We were hoping you could tell us."

"Well, I remember the invisible guy saying 'Holy fuck' when he started getting dopey from the drugged drink. Does that help?"

It didn't help. Eventually, they got tired of hearing the same replies to the same questions and I was dismissed. I got a courtesy lift back to my trailer park and was instructed not to leave town.

I smoked my last cigarette the next morning. Before I lit it I savored its aroma. The tobacco companies know how to put together an enticing package. All those flavoring agents they spray on the tobacco combine to work magic on your nose. And when the stuff inside got fiery, it sprang the locks to all those secret passageways leading to your brain's deepest pleasure centers. I smoked Kenny's final cigarette and snuffed out the butt. I knew it would not be long before the tantrums would start to rage inside my skull.

The third time Kenny's cell phone rang was the charm. It was Fresno's favorite comedienne.

"It's me," she said. "We need to talk. I'll pick you up in an hour."

She was a half-hour late. I didn't mind; I had nowhere else to go. She honked her horn, I hopped into her Mercedes, and she drove back to the park where we had dined on ribs a few days before. We didn't get out of her car.

"How's life in the trailer park?" she inquired with a noticeable lack of warmth.

"I can't complain."

"Why the hell not?"

"Because I'm visible again."

"Why do you keep feeling your pockets?"

"Because I quit smoking and the news hasn't reached my hands yet."

"I can't believe you haven't gotten rid of that stupid hair-cut."

"I have to keep on looking like Kenny, Tara. The FBI is still interested in us."

"Tell me about it. They raided Henry's offices this morning."

"Henry your ex-husband?"

"The same. They seized computers, hard drives, files–the works."

"Why?"

"They figured out you and I didn't have the smarts to build an invisibility machine, so they did some research and came up with Henry."

I tried to suppress the laugh, but it sneaked out anyway. Tara glared at me, but soon was chuckling along.

"Yeah, it was a wild time this morning up in Sunnyvale, let me tell you. Henry lost a great deal of face with his colleagues."

"Well, that'll keep the FBI busy for a while. Did you take back the monitor?"

"My dad did."

"Will he mention it if the FBI drops by?"

"My father's Bulgarian. We have an inbred distrust of all authority figures. Oh, I tossed Axel's bag, gun, and laptop into Newport Bay."

There went the rest of my old life.

"Good, Tara. Now all we have to do is sit tight."

I glanced over at her. She was looking most attractive in her summery blouse and short skirt.

"I refuse to address you as Kenny."

"Call me Jack. I found out my full name is Kenneth John Tinker. Did you do a pregnancy test?"

"That really isn't any of your business now."

"Don't say that, Tara. It would still be my kid."

"Wrong. It would be Axel Weston's."

"Axel Weston is sitting beside you, Tara. He's right here.

He still loves you. He's just got a big handicap now."

"Yeah. He's got a handicap the size of a fucking elephant."

The next day I spent drinking coffee and observing my brain thrash around inside my head. Kenny was probably the sort of guy who had smoked since he was six. The habit was deeply, deeply ingrained. I couldn't do anything more demanding than pump some iron and look through Kenny's effects in the trailer. A black woman with a sexy voice phoned to tell me I was a "first class shit" and that she hoped I would "rot in hell forever." I didn't take it personally; I figured it was the only aspect of Kenny's life that qualified as first class.

That evening I took Kenny's mom out to dinner at a steak house in Newport Beach that Tara recommended. It seemed to me I owed her something for depriving her of her son, however cretinous he may have been. Kenny clearly hadn't inherited his aversion to alcohol from her. She downed three gimlets before the food arrived and then drank most of a bottle of cabernet. I sampled the wine, but it was ghastly—even worse than beer. I stuck to tonic water without the gin.

Mom had lots of issues with her son, but the alcohol helped her relax and I got her to reminisce about Kenny's childhood, his dad, other relatives, previous homes, etc. I started out sympathizing with her situation, but by the end of the evening had concluded that Kenny's bad seed had not fallen very far from her polluted tree. The widow Mrs. Tinker was thoroughly and insidiously nasty. By the time I dropped her off at her house, I was of the opinion that Kenny had demonstrated remarkable restraint in only breaking one of her arms.

The next morning I got another free ride to Santa Ana. My buddies the G-men were looking even more haggard than before. Clearly, it wasn't as much fun having an invisible man around if you didn't know how he got that way. As I had anticipated, they invited me back to play the game "I'm More

Kenny Than You Are." The invisible Kenny had been giving them lots of facts to prove he was who he claimed to be. This must have irritated them big time, especially since they probably weren't learning much about invisibility from Henry's computers.

"Where was your father born, Ken?" asked the chief agent.

That was an easy one. I was ready for it.

"Duluth, Minnesota. Dad was a machinist. He moved out here because of all the aerospace work. He couldn't take the cold."

I smiled. The two agents looked at each other, clearly perplexed.

The game continued for about an hour. I didn't score 100 percent on their questions (few of us are gifted with total recall), but it was clear I had an excellent command of the salient details of Kenny's life. I attributed this to my years of digging for facts as a journalist. They appeared to attribute it to the fact that they had two Kenny Tinkers on their hands.

"OK, Ken," said the G-man, "how do you think Axel Weston knows so much about your goddam life?"

"Shit if I know. Damn! I feel like my privacy's been invaded. I think you should arrest that sucker for identity theft!"

Tara called two days later.

"What are you doing, Jack?"

"Not much. Missing you."

"Want to help me unpack?"

"Sure. Where are you?"

"The house on Amalfi Drive. Do you remember the address?"

"How could I forget it? I'll get there as soon as I can."

"Take your time. I'll be here all day."

The 405 freeway was not excessively clogged. I exited in Santa Monica and got a haircut in a shop on Wilshire. The barber and I were both pleased to see the last of Kenny's mullet. When he finished, he held up a hand mirror so I could inspect the job front and back. Not bad. From certain angles Kenny looked almost handsome. He had even features and no glaring defects. His eyes were a pleasant hazel-brown. The ochre smile had been brushed away. The new mustache was growing well and lent a certain maturity to his face. As long as he kept his shirt on he did not flash TRAILER TRASH in bright neon.

Tara opened the door when I knocked. She did not rush into my arms, but she appeared somewhat approving as she inspected the new me.

"What do you think?" I asked.

"Well, now I can look at you without feeling my skin crawl."

In small baby steps was progress made.

She took me on a tour of her new house, crowded floor to ceiling with boxes and household stuff. The rooms were large, airy, and well lit. Many windows looked out on the verdant rear garden and pool area. Some decorator, though, had been given too free a reign in the kitchen, which featured sky-blue cabinets and lavender appliances.

"What do you suppose they were thinking?" inquired Tara, opening her purple refrigerator to get me a Coke. "Were they insane or just excessively medicated?"

"I vote for color blind."

"Well, now you see why the rent was so cheap."

"I'm not sure $72,000 a year qualifies as cheap, Tara. Are you going to change it?"

"Certainly not. I think it's hilarious. My act should be so funny."

Tara made BLTs for lunch, then we set to work on her stacks of stuff. My strong new body was ideal for lugging, carting, hoisting, and arranging. By dinnertime we had made a significant dent in the disorder. Neither of us was dressed for any place fancy, so Tara took me out to a Thai restaurant a few miles away. We had a pleasant meal–our first in a public place. We went back to her house and sat on her sofa with our feet up on the coffee table. She did not pull away when I took her hand.

"What am I going to do with you, Jack?"

"Love me someday if you can."

"That's like asking Golda Meir to fall in love with Adolph Hitler."

She leaned toward me and sniffed.

"You don't smell disgusting any more."

"I'm a pretty nice guy. I've been working on my self-esteem issues."

"You had a lot of those, Jack. And for good reason."

"Any news on the baby front?"

"April 15. He's going to be a tax-day baby."

She wouldn't let me kiss her, but she said I could come back tomorrow to help finish the unpacking.

I was back after rush-hour the next day. I hoped my aging Grand Prix was up to all those freeway miles. Tara and Axel had barely been able to keep their hands off each other for more than five minutes at a time; I felt the same magnetic pull as I unpacked her boxes and put away her towels. Every time we passed I wanted to reach out and grab her.

It was a warm day. After lunch Tara asked me if I wanted to join her for a swim in her new pool.

"I can't, Tara."

"Why not, Jack?"

"Can't take off my shirt."

"Oh. That's right. Well, you could leave your shirt on."

We found some swim trunks in the pool house that would fit me. I went into the pool in my long-sleeve shirt and swim trunks over my athletic supporter. Tara changed into a sexy bikini and joined me. Nice, but I preferred her previous swim attire in Mendocino.

We embraced in the water and she let me kiss her.

"That's not too awful if I keep my eyes closed," she commented.

"I love you, Tara," I said, holding her close.

The words came easy this time and didn't sound phoney.

"Oh, God, Jack. This is so weird."

"Well, most relationships are a love-hate thing."

"The hate I've got, Jack. It's the love I'm working on."

I kissed her again.

"Now I suppose you want to rape me," she said.

"Do you have a condom, darling? We don't dare do it without one."

"Condom nothing, Jack. I'd prefer a sexual surrogate."

Tara scrounged up a condom. We closed the blinds in her bedroom, stripped off our wet garments, and–still damp–embraced gingerly on her bed.

"You'll have to put on the condom yourself, Jack. I'm keeping my eyes shut."

"Good, darling. I was hoping you'd do that."

Kenny's equipment had reached its maximum size. Some effort was required to stretch the condom over the thick shaft. Praying the latex wouldn't break, I applied myself to the task at hand.

"Damn, Jack, how many of them are you?"

"Uh, just me. Are you OK?"

"I'm more than OK. Don't stop."

When we finished, Tara opened her eyes and kissed me.

"What was all that bouncing against my bottom?"

"My balls I'm afraid. I've never seen such droopy ones."

"Can they be–you know–adjusted?"

"I have no idea. I doubt it."

"I'm making an appointment with a plastic surgeon for you, Jack. We have to get those tattoos removed."

"It's fine by me, darling. The sooner the better."

"What the fuck is that writing on your dick?"

I showed her my ornamentation and told her she would have to get used to it. No way was I having any painful laser work done on that part.

We had dinner in an Italian restaurant in Westwood. Tara sipped her wine and said her mother was going to kill her.

"Why, darling?"

"You remember how I told you my friends in Costa Mesa kept me posted on the latest Kenny Stinker outrages?"

"Yeah."

"Well, gossipy Tara always called her mom to relay the latest dirt. My parents despise you more than I did."

"You could introduce me as Kenny's twin brother Jack."

"Won't work, darling. It's probably all over the Orange County grapevine that we've slept together. Oh, it's going to be ugly. They'll think I've lost my fucking mind. It was enough of a stretch for them when I was planning to marry that senior citizen Richard."

"We should get married before the baby arrives."

"Is that a proposal?"

"It is if you'll have me. I should advise you that I'm unemployed and living in a trailer."

"How do we explain that to my parents? God, it's a good thing I'm knocked up. Otherwise, Jack, you'd be a dead man for sure."

"So will you have me?"

"Yes, Jack. If you're alive on our wedding day, I will marry you."

I spent the night with her and moved in my stuff (what little I had) the next day. Kenny's trailer I abandoned for the park management to deal with. They could have the pleasure of opening that refrigerator door. I did pack along his bench and weights. I saw no point in letting all that sinewy muscle go to flab–especially if I'd soon have to fight off Mr. Yordanyotov's paid assassins.

Tara put me on her health plan, and I got checked out by a doctor. The pinworms had cleared up, and blood tests revealed I was disease-free. A dentist did some minor tinkering in my mouth and told me to keep up the good work. The first plastic surgeon we consulted declined the job (the swastika was too objectionable), but a guy named Steve in Studio City took me on. I think he may have been Desma's Steve. I lay on his table and cursed Kenny as Steve barbecued my flesh with his laser beam. He toasted a huge patch on my shoulder because there was no point in replacing a swastika tattoo with a swastika-shaped scar. It hurt like hell, cost Tara a bundle, and required many sessions.

Tara's parents kept bugging her to invite them up to see her new house. One Saturday morning she got up the courage and dropped the bomb. Thank God, she did it over the phone. She started with the news that she was pregnant. I could hear the squawks from the phone across the room. Then she said she was in love with the father and engaged to be married. The squawking subsided.

"Actually, Mom," Tara continued, "you know the guy I'm going to marry. No, it's not Richard. I need to tell you first that this fellow has really changed. Yeah, he's matured. He's like a totally different person. You have to keep that in mind. Also, please remember that he's the father of your first grandchild. That fact cannot be changed. The deed is done. There's no use trying to talk me out of this, and I'm not insane or on drugs. I know what I'm doing. I haven't been taken over by some cult. No, I'm not trying to alarm you, Mom, I just want you to keep an open mind here. Yes, I'm getting to his name. His name is, uh, Ken. Yes, that's his first name, but I call him Jack. Nice, huh? His last name? Uh, well . . . his last name is, uh, Tinker."

An ominous silence in the room. No squawking from the phone.

"What's happening?" I whispered.

Tara put her hand over the receiver. "She's either dead or off informing my father."

An explosion of bellowing from the phone. The conversation went on for another two hours. I finally had to leave the room and go sit by the pool and pick at my tattoo scabs. I sensed I was destined for some serious in-law trouble.

We met them the next day for brunch. We didn't go to their house, but agreed to meet on neutral turf at a Huntington Beach restaurant. Tara warned her father ahead of time that if there was any physical violence, we would leave and they would not be invited to our wedding or their grandchild's christening. For the occasion I wore all new clothes, purchased at great expense in Beverly Hills, and I looked as decent and respectable as a Tinker could.

The first words out of Tara's mother's mouth as we approached their table were, "Oh, God! I had prayed it was some other Ken Tinker!"

She was white as a sheet; her husband, on the other hand, was an unnatural shade of red. He glared at me like I was the Antichrist come to brunch. Tara smiled bravely and made the introductions. Neither of my future in-laws deigned to shake my outstretched hand. I withdrew it awkwardly and placed it around their only daughter's semi-bare shoulder. A fresh outrage against decency for them to swallow.

Somehow I got through the next 10 minutes. My mouth worked and I was capable of ordering. I requested the coconut french toast and coffee. I sensed my order may have put Tara's parents off coconut for life.

"I hope you don't name the baby Baxter," said Tara's mother, making a veiled allusion to that brave martyred hamster of long ago.

"Actually, we were thinking of Axel," said Tara brightly.

"Like the car part?" grunted her dad, still beaming daggers in my direction.

"Spelled differently," replied Tara. "God, I hope I can keep my breakfast down. I've been throwing up a lot lately."

More daggers flashed at the villain responsible. I sipped my coffee and longed for my former invisibility.

My breakfast arrived and went untouched as I got the full Bulgarian father's grilling: job, income, family background, work history, future plans, religion, etc. Very few of my halting replies were judged to be at all satisfactory. Both parents obviously concluded I was a vile deadbeat planning to sponge off their daughter. That judgement seemed not far off the mark. Tara was affluent, she was supporting me, and I had no real prospects for altering the situation. Hating me with a passion was a perfectly reasonable response, even if I weren't a known Halloween poisoner.

The next hour made even Fresno time seem fast. The minutes dragged by like snails on quaaludes. Still, the moment came when Tara's dad grudgingly paid the bill, the last coffee was sipped, resentful good-byes were said in the parking lot, and normal life got switched back on.

"Well, that went better than I expected," said Tara from the passenger's seat, as I piloted us away in her Mercedes.

"They hate my guts!"

"Well, that's to be expected. But you did good, darling. You were articulate and mostly coherent. I think you made a good first impression, all things considered."

"Your father wanted to strangle me with his bare hands. He ordered steak and eggs just so he could jab at me with that steak knife."

"He was just gesturing, Jack. Bulgarians always talk with their hands. Give them time, darling. I hated you until a few weeks ago. We need time for your charm to work its magic."

We decided on a November wedding. I signed a not-too-onerous prenup (Tara's manager Matt insisted on it), and an announcement was released to the media. Not surprisingly, this sent the tabloids scurrying off for dirt. All of Kenny's arrests and scrapes were dragged out and picked over. The *Los Angeles Times* ran a sober, two-part feature about women in the entertainment world and their difficulty in finding appropriate partners. They ran my photo both days. Paparazzi descended on once-peaceful Amalfi Drive, alienating our neighbors. (Some no doubt were there representing my old pal Jeremy.)

A half-dozen of Tara's friends called and offered her shelter and help in seeking counseling. Several sent her articles on the Stockholm syndrome and manuals on self-defense for domestic violence victims. Richard phoned up drunk and offered to pay to have me snuffed. A tabloid TV show dug deepest of all and came up with two hardcore porno films in which Tara's betrothed had appeared. That made the papers around the globe. You can imagine how that revelation was received in certain Costa Mesa households.

Tara didn't seem to mind. She went on the Tonight Show and cracked jokes about her boyfriend the porn star. I had nothing else to do, so I started helping her deal with all the demands on her time. I suggested some jokes, a couple of which she tried out in her act. One got a big laugh in Seattle. I helped out with the wedding plans, and worked on being charming at the many public and private functions to which we were invited. Gradually, some of her friends came to view me as something more than a bad joke with a big dick.

Once in a while Tara would slip into one of her black moods, and I would retreat to the pool house to work on my new screenplay. This one might go somewhere someday; it's about a guy who's invisible.

Our G-men buddies dropped by one last time to see if we were ready to confess to being masters of invisibility. We weren't. We pointed out that it wasn't a crime for a comedy star to marry the guy she hired to help her move. We said we did not appreciate being harassed by the government and had lawyers who were willing to make that point in court. They sighed and went away. I suspected their invisible Kenny was getting on their nerves. They also were frustrated by their inability to track down Claudia. They probably wished they'd never been dragged into this invisibility mess in the first place.

We were not invited to any Halloween parties. We went to the movies that night and did not pass out candy. I could sense it was not going to be my favorite holiday.

We got married in Mendocino the week before Thanksgiving. We reserved the entire inn for the occasion. It was a stressful three-day affair, but everything went off as planned. People seemed to have a good time, all the media commotion helped the local economy, and nobody walked off a cliff, although my in-laws may have been tempted. Many of the assembled Yordanyotovs wept throughout the ceremony, some possibly from happiness. I felt a little guilty not inviting Kenny's mom, but what could she expect from such a worthless son? Tara was a beautiful bride and didn't show excessively in her pale lavender dress, which she liked to point out matched her appliances.

We went to Bali for our honeymoon where nobody knew us from Adam. We had a blissful two weeks being ordinary tourists. The weather was great, and Tara experienced a breakthrough one afternoon on a serene beach under a tropical sun. She revealed that she at last could look at me without the slightest cringe.

When we returned to L.A. this letter was waiting in Tara's stack of mail:

> Dear Tara,
>
> I hope this reaches you. I have a sense that you know a Mr. A.W. Tell him that I did not appreciate being ditched that morning. I was pissed as hell, but everything turned out OK. I met a nice drawbridge attendant in a location I'd rather not mention. David is one inch shy of seven feet tall and makes me feel almost petite. His middle name is Bruce–is that destiny or what? He helped me say certain words and overcome a problem I'd been having. Anyway, I'm stuck on the big galoot and he likes me too. The river life is grand, so please don't visit here and screw things up for me.
>
> Fondly,
>
> C.

We had Christmas dinner in Costa Mesa with my in-laws. I felt a little queasy after the meal, but it turned out to be nerves, not poisoning. Presents were opened and I expressed heartfelt appreciation for my gift: a hardbound book offering 500 proven tips for the job-seeker. I had done a little better back at Amalfi Drive that morning. Parked in the driveway was a gleaming 1949 yellow Ford convertible. I nearly died from shock as I untied the big red bow.

The tax baby arrived a little early on April 14. He was a lusty eight-pounder entirely visible to the naked eye. We named him Axel Jack over the protests of my in-laws, who said it sounded like an automotive tool.

The little bastard bellows like a banshee and produces more foul effluent than your average pig farm. I suggested to his mom that we chain him up on the patio and hose him down hourly. I took a knife-making class at the JC and decided I really liked working with metal. A couple of buddies I met there say they might be able to get me a job as an apprentice machinist. I'm letting my hair grow out and really like the down-to-the-shoulder length in the back. Kind of freaks out my old lady though. Wait til she sees the tattoo I'm planning to get over that scar on my shoulder. The Ford was flashy, but not making it as a daily driver. So I traded it in on a late-model Grand Prix. While I was at it, I got the phone number of the foxy salesgal who arranged the deal. No way I'm going to stay home and play babysitter while the old lady is off for weeks entertaining the rubes. She can think again if she thinks she can play this dude for a patsy.

Got you worried yet? Relax. Strike that last graph; it's just a bit of Kenny Tinker leg-pulling. Since I'm married to a comic, people expect me to be amusing as well. Still, there are days when I really feel like muscling a party guest or dabbling in some minor poisoning. But I suppose we all have to express our inner Kenny.

Made in the USA
Lexington, KY
03 February 2012